'Dick's plastic realities tell us more than we'll ever want to know about the inside of our heads and the view looking out. In his tortured topographies of worlds never made, we see mindscapes that we ourselves, in our madder moments, have glimpsed and thought real. Dick travelled out there on our behalf. It is our duty to read the reports he sent home.' *James Lovegrove*

'Dick quietly produced serious fiction in a popular form and there can be no greater praise.' *Michael Moorcock*

'One of the most original practitioners writing any kind of fiction, Philip K. Dick made most of the European avant-garde seem navel-gazers in a cul-de-sac.' *Sunday Times*

'The most consistently brilliant SF writer in the world' *John Brunner*

'Dick's abundant storytelling gifts and the need to express his inner struggles combined to produce some of the most groundbreaking novels and ideas to emerge from SF in the fifties and sixties' *Waterstone's Guide to Science Fiction, Fantasy and Horror*

'In all his work he was astonishingly intimate, self exposed, and very dangerous. He was the funniest sf writer of his time, and perhaps the most terrifying, His dreads were our own, spoken as we could not have spoken them' *The Encyclopedia of Science Fiction*

Also by Philip K. Dick

NOVELS
Solar Lottery (1955)
The World Jones Made (1956)
The Man Who Japed (1956)
The Cosmic Puppets (1957)
Eye in the Sky (1957)
Dr Futurity (1959)
Time Out of Joint (1959)
Vulcan's Hammer (I960)
The Man in the High Castle (1962)
The Game-Players of Titan (1963)
The Penultimate Truth (1964)
The Simulacra (1964)
Martian Time-Slip (1964)
Clans of the Alphane Moon (1964)
The Three Stigmata of Palmer Eldritch (1965)
The Ganymede Takeover (with Ray F. Nelson) (1967)
Now Wait for Last Year (1966)
The Crack in Space (1966)
The Zap Gun (1967)
Counter-Clock World (1967)
Do Androids Dream of Electric Sheep? (1968)
Galactic Pot-Healer (1969)
Ubik (1969)
Our Friends From Frolix 8 (1970)
A Maze of Death (1970)
We Can Build You (1972)
Flow My Tears, The Policeman Said (1974)
Confessions of a Crap Artist (1975)
Deus Irae (with Roger Zelazny) (1976)
A Scanner Darkly (1977)
The Divine Invasion (1981)
Valis (1981)
The Transmigration of Timothy Archer (1982)
Lies, Inc (1984)
The Man Whose Teeth Were All Exactly Alike (1984)
Puttering About in a Small Land (1985)
In Milton Lumky Territory (1985)
Radio Free Albemuth (1985)
Humpty Dumpty in Oakland (1986)
Mary and the Giant (1987)
The Broken Bubble (1988)

SHORT STORY COLLECTIONS
The Variable Man (1957)
A Handful of Darkness (1966)
The Turning Wheel (1977)
The Best of Philip K. Dick (1977)
The Golden Man (1980)
Minority Report (2002)

THE COLLECTED STORIES OF PHILIP K. DICK
1. Beyond Lies the Wub (1987)
2. Second Variety (1987)
3. The Father Thing (1987)
4. Minority Report (1987)
5. We Can Remember it for you Wholesale (1987)

Dr Bloodmoney

Philip K. Dick

This edition published in Great Britain in 2007 by
Gollancz
An imprint of the Orion Publishing Group
Orion House, 5 Upper St Martin's Lane, London WC2H 9EA

10 9 8 7 6 5 4 3 2 1

A CIP catalogue record for this book
is available from the British Library

ISBN-13 978 0 57507 994 6
ISBN-10 0 575 07994 0

Typeset at The Spartan Press Ltd,
Lymington, Hants

Printed and bound at
Mackays of Chatham plc, Chatham, Kent

www. orionbooks.co.uk

One

Early in the bright sun-yellowed morning, Stuart McConchie swept the sidewalk before Modern TV Sales & Service, hearing the cars along Shattuck Avenue and the secretaries hurrying on high heels to their offices, all the stirrings and fine smells of a new week, a new time in which a good salesman could accomplish things. He thought about a hot roll and coffee for his second breakfast, along about ten. He thought of customers whom he had talked to returning to buy, all of them perhaps today, his book of sales running over, like that cup in the Bible. As he swept he sang a song from a new Buddy Greco album and he thought too how it might feel to be famous, a world-famous great singer that everyone paid to see at such places as Harrah's in Reno or the fancy expensive clubs in Las Vegas which he had never seen but heard so much about.

He was twenty-six years old and he had driven, late on certain Friday nights, from Berkeley along the great ten-lane highway to Sacramento and across the Sierras to Reno, where one could gamble and find girls; he worked for Jim Fergesson, the owner of Modern TV, on a salary and commission basis, and being a good salesman he made plenty. And anyhow this was 1981 and business was not bad. Another good year, booming from the start, where America got bigger and stronger and everybody took more home.

'Morning, Stuart.' Nodding, the middle-aged jeweler from across Shattuck Avenue passed by. Mr Crody, on his way to his own little store.

All the stores, the offices, opening, now; it was after nine and even Doctor Stockstill, the psychiatrist and specialist in psychosomatic disorders, appeared, key in hand, to start up his high-paying enterprise in the glass-sided office building which the insurance company had built with a bit of its surplus money. Doctor Stockstill had parked his foreign car in the lot; he could afford to pay five dollars a day. And now came the tall, long-legged pretty secretary of Doctor Stockstill's, a head taller than he. And, sure enough as Stuart watched, leaning on his broom, the furtive first nut of the day sidled guiltily toward the psychiatrist's office.

It's a world of nuts, Stuart thought, watching. Psychiatrists make a lot. If I had to go to a psychiatrist I'd come and go by the back door. Nobody'd see me and jeer. He thought, Maybe some of them do; maybe Stockstill has a back door. For the sicker ones, or rather (he corrected his thought) the ones who don't want to make a spectacle out of themselves; I mean the ones who simply have a problem, for instance worry about the Police Action in Cuba, and who aren't nuts at all, just – concerned.

And he was concerned, because there was still a good chance that he might be called up for the Cuban War, which had now become bogged down in the mountains once more, despite the new little antipersonnel bombs that picked out the greasy gooks no matter how well dug in. He himself did not blame the president – it wasn't the president's fault that the Chinese had decided to honor their pact. It was just that hardly anyone came home from fighting the greasy gooks free of virus bone infections. A thirty-year-old combat veteran returned looking like some dried mummy left out of doors to hang for a century . . . and it was hard for Stuart McConchie to imagine himself picking up once more after that, selling stereo TV again, resuming his career in retail selling.

'Morning, Stu,' a girl's voice came, startling him. The small, dark-eyed waitress from Edy's candy store. 'Day dreaming so early?' She smiled as she passed on by along the sidewalk.

'Heck no,' he said, again sweeping vigorously.

Across the street the furtive patient of Doctor Stockstill's, a man black in color, black hair and eyes, light skin, wrapped tightly in a big overcoat itself the color of deep night, paused to light a cigarette and glance about. Stuart saw the man's hollow face, the staring eyes and the mouth, especially the mouth. It was drawn tight and yet the flesh hung slack, as if the pressure, the tension there, had long ago ground the teeth and the jaw away; the tension remained there in that unhappy face, and Stuart looked away.

Is that how it is? he wondered. To be crazy? Corroded away like that, as if devoured by . . . he did not know what by. Time or perhaps water; something slow but which never stopped. He had seen such deterioration before, in watching the psychiatrist's patients come and go, but never this bad, never this complete.

The phone rang from inside Modern TV, and Stuart turned to hurry toward it. When next he looked out onto the street the black-wrapped man had gone, and once more the day was regaining its brightness, its promise and smell of beauty. Stuart shivered, picked up his broom.

I know that man, he said to himself. I've seen his picture or he's come into the store. He's either a customer – an old one, maybe even a friend of Fergesson's – or he's an important celebrity.

Thoughtfully, he swept on.

To his new patient, Doctor Stockstill said, 'Cup of coffee? Or tea or Coke?' He read the little card which Miss Purcell had placed on his desk, 'Mr Tree,' he said aloud. 'Any relation to the famous English literary family? Iris Tree, Max Beerbohm . . .'

In a heavily-accented voice Mr Tree said, 'That is not actually my name, you know.' He sounded irritable and impatient. 'It occurred to me as I talked to your girl.'

Doctor Stockstill glanced questioningly at his patient.

'I am world-famous,' Mr Tree said. 'I'm surprised you don't recognize me; you must be a recluse or worse.' He ran a hand shakily through his long black hair. 'There are thousands, even millions of people in the world, who hate me and would like to destroy me. So naturally I have to take steps; I have to give you a made-up name.' He cleared his throat and smoked rapidly at his cigarette; he held the cigarette European style, the burning end within, almost touching his palm.

Oh my god, Doctor Stockstill thought. This man, I do recognize him. This is Bruno Bluthgeld, the physicist. And he is right; a lot of people both here and in the East would like to get their hands on him because of his miscalculation back in 1972. Because of the terrible fall-out from the high-altitude blast which wasn't supposed to hurt anyone; Bluthgeld's figures *proved* it in advance.

'Do you want me to know who you are?' Doctor Stockstill asked. 'Or shall we accept you simply as "Mr Tree"? It's up to you; either way is satisfactory to me.'

'Let's simply get on,' Mr Tree grated.

'All right.' Doctor Stockstill made himself comfortable, scratched with his pen against the paper on his clipboard. 'Go ahead.'

'Does an inability to board an ordinary bus – you know, with perhaps a dozen persons unfamiliar to you – signify anything?' Mr Tree watched him intently.

'It might,' Stockstill said.

'I feel they're staring at me.'

'For any particular reason?'

'Because,' Mr Tree said, 'of the disfiguration of my face.'

Without an overt motion, Doctor Stockstill managed to glance up and scrutinize his patient. He saw this middle-aged man, heavy-set, with black hair, the stubble of a beard dark against his unusually white skin. He saw circles of fatigue and tension beneath the man's eyes, and the expression in the eyes, the despair. The physicist had bad skin and he needed a haircut, and his entire face was marred by the worry within him . . . but there was no 'disfiguration.' Except for the strain visible there, it was an ordinary face; it would not have attracted notice in a group.

'Do you see the blotches?' Mr Tree said hoarsely. He pointed at his cheeks, his jaw. 'The ugly marks that set me apart from everybody?'

'No,' Stockstill said, taking a chance and speaking directly.

'They're there,' Mr Tree said. 'They're on the inside of the skin, of course. But people notice them anyhow and stare. I can't ride on a bus or go into a restaurant or a theater; I can't go to the San Francisco opera or the ballet or the symphony orchestra or even a nightclub to watch one of those folk singers; if I do succeed in getting inside I have to leave almost at once because of the staring. And the remarks.'

'Tell me what they say.'

Mr Tree was silent.

'As you said yourself,' Stockstill said, 'you are world-famous – and isn't it natural for people to murmur when a world-famous personage comes in and seats himself among them? Hasn't this been true for years? And there is controversy about your work, as you pointed out . . . hostility and perhaps one hears disparaging remarks. But everyone in the public eye—'

'Not that,' Mr Tree broke in. 'I expect that; I write articles and appear on the TV, and I expect that; I know that. This – has to do with my private life. My most innermost thoughts.' He gazed at Stockstill and said, 'They read my thoughts and they tell me about my private personal life, in every detail. They have access to my brain.'

Paranoia sensitiva, Stockstill thought, although of course there have to be tests . . . the Rorschach in particular. It could be advanced insidious schizophrenia; these could be the final stages of a lifelong illness process. Or—

'Some people can see the blotches on my face and read my personal thoughts more accurately than others,' Mr Tree said. 'I've noted quite a spectrum in ability – some are barely aware, others seem to make an instantaneous Gestalt of my differences, my stigmata. For example, as I came up the sidewalk to your office, there was a Negro sweeping on the other side . . . he stopped work and concentrated on me, although of course he was too far away to jeer at me. Nevertheless, he saw. It's typical of lower-class people, I've noticed. More so than educated or cultured people.'

'I wonder why that is,' Stockstill said, making notes.

'Presumably, you would know, if you're competent at all. The woman who recommended you said you were exceptionally able.' Mr Tree eyed him, as if seeing no sign of ability as yet.

'I think I had better get a background history from you,' Stockstill said. 'I see that Bonny Keller recommended me. How is Bonny? I haven't seen her since last April or so . . . did her husband give up his job with that rural grammar school as he was talking about?'

'I did not come here to discuss George and Bonny Keller,' Mr Tree said. 'I am desperately pressed, Doctor. They may decide to complete their destruction of me any time now; this harassment has gone on for so long now that—' He broke off.

'Bonny thinks I'm ill, and I have great respect for her.' His tone was low, almost inaudible. 'So I said I'd come here, at least once.'

'Are the Kellers still living up in West Marin?'

Mr Tree nodded.

'I have a summer place up there,' Stockstill said. 'I'm a sailing buff; I like to get out on Tomales Bay every chance I get. Have you ever tried sailing?'

'No.'

'Tell me when you were born and where.'

Mr Tree said, 'In Budapest, in 1934.'

Doctor Stockstill, skillfully questioning, began to obtain in detail the life-history of his patient, fact by fact. It was essential for what he had to do: first diagnose and then, if possible, heal. Analysis and then therapy. A man known all over the world who had delusions that strangers were staring at him – how in this case could reality be sorted out from fantasy? What was the frame of reference which would distinguish them one from the other?

It would be so easy, Stockstill realized, to find pathology here. So easy – and so tempting. A man this hated . . . I share their opinion, he said to himself, the *they* that Bluthgeld – or rather Tree – talks about. After all, I'm part of society too, part of the civilization menaced by the grandiose, extravagant miscalculations of this man. It could have been – could someday be – my children blighted because this man had the arrogance to assume that he could not err.

But there was more to it than that. At the time, Stockstill had felt a twisted quality about the man; he had watched him being interviewed on TV, listened to him speak, read his fantastic anti-communist speeches – and come to the tentative conclusion that Bluthgeld had a profound hatred for people, deep and pervasive enough to make him want, on some unconscious level, to err, to make him want to jeopardize the lives of millions.

No wonder that the Director of the FBI, Richard Nixon, had spoken out so vigorously against 'militant amateur anti-communists in high scientific circles.' Nixon had been alarmed, too, long before the tragic error of 1972. The elements of paranoia, with the delusions not only of reference but of grandeur, had been palpable; Nixon, a shrewd judge of men, had observed them, and so had many others.

And evidently they had been correct.

'I came to America,' Mr Tree was saying, 'in order to escape the Communist agents who wanted to murder me. They were after me even then . . . so of course were the Nazis. They were all after me.'

'I see,' Stockstill said, writing.

'They still are, but ultimately they will fail,' Mr Tree said hoarsely, lighting a new cigarette. 'For I have God on my side; He sees my need and often He has spoken to me, giving me the wisdom I need to survive my pursuers. I am at present at work on a new project, out at Livermore; the results of this will be definitive as regards our enemy.'

Our enemy, Stockstill thought. Who is our enemy . . . isn't it you, Mr Tree? Isn't it you sitting here rattling off your paranoid delusions? How did you ever get the high post that you hold? Who is responsible for giving you power over the lives of others – and letting you keep that power even after the fiasco of 1972? You – and they – are surely our enemies.

All our fears about you are confirmed; you are deranged, your presence here proves it. Or does it? Stockstill thought, No, it doesn't, and perhaps I should disqualify myself; perhaps it is unethical for me to try to deal with you. Considering the way I feel . . . I can't take a detached, disinterested position regarding you; I can't be genuinely scientific, and hence my analysis, my diagnosis, may well prove faulty.

'Why are you looking at me like this?' Mr Tree was saying.

'Beg pardon?' Stockstill murmured.

'Are you repelled by my disfigurations?' Mr Tree said.

'No-no,' Stockstill said. 'It isn't that.'

'My thoughts, then? You were reading them and their disgusting character causes you to wish I had not consulted you?' Rising to his feet, Mr Tree moved abruptly toward the office door. 'Good day.'

'Wait.' Stockstill came after him. 'Let's get the biographical material concluded, at least; we've barely begun.'

Mr Tree, eyeing him, said presently, 'I have confidence in Bonny Keller; I know her political opinions . . . she is not a part of the international Communist conspiracy seeking to kill me at any opportunity.' He reseated himself, more composed, now. But his posture was one of wariness; he would not permit himself to relax a moment in Stockstill's presence, the psychiatrist knew. He would not open up, reveal himself candidly. He would continue to be suspicious – and perhaps rightly, Stockstill thought.

As he parked his car Jim Fergesson, the owner of Modern TV, saw his salesman Stuart McConchie leaning on his broom before the shop, not sweeping but merely daydreaming or whatever it was he did. Following McConchie's gaze he saw that the salesman was enjoying not the sight of some girl passing by or some unusual car – Stu liked girls and cars, and that was normal – but was instead looking in the direction of patients entering the office of the doctor across the street. That wasn't normal. And what business of McConchie's was it anyhow?

'Look,' Fergesson called as he walked rapidly toward the

entrance of his shop. 'You cut it out; someday maybe you'll be sick, and how'll you like some goof gawking at you when you try to seek medical help?'

'Hey,' Stuart answered, turning his head, 'I just saw some important guy go in there but I can't recall who.'

'Only a neurotic watches over other neurotics,' Fergesson said, and passed on into the store, to the register, which he opened and began to fill with change and bills for the day ahead.

Anyhow, Fergesson thought, wait'll you see what I hired for a TV repairman; you'll really have something to stare at.

'Listen, McConchie,' Fergesson said. 'You know that kid with no arms and legs that comes by on that cart? That phocomelus with just those dinky flippers whose mother took that drug back in the early '60s? The one that always hangs around because he wants to be a TV repairman?'

Stuart, standing with his broom, said, 'You hired him.'

'Yeah, yesterday while you were out selling.'

Presently McConchie said, 'It's bad for business.'

'Why? Nobody'll see him; he'll be downstairs in the repair department. Anyhow you have to give those people jobs; it isn't their fault they have no arms or legs, it's those Germans' fault.'

After a pause Stuart McConchie said, 'First you hire me, a Negro, and now a phoce. Well, I have to hand it to you, Fergesson; you're trying to do right.'

Feeling anger, Fergesson said, 'I not only try, I do; I'm not just daydreaming, like you. I'm a man who makes up his mind and acts.' He went to open the store safe. 'His name is Hoppy. He'll be in this morning. You ought to see him move stuff with his electronic hands; it's a marvel of modern science.'

'I've seen,' Stuart said.

'And it pains you.'

Gesturing, Stuart said, 'It's – unnatural.'

Fergesson glared at him. 'Listen, don't say anything along the lines of razzing to the kid; if I catch you or any of the other salesmen or anybody who works for me—'

'Okay,' Stuart muttered.

'You're bored,' Fergesson said, 'and boredom is bad because it means you're not exerting yourself fully; you're slacking off, and on my time. If you worked hard, you wouldn't have time to lean on that broom and poke fun at poor sick people going to the doctor. I forbid you to stand outside on the sidewalk ever again; if I catch you you're fired.'

'Oh Christ, how am I supposed to come and go and go eat? How do I get into the store in the first place? Through the wall?'

'You can come and go,' Fergesson decided, 'but you can't loiter,'

Glaring after him dolefully, Stuart McConchie protested, 'Aw cripes!'

Fergesson however paid no attention to his TV salesman; he began turning on displays and signs, preparing for the day ahead.

Two

The phocomelus Hoppy Harrington generally wheeled up to Modern TV Sales & Service about eleven each morning. He generally glided into the shop, stopping his cart by the counter, and if Jim Fergesson was around he asked to be allowed to go downstairs to watch the two TV repairmen at work. However, if Fergesson was not around, Hoppy gave up and after a while wheeled off, because he knew that the salesmen would not let him go downstairs; they merely ribbed him, gave him the runaround. He did not mind. Or at least as far as Stuart McConchie could tell, he did not mind.

But actually, Stuart realized, he did not understand Hoppy, who had a sharp face with bright eyes and a quick, nervous manner of speech which often became jumbled into a stammer. He did not understand him *psychologically*. Why did Hoppy want to repair TV sets? What was so great about that? The way the phoce hung around, one would think it was the most exalted calling of all. Actually, repair work was hard, dirty, and did not pay too well. But Hoppy was passionately determined to become a TV repairman, and now he had succeeded, because Fergesson was determined to do right by all the minority groups in the world. Fergesson was a member of the American Civil Liberties Union and the NAACP and the Help for the Handicapped League – the latter being, as far as Stuart could tell, nothing but a lobby group on an international scale, set up to promote soft berths for all the victims of modern medicine and science, such as the multitude from the Bluthgeld Catastrophe of 1972.

And what does that make me? Stuart asked himself as he sat upstairs in the store's office, going over his sales book, I mean, he thought, with a phoce working here . . . that practically makes me a radiation freak, too, as if being colored was a sort of early form of radiation burn. He felt gloomy thinking about it.

Once upon a time, he thought, all the people on Earth were white, and then some horse's ass set off a high-altitude bomb back say around ten thousand years ago, and some of us got seared and it was permanent; it affected our genes. So here we are today.

Another salesman, Jack Lightheiser, came and sat down at the desk across from him and lit a Corona cigar. 'I hear Jim's hired that kid on the cart,' Lightheiser said. 'You know why he did it, don't you? For publicity. The SF newspapers'll write it up. Jim loves getting his name in the paper. It's a smart move, when you get down to it. The first retail dealer in the East Bay to hire a phoce.'

Stuart grunted.

'Jim's got an idealized image of himself,' Lightheiser said. 'He isn't just a merchant; he's a modern Roman, he's civic-minded. After all, he's an educated man – he's got a master's degree from Stanford.'

'That doesn't mean anything any more,' Stuart said. He himself had gotten a master's degree from Cal, back in 1975, and look where it had got him.

'It did when he got it,' Lightheiser said. 'After all, he graduated back in 1947; he was on that GI Bill they had.'

Below them, at the front door of Modern TV, a cart appeared, in the center of which, at a bank of controls, sat a slender figure. Stuart groaned and Lightheiser glanced at him.

'He's a pest,' Stuart said.

'He won't be when he gets started working,' Lightheiser said. 'The kid is all brain, no body at all, hardly. That's a powerful mind he's got, and he also has ambition. God, he's only seventeen years old and what he wants to do is work, get out of school and work. That's admirable.'

The two of them watched Hoppy on his cart; Hoppy was wheeling toward the stairs which descended to the TV repair department.

'Do the guys downstairs know, yet?' Stuart asked.

'Oh sure, Jim told them last night. They're philosophical; you know how TV repairmen are – they griped about it but it doesn't mean anything; they gripe all the time anyhow.'

Hearing the salesman's voice, Hoppy glanced sharply up. His thin, bleak face confronted them; his eyes blazed and he said stammeringly, 'Hey, is Mr Fergesson in right now?'

'Naw,' Stuart said.

'Mr Fergesson hired me,' the phoce said.

'Yeah,' Stuart said. Neither he nor Lightheiser moved; they remained seated at the desk, gazing down at the phoce.

'Can I go downstairs?' Hoppy asked.

Lightheiser shrugged.

'I'm going out for a cup of coffee,' Stuart said, rising to his feet. 'I'll be back in ten minutes; watch the floor for me, okay?'

'Sure,' Lightheiser said, nodding as he smoked his cigar.

When Stuart reached the main floor he found the phoce still there; he had not begun the difficult descent down to the basement.

'Spirit of 1972,' Stuart said as he passed the cart.

The phoce flushed and stammered, 'I was born in 1964; it had nothing to do with that blast.' As Stuart went out the door onto the sidewalk the phoce called after him anxiously, 'It was that drug, that thalidomide. Everybody knows that.'

Stuart said nothing; he continued on toward the coffee shop.

It was difficult for the phocomelus to maneuver his cart down the stairs to the basement where the TV repairmen worked at their benches, but after a time he managed to do so, gripping the handrail with the manual extensors which the US Government had thoughtfully provided. The extensors were really not much good; they had been fitted years ago, and were not only partly wornout but were – as he knew from reading the current literature on the topic – obsolete. In theory, the Government was bound to replace his equipment with the more recent models; the Remington Act specified that, and he had written the senior California senator, Alf M. Partland, about it. As yet, however, he had received no answer. But he was patient. Many times he had written letters to US Congressmen, on a variety of topics, and often the answers were tardy or merely mimeographed and sometimes there was no answer at all.

In this case, however, Hoppy Harrington had the law on his side, and it was only a matter of time before he compelled someone in authority to give him that which he was entitled to. He felt grim about it, patient and grim. They *had* to help him, whether they wanted to or not. His father, a sheep rancher in the Sonoma Valley, had taught him that: taught him always to demand what he was entitled to.

Sound blared. The repairmen at work; Hoppy paused, opened the door and faced the two men at the long, littered bench with its instruments and meters, its dials and tools and television sets in all stages of decomposition. Neither repairman noticed him.

'Listen,' one of the repairmen said all at once, startling him. 'Manual jobs are looked down on. Why don't you go into something mental, why don't you go back to school and get a degree?' The repairman turned to stare at him questioningly.

No, Hoppy thought. I want to work with – my hands.

'You could be a scientist,' the other repairman said, not ceasing his work; he was tracing a circuit, studying his voltmeter.

'Like Bluthgeld,' Hoppy said.

The repairman laughed at that, with sympathetic understanding.

'Mr Fergesson said you'd give me something to work on,' Hoppy said. 'Some easy set to fix, to start with. Okay?' He waited, afraid that they were not going to respond, and then one of them pointed to a record changer. 'What's the matter with it?' Hoppy said, examining the repair tag. 'I know I can fix it.'

'Broken spring,' one of the repairmen said. 'It won't shut off after the last record.'

'I see,' Hoppy said. He picked up the record changer with his two manual extensors and rolled to the far end of the bench, where there was a cleared space. 'I'll work here.' The repairmen did not protest, so he picked up pliers. This is easy, he thought to himself. I've practiced at home; he concentrated on the record changer but also watching the two repairmen out of the corner of his eye. I've practiced many times; it nearly always works, and all the time it's better, more accurate. More predictable. A spring is a little object, he thought, as little as they come. So light it almost blows away. I see the break in you, he thought. Molecules of metal not touching, like before. He concentrated on that spot, holding the pliers so that the repairman nearest him could not see; he pretended to tug at the spring, as if trying to remove it.

As he finished the job he realized that someone was standing behind him, had come up to watch; he turned, and it was Jim Fergesson, his employer, saying nothing but just standing there with a peculiar expression on his face, his hands stuck in his pockets.

'All done,' Hoppy said nervously.

Fergesson said, 'Let's see.' He took hold of the changer, lifted it up into the overhead fluorescent light's glare.

Did he see me? Hoppy wondered. Did he understand and if so, what does he think? Does he mind, does he really care? Is he – horrified?

There was silence as Fergesson inspected the changer.

'Where'd you get the new spring?' he asked suddenly.

'I found it lying around,' Hoppy said, at once.

It was okay. Fergesson, if he had seen, had not understood. The phocomelus relaxed and felt glee, felt a superior pleasure take the place of his anxiety; he grinned at the two repairmen, looked about for the next job expected of him.

Fergesson said, 'Does it make you nervous to have people watch you?'

'No,' Hoppy said. 'People can stare at me all they want; I know I'm different. I've been stared at since I was born.'

'I mean when you work.'

'No,' he said, and his voice sounded loud – perhaps too loud – in his ears. 'Before I had a cart,' he said, 'before the Government provided me anything, my dad used to carry me around on his back, in a sort of knapsack. Like a papoose.' He laughed uncertainly.

'I see,' Fergesson said.

'That was up around Sonoma,' Hoppy said. 'Where I grew up. We had sheep. One time a ram butted me and I flew through the air. Like a ball.' Again he laughed; the two repairmen regarded him silently, both of them pausing in their work.

'I'll bet,' one of them said after a moment, 'that you rolled when you hit the ground.'

'Yes,' Hoppy said, laughing. They all laughed, now, himself and Fergesson and the two repairmen; they imagined how it looked, Hoppy Harrington, seven years old, with no arms or legs, only a torso and head, rolling over the ground, howling with fright and pain – but it was funny; he knew it. He told it so it would be funny; he made it become that way.

'You're a lot better set up now, with your cart,' Fergesson said.

'Oh yes,' he said. 'And I'm designing a new one, my own design; all electronic – I read an article on brain-wiring, they're using it in Switzerland and Germany. You're wired directly to the motor centers of the brain so there's no lag; you move even quicker than – a regular physiological structure.' He started to say, *than a human*. 'I'll have it perfected in a couple of years,' he said, 'and it'll be an improvement even on the Swiss models. And then I can throw away this Government junk.'

Fergesson said in a solemn, formal voice, 'I admire your spirit.'

Laughing, Hoppy said with a stammer, 'Th-thanks, Mr Fergesson.'

One of the repairmen handed him a multiplex FM tuner. 'It drifts. See what you can do for the alignment.'

'Okay,' Hoppy said, taking it in his metal extensors. 'I sure will. I've done a lot of aligning, at home; I'm experienced with that.' He had found such work easiest of all: he barely had to concentrate on the set. It was as if the task were made to order for him and his abilities.

*

Reading the calendar on her kitchen wall, Bonny Keller saw that this was the day her friend Bruno Bluthgeld saw her psychiatrist Doctor Stockstill at his office in Berkeley. In fact, he had already seen Stockstill, had had his first hour of therapy and had left. Now he no doubt was driving back to Livermore and his own office at the Radiation Lab, the lab at which she had worked years ago before she had gotten pregnant: she had met Doctor Bluthgeld, there, back in 1975. Now she was thirty-one years old and living in West Marin; her husband George was now vice-principal of the local grammar school, and she was very happy.

Well, not *very* happy. Just moderately – tolerably – happy. She still took analysis herself – once a week now instead of three times – and in many respects she understood herself, her unconscious drives and paratactic systematic distortions of the reality situation. Analysis, six years of it, had done a great deal for her, but she was not cured. There was really no such thing as being cured; the 'illness' was life itself, and a constant growth (or rather a viable growing adaptation) had to continue, or psychic stagnation would result.

She was determined not to become stagnant. Right now she was in the process of reading *The Decline of the West* in the original German; she had gotten fifty pages read, and it was well worth it. And who else that she knew had read it, even in the English?

Her interest in German culture, in its literary and philosophical works, had begun years ago through her contact with Doctor Bluthgeld. Although she had taken three years of German in college, she had not seen it as a vital part of her adult life; like so much that she had carefully learned, it had fallen into the unconscious, once she had graduated and gotten a job. Bluthgeld's magnetic presence had reactivated and enlarged many of her academic interests, her love of music and art . . . she owed a great deal to Bluthgeld, and she was grateful.

Now, of course, Bluthgeld was sick, as almost everyone at Livermore knew. The man had profound conscience, and he had never ceased to suffer since the error of 1972 – which, as they all knew, all those who had been a part of Livermore in those days, was not specifically his fault; it was not his personal burden, but he had chosen to make it so, and because of that he had become ill, and more ill with each passing year.

Many trained people, and the finest apparati, the foremost computers of the day, had been involved in the faulty calculation – not faulty in terms of the body of knowledge available in 1972 but faulty in relationship to the reality situation. The enormous masses of radioactive clouds had not drifted off but had been attracted by the Earth's gravitational field, and had returned to the atmosphere; no one had been more surprised than the staff at Livermore. Now, of course, the Jamison-French Layer was more completely understood; even the popular magazines such as *Time* and *US News* could lucidly explain what had gone wrong and why. But this was nine years later.

Thinking of the Jamison-French Layer, Bonny remembered the event of the day, which she was missing. She went at once to the TV set in the living room and switched it on. Has it been fired off yet? she wondered, examining her watch. No, not for another half hour. The screen lighted, and sure enough, there was the rocket and its tower, the personnel, trucks, gear; it was decidedly still on the ground, and probably Walter Dangerfield and Mrs Dangerfield had not even boarded it yet.

The first couple to emigrate to Mars, she said to herself archly, wondering how Lydia Dangerfield felt at this moment . . . the tall blond woman, knowing that their chances of getting to Mars were computed at only about sixty per cent. Great equipment, vast diggings and constructions, awaited them, but so what if they were incinerated along the way? Anyhow, it would impress the Soviet bloc, which had failed to establish its colony on Luna; the Russians had cheerfully suffocated or starved – no one knew exactly for sure. In any case, the colony was gone. It had passed out of history as it had come in, mysteriously.

The idea of NASA sending just a couple, one man and his wife, instead of a group, appalled her; she felt instinctively that they were courting failure by not randomizing their bets. It should be a few people leaving New York, a few leaving California, she thought as she watched on the TV screen the technicians giving the rocket last-minute inspections. What do they call that? Hedging your bets? Anyhow, not all the eggs should be in this one basket . . . and yet this was how NASA had always done it: one astronaut at a time from the beginning, and plenty of publicity. When Henry Chancellor, back in 1967, had burned to particles in his space platform, the entire world had watched on TV – grief-stricken, to be sure, but nonetheless they had been permitted to watch. And the public reaction had set back space exploration in the West five years.

'As you can see now,' the NBC announcer said in a soft but urgent voice, 'final preparations are being made. The arrival of Mr and Mrs Dangerfield is expected momentarily. Let us review just for the sake of the record the enormous preparations made to insure—'

Blah, Bonny Keller said to herself, and, with a shudder, shut off the TV. I can't watch she said to herself.

On the other hand, what was there to do? Merely sit biting her nails for the next six hours – for the next two weeks, in fact? The only answer would have been *not* to remember that this was the day the First Couple was being fired off. However, it was too late now not to remember.

She liked to think of them as that, the *first couple* . . . like something out of a sentimental, old-time, science-fiction story. Adam and Eve, once over again, except that in actuality Walt Dangerfield was no Adam; he had more the quality of the last, not the first man, with his wry, mordant wit, his halting, almost cynical manner of speech as he faced the reporters. Bonny admired him; Dangerfield was no punk, no crewcut-haired young blond automaton, hacking away at the Air Forces' newest task. Walt was a real person, and no doubt that was why NASA had selected him. His genes – they were probably stuffed to overflowing with four thousand years of culture, the heritage of mankind built right in. Walt and Lydia would found a Nova Terra . . . there would be lots of sophisticated little Dangerfields strolling about Mars, declaiming intellectually and yet with that amusing trace of sheer jazziness that Dangerfield had.

'Think of it as a long freeway,' Dangerfield had once said in an interview, answering a reporter's query about the hazards of the trip. 'A million miles of ten lanes . . . with no oncoming traffic, no slow trucks. Think of it as being four o'clock in the morning . . . just your vehicle, no others. So like the guys say, what's to worry?' And then his good smile.

Bending, Bonny turned the TV set back on.

And there, on the screen, was the round, bespectacled face of Walt Dangerfield; he wore his space suit – all but the helmet – and beside him stood Lydia, silent, as Walt answered questions.

'I hear,' Walt was drawling, with a chewing-movement of his jaw as if he were masticating the question before answering, 'that there's a LOL in Boise, Idaho, who's worried about me.' He glanced up, as someone in the rear of the room asked something. 'A LOL?' Walt said, 'Well, – that was the great now-departed Herb Caen's term for Little Old Ladies . . . there's always one of them, everywhere. Probably there's one on Mars already, and we'll be living down the street from her. Anyhow, this one in Boise, or so I understand, is a little nervous about Lydia and myself, afraid something might happen to us. So she's sent us a good luck charm.' He displayed it, holding it clumsily with the big gloved fingers of his suit. The reporters all murmured with amusement. 'Nice, isn't it?' Dangerfield said. 'I'll tell you what it does; it's good for rheumatism.' The reporters laughed. 'In case we get rheumatism while we're on Mars. Or is it gout? I think it's gout, she said in her letter.' He glanced at his wife. 'Gout, was it?'

I guess, Bonny thought, they don't make charms to ward off meteors or radiation. She felt sad, as if a premonition had come over her. Or was it just because this was Bruno Bluthgeld's day at the psychiatrist's? Sorrowful thoughts emanating from that fact, thoughts about death and radiation and miscalculation and terrible, unending illness.

I don't believe Bruno has become a paranoid schizophrenic, she said to herself. This is only a situation deterioration, and with the proper psychiatric help – a few pills here and there – he'll be okay. It's an endocrine disturbance manifesting itself physically, and they can do wonders with that; it's not a character defect, a psychotic constitution, unfolding itself in the face of stress.

But what do I know, she thought gloomily. Bruno had to practically sit there and tell us 'they' were poisoning his drinking water before either George or I grasped how ill he was . . . he merely seemed depressed.

Right this moment she could imagine Bruno with a prescription for some pill which stimulated the cortex or suppressed the diencephalon; in any case the modern Western equivalent for contemporary Chinese herbal medicine would be in action, altering the metabolism of Bruno's brain, clearing away the delusions like so many cobwebs. And all would be well again; she and George and Bruno would be together again with their West Marin Baroque Recorder Consort, playing Bach and Handel in the evenings . . . it would be like old times. Two wooden Black Forest (genuine) recorders and then herself at the piano. The house full of baroque music and the smell of home-baked bread, and a bottle of Buena Vista wine from the oldest winery in California . . .

On the television screen Walt Dangerfield was wisecracking in his adult way, a sort of Voltaire and Will Rogers combined. 'Oh yeah,' he was saying to a lady reporter who wore a funny large hat. 'We expect to uncover a lot of strange life forms on Mars.' And he eyed her hat, as if saying, 'There's one now, I think.' And again, the reporters all laughed. 'I think it moved,' Dangerfield said, indicating the hat to his quiet, cool-eyed wife. 'It's coming for us, honey.'

He really loves her, Bonny realized, watching the two of them. I wonder if George ever felt toward me the way Walt Dangerfield feels toward his wife; I doubt it, frankly. If he did, he never would have allowed me to have those two therapeutic abortions. She felt even more sad, now, and she got up and walked away from the TV set, her back to it.

They ought to send George to Mars, she thought with bitterness. Or better yet, send us all, George and me and the Dangerfields; George can have an affair with Lydia Dangerfield – if he's able – and I can bed down with Walt; I'd be a fair to adequate partner in the great adventure. Why not?

I wish something would happen, she said to herself. I wish Bruno would call and say Doctor Stockstill had cured him, or I wish Dangerfield would suddenly back out of going, or the Chinese would start World War Three, or George would really hand the school board back that awful contract as he's been saying he's going to. Something, anyhow. Maybe, she thought, I ought to get out my potter's wheel and pot; back to so-called creativity, or anal play or whatever it is. I could make a lewd pot. Design it, fire it in Violet Clatt's kiln, sell it down in San Anselmo at Creative Artworks, Inc., that society ladies' place that rejected my welded jewelry last year. I know they'd accept a lewd pot if it was a *good* lewd pot.

At Modern TV, a small crowd had collected in the front of the store to watch the large stereo color TV set, the Dangerfields' flight being shown to all Americans everywhere, in their homes and at their places of work. Stuart McConchie stood with his arms folded, back of the crowd, also watching.

'The ghost of John L. Lewis,' Walt Dangerfield was saying in his dry way, 'would appreciate the true meaning of portal to portal pay . . . if it hadn't been for him, they'd probably be paying me about five dollars to make this trip, on the grounds that my job doesn't actually begin until I get there.' He had a sobered expression, now; it was almost time for him and Lydia to enter the cubicle of the ship. 'Just remember this . . . if something happens to us, if we get lost, don't come out looking for us. Stay home and I'm sure Lydia and I will turn up somewhere.'

'Good luck,' the reporters were murmuring, as officials and technicians of NASA appeared and began bundling the Dangerfields off, out of view of the TV cameras.

'Won't be long,' Stuart said to Lightheiser, who now stood beside him, also watching.

'He's a sap to go,' Lightheiser said, chewing on a toothpick. 'He'll never come back; they make no bones about that.'

'Why should he want to come back?' Stuart said. 'What's so great about it here?' He felt envious of Walt Dangerfield; he wished it was he, Stuart McConchie, up there before the TV cameras, in the eyes of the entire world.

Up the stairs from the basement came Hoppy Harrington on his cart, wheeling eagerly forward. 'Have they shot him off?' he asked Stuart in a nervous quick voice, peering at the screen. 'He'll be burned up; it'll be like that time in '65; I don't remember it, naturally, but—'

'Shut up, will you,' Lightheiser said softly, and the phocomelus, flushing, became silent. They all watched, then, each with his own private thoughts and reactions as on the TV screen the last inspection team was lifted by an overhead boom from the nose cone of the rocket. The count-down would soon begin; the rocket was fueled, checked over, and now the two people were entering it. The small group around the TV set stirred and murmured.

Sometime later today, sometime in the afternoon, their waiting would be rewarded, because Dutchman IV would take off; it would orbit the Earth for an hour or so, and the people would stand at the TV screen watching that, seeing the rocket go around and around, and then finally the decision would be made and someone below in the block-house would fire off the final stage and the orbiting rocket would change trajectory and leave the world. They had seen it before; it was much like this every time, but this was new because the people in this one this time would never be returning. It was well worth spending a day in front of the set; the crowd of people was ready for the wait.

Stuart McConchie thought about lunch and then after that he would come back here and watch again; he would station himself here once more, with the others. He would get little or no work done today, would sell no TV sets to anybody. But this was more important. He could not miss this. That might be me up there someday, he said to himself; maybe I'll emigrate later on when I'm earning enough to get married, take my wife and kids and start a new life up there on Mars, when they get a really good colony going, not just machines.

He thought of himself in the nose cone, like Walt Dangerfield, strapped next to a woman of great physical attractiveness. Pioneers, he and her, founding a new civilization on a new planet. But then his stomach rumbled and he realized how hungry he was; he could not postpone lunch much longer.

Even as he stood watching the great upright rocket on the TV screen, his thoughts turned toward soup and rolls and beef stew and apple pie with ice cream on it, up at Fred's Fine Foods.

Three

Almost every day Stuart McConchie ate lunch at the coffee shop up the street from Modern TV. Today, as he entered Fred's Fine Foods, he saw to his irritation that Hoppy Harrington's cart was parked in the back, and there was Hoppy eating his lunch in a perfectly natural and easygoing manner, as if he were used to coming here. Goddamn, Stuart thought. He's taking over; the phoces are taking over. And I didn't even see him leave the store.

However, Stuart seated himself in a booth and picked up the menu. He can't drive me off, he said to himself as he looked to see what the special of the day was, and how much it cost. The end of the month had arrived, and Stuart was nearly broke. He looked ahead constantly to his twice-monthly paycheck; it would be handed out personally by Fergesson at the end of the week.

The shrill sound of the phoce's voice reached Stuart as he sipped his soup; Hoppy was telling a yarn of some sort, but to whom? To Connie, the waitress? Stuart turned his head and saw that both the waitress and Tony the frycook were standing near Hoppy's cart, listening, and neither of them showed any revulsion toward the phoce.

Now Hoppy saw and recognized Stuart. 'Hi!' he called.

Stuart nodded and turned away, concentrating on his soup.

The phoce was telling them all about an invention of his, some kind of electronic contraption he had either built or intended to build – Stuart could not tell which, and he certainly did not care. It did not matter to him what Hoppy built, what crazy ideas emanated from the little man's brain. No doubt it's something sick, Stuart said to himself. Some crank gadget, like a perpetual motion machine . . . maybe a perpetual motion cart for him to ride on. He laughed at that idea, pleased with it. I have to tell that to Lightheiser, he decided. Hoppy's perpetual motion – and then he thought, His phocomobile. At that, Stuart laughed aloud.

Hoppy heard him laugh, and evidently thought he was laughing at something which he himself was saying. 'Hey, Stuart,' he called, 'come on over and join me and I'll buy you a beer.'

The moron, Stuart thought. Doesn't he know Fergesson would never let us have a beer on our lunch hour? It's a rule; if we have a beer we're supposed to never come back to the store and he'll mail us our check.

'Listen,' he said to the phoce, turning around in his seat, 'when you've worked for Fergesson a little longer you'll know better than to say something stupid like that.'

Flushing, the phoce murmured, 'What do you mean?'

The frycook said, 'Fergesson don't allow his employees to drink; it's against his religion, isn't it, Stuart?'

'That's right,' Stuart said, 'And you better learn that.'

'I wasn't aware of that,' the phoce said, 'and anyhow I wasn't going to have a beer myself. But I don't see what right an employer has to tell his employees what they can't have on their own time. It's their lunch hour and they should have a beer if they want it.' His voice was sharp, full of grim indignation. He was no longer kidding.

Stuart said, 'He doesn't want his salesmen coming in smelling like a brewery; I think that's his right. It'd offend some old lady customer.'

'I can see that for the salesmen like you,' Hoppy said, 'but

I'm not a salesman; I'm a repairman, and I'd have a beer if I wanted it.'

The frycook looked uneasy. 'Now look, Hoppy—' he began.

'You're too young to have a beer,' Stuart said. Now everyone in the place was listening and watching.

The phoce had flushed a deep red. 'I'm of age,' he said in a quiet, taut voice.

'Don't serve him any beer,' Connie, the waitress, said to the frycook. 'He's just a kid.'

Reaching into his pocket with his extensor, Hoppy brought out his wallet; he laid it open on the counter. 'I'm twenty-one,' he said.

Stuart laughed. 'Bull.' He must have some phony identification in there, he realized. The nut printed it himself or forged it or something. He has to be exactly like everyone; he's got an obsession about it.

Examining the identification in the wallet, the frycook said, 'Yeah, it says he's of age. But Hoppy, remember that other time you were in here and I served you a beer remember—'

'You have to serve me,' the phoce said.

Grunting, the frycook went and got a bottle of Hamm's beer, which he placed, unopened, before Hoppy.

'An opener,' the phoce said.

The frycook went and got an opener; he tossed it on the counter, and Hoppy pried open the bottle.

Taking a deep breath, the phoce drank the beer.

What's going on? Stuart wondered, noticing the way that the frycook and Connie – and even a couple of the patrons – were watching Hoppy. Does he pass out or something? Goes berserk, maybe? He felt repelled and at the same time deeply uneasy. I wish I was through with my food, he thought; I wish I was out of here. Whatever it is, I don't want to be a witness to it. I'm going back to the shop and watch the rocket again, he decided. I'm going to watch Dangerfield's flight, something vital to America, not this freak; I don't have time to waste on this.

But he stayed where he was, because something was happening, some peculiar thing involving Hoppy Harrington; he could not draw his attention away from it, try as he might.

In the center of his cart the phocomelus had sunk down, as if he were going to sleep. He lay with his head resting on the tiller which steered the cart, and his eyes became almost shut; his eyes had a glazed look.

'Jeez,' the frycook said. 'He's doing it again.' He appealed around to the rest of them, as if asking them to do something, but no one stirred; they all stood or sat where they were.

'I knew he would,' Connie said in a bitter, accusing voice.

The phoce's lips trembled and in a mumble he said, 'Ask me. Now somebody ask me.'

'Ask you what?' the frycook said angrily. He made a gesture of disgust, turned and walked away, back to his grill.

'Ask me,' Hoppy repeated, in a dull, far-off voice, as if he were speaking in a kind of fit. Watching, Stuart realized that it was a fit, a kind of epilepsy. He yearned to be out of the place and away, but still he could not stir; he still, like the others, had to go on watching.

Connie said to Stuart, 'Can't you push him back to the store? Just start pushing!' She glowered at him, but it wasn't his fault; Stuart shrank away and gestured to show his helplessness.

Mumbling, the phoce flopped about on his cart, his plastic and metal manual extensors twitching. 'Ask me about it,' he was saying. 'Come on, before it's too late; I can tell you now, I can see.'

At his grill the frycook said loudly, 'I wish one of you guys would ask him. I wish you'd get it over with; I know somebody's going to ask him and if you don't I will – I got a couple of questions.' He threw down his spatula and made his way back to the phoce. 'Hoppy,' he said loudly, 'you said last time it was all dark. Is that right? No light at all?'

The phoce's lips twitched. 'Some light. Dim light. Yellow, like it's about burned out.'

Beside Stuart appeared the middle-aged jeweler from across the street. 'I was here last time,' he whispered to Stuart. 'Want to know what it is he sees? I can tell you; listen, Stu, he sees *beyond.*'

'Beyond what?' Stuart said, standing up so that he could watch and hear better; everyone had moved closer, now, so as not to miss anything.

'You know,' Mr Crody said. 'Beyond the grave. The afterlife. You can laugh, Stuart, but it's true; when he has a beer he goes into this trance, like you see him in now and he has occult vision or something. You ask Tony or Connie and some of these other people; they were here, too.'

Now Connie was leaning over the slumped, twitching figure in the center of the cart. 'Hoppy, what's the light from? Is it God?' She laughed nervously. 'You know, like in the Bible. I mean, is it true?'

Hoppy said mumblingly, 'Gray, darkness. Like ashes. Then a great flatness. Nothing but fires burning, light is from the burning fires. They burn forever. Nothing alive.'

'And where are you?' Connie asked.

'I'm – floating,' Hoppy said. 'Floating near the ground . . . no, now I'm very high. I'm weightless, I don't have a body any more so I'm high up, as high as I want to be. I can hang here, if I want; I don't have to go back down. I like it up here and I can go around the Earth forever. There it is down below me and I can just keep going around and around.'

Going up beside the cart, Mr Crody the jeweler said, 'Uh,

Hoppy, isn't there anybody else? Are each of us doomed to isolation?'

Hoppy mumbled, 'I – see others, now. I'm drifting back down, I'm landing among the grayness. I'm walking about.'

Walking, Stuart thought. On what? Legs but no body; what an afterlife. He laughed to himself. What a performance, he thought. What crap. But he, too, came up beside the cart, now, squeezing in to be able to see.

'Is it that you're born into another life, like they teach in the East?' an elderly lady customer in a cloth coat asked.

'Yes,' Hoppy said, surprisingly. 'A new life. I have a different body; I can do all kinds of things.'

'A step up,' Stuart said.

'Yes,' Hoppy mumbled. 'A step up. I'm like everybody else; in fact I'm better than anybody else. I can do anything they can do and a lot more. I can go wherever I want, and they can't. They can't move.'

'Why can't they move?' the frycook demanded.

'Just can't,' Hoppy said. 'They can't go into the air or on roads or ships; they just stay. It's all different from this. I can see each of them, like they're dead, like they're pinned down and dead. Like corpses.'

'Can they talk?' Connie asked.

'Yes,' the phoce said, 'they can converse with each other. But – they have to—' He was silent, and then he smiled; his thin, twisted face showed joy. 'They can only talk through me.'

I wonder what that means, Stuart thought. It sounds like a megalomaniacal daydream, where he rules the world. Compensation because he's defective . . . just what you'd expect a phoce to imagine.

It did not seem so interesting to Stuart, now that he had realized that. He moved away, back toward his booth, where his lunch waited.

The frycook was saying, 'Is it a good world, there? Tell me if it's better than this or worse.'

'Worse,' Hoppy said. And then he said, 'Worse for you. It's what everybody deserves; it's justice.'

'Better for you, then,' Connie said, in a questioning way.

'Yes,' the phoce said.

'Listen,' Stuart said to the waitress from where he sat, 'can't you see it's just psychological compensation because he's defective? It's how he keeps going, imagining that. I don't see how you can take it seriously.'

'I don't take it seriously,' Connie said. 'But it's interesting; I've read about mediums, like they're called. They go into trances and can commune with the next world, like he's doing. Haven't you ever heard of that? It's a scientific fact, I think. Isn't it, Tony?' She turned to the frycook for support.

'I don't know,' Tony said moodily, walking slowly back to his grill to pick up his spatula.

The phoce, now, seemed to have fallen deeper into his beer-induced trance; he seemed asleep, in fact, no longer seeing anything or at least no longer conscious of the people around him or attempting to communicate his vision – or whatever it was – to them. The séance was over.

Well, you never know, Stuart said to himself. I wonder what Fergesson would say to this; I wonder if he'd want somebody who's not only physically crippled but an epileptic or whatever working for him. I wonder if I should or shouldn't mention this to him when I get back to the store. If he hears he'll probably fire Hoppy right on the spot; I wouldn't blame him. So maybe I better not say anything, he decided.

The phoce's eyes opened. In a weak voice he said, 'Stuart.'

'What do you want?' Stuart answered.

'I—' The phoce sounded frail, almost ill, as if the

experience had been too much for his weak body. 'Listen, I wonder . . .' He drew himself up, then rolled his cart slowly over to Stuart's booth. In a low voice he said, 'I wonder, could you push me back to the store? Not right now but when you're through eating. I'd really appreciate it.'

'Why?' Stuart said. 'Can't you do it?'

'I don't feel good,' the phoce said.

Stuart nodded. 'Okay. When I'm finished eating.'

'Thanks,' the phoce said.

Ignoring him stonily, Stuart continued eating. I wish it wasn't obvious I know him, he thought to himself. I wish he'd wheel off and wait somewhere else. But the phoce had sat down, rubbing his forehead with the left extensor, looking too spent to move away again, even to his place at the other end of the coffee shop.

Later, as Stuart pushed the phoce in his cart back up the sidewalk toward Modern TV, the phoce said in a low voice,

'It's a big responsibility, to see beyond.'

'Yeah,' Stuart murmured, maintaining his remoteness, doing his duty only, no more; he pushed the cart and that was all. Just because I'm pushing you, he thought, doesn't mean I have to converse with you.

'The first time it happened,' the phoce went on, but Stuart cut him off.

'I'm not interested.' He added, 'I just want to get back and see if they fired off the rocket yet. It's probably in orbit by now.'

'I guess so,' the phoce said.

At the intersection they waited for the light to change.

'The first time it happened,' the phoce said, 'it scared me.' As Stuart pushed him across the street he went on, 'I knew right away what it was I was seeing. The smoke and the fires . . . everything all smudged. Like a mining pit or a place where they process slag. Awful.' He shuddered. 'But is this so terrific the way it is now? Not for me.'

'I like it,' Stuart said shortly.

'Naturally,' the phoce said. 'You're not a biological sport.'

Stuart grunted.

'You know what my earliest memory from childhood is?' the phoce said in a quiet voice. 'Being carried to church in a blanket. Laid out on a pew like a—' His voice broke. 'Carried in and out in that blanket, inside it, so no one could see me. That was my mother's idea. She couldn't stand my father carrying me on his back, where people could see.'

Stuart grunted.

'This is a terrible world,' the phoce said. 'Once you Negroes had to suffer; if you lived in the South you'd be suffering now. You forget all about that because they let you forget, but me – they don't let me forget. Anyhow, I don't want to forget, about myself I mean. In the next world it all will be different. You'll find out because you'll be there, too.'

'No,' Stuart said. 'When I die I'm dead; I don't have a soul.'

'You, too,' the phoce said, and he seemed to be gloating; his voice had a malicious, cruel tinge of relish. 'I know.'

'How do you know?'

'Because,' the phoce said, 'one time I saw you.'

Frightened in spite of himself, Stuart said, 'Aw—'

'One time,' the phoce insisted, more firmly now. 'It was you; no doubt about it. Want to know what you were doing?'

'Naw.'

'You were eating a dead rat raw.'

Stuart said nothing, but he pushed the cart faster and faster, down the sidewalk as fast as he could go, back to the store.

★

When they got back to the store they found the crowd of people still in front of the TV set. And the rocket had been fired off; it had just left the ground, and it was not known yet if the stages had performed properly.

Hoppy wheeled himself back downstairs to the repair department and Stuart remained upstairs before the set. But the phoce's words had upset him so much that he could not concentrate on the TV screen; he wandered off, and then, seeing Fergesson in the upstairs office, walked that way.

At the office desk, Fergesson sat going over a pile of contracts and charge tags. Stuart approached him 'Listen. That goddam Hoppy—'

Fergesson glanced up from his tags.

'Forget it,' Stuart said, feeling discouraged.

'I watched him work,' Fergesson said. 'I went downstairs and watched him when he didn't know I was. I agree there's something unsavory about it. But he's competent; I looked at what he'd done, and it was done right, and that's all that counts.' He scowled at Stuart.

'I said forget it,' Stuart said.

'Did they fire the rocket off?'

'Just now.'

'We haven't moved a single item today, because of that circus,' Fergesson said.

'Circus!' He seated himself in the chair opposite Fergesson, in such a manner that he could watch the floor below them. 'It's history!'

'It's a way of you guys standing around doing nothing.' Once more Fergesson sorted through the tags.

'Listen, I'll tell you what Hoppy did.' Stuart leaned toward him. 'Up at the café, at Fred's Fine Foods.'

Fergesson eyed him, pausing in his work.

'He had a fit,' Stuart said 'He went nuts.'

'No kidding.' Fergesson looked displeased.

'He passed out because – he had a beer. And he saw beyond the grave. He saw me eating a dead rat. And it was raw. So he said.'

Fergesson laughed.

'It's not funny.'

'Sure it is. He's razzing you back for all the razzing you dish out and you're so dumb you get taken in.'

'He really saw it,' Stuart said stubbornly.

'Did he see me?'

'He didn't say. He does that up there all the time; they give him beers and he goes into his trance and they ask questions. About what it's like. I just happened to be there, eating lunch. I didn't even see him leave the store; I didn't know he would be there.'

For a moment Fergesson sat frowning and pondering, and then he reached out and pressed the button of the intercom which connected the office with the repair department. 'Hoppy, wheel up here to the office; I want to talk to you.'

'It wasn't my intention to get him into trouble,' Stuart said.

'Sure it was,' Fergesson said. 'But I still ought to know; I've got a right to know what my employees are doing when they're in a public place acting in a fashion that might throw discredit on the store.'

They waited, and after a time they heard the labored sound of the cart rolling up the stairs to the office.

As soon as he appeared, Hoppy said, 'What I do on my lunch hour is my own business, Mr Fergesson. That's how I feel.'

'You're wrong,' Fergesson said. 'It's my business, too. Did you see me beyond the grave, like you did Stuart? What was I doing? I want to know, and you better give me a good answer or you're through here, the same day you were hired.'

The phoce, in a low, steady voice, said, 'I didn't see you, Mr Fergesson, because your soul perished and won't be reborn.'

For a while Fergesson studied the phoce. 'Why is that?' he asked finally.

'It's your fate,' Hoppy said.

'I haven't done anything criminal or immoral.'

The phoce said, 'It's the cosmic process, Mr Fergesson. Don't blame me.' He became silent, then.

Turning to Stuart, Fergesson said, 'Christ. Well, ask a stupid question, get a stupid answer.' Returning to the phoce he said, 'Did you see anybody else I know, like my wife? No, you never met my wife. What about Lightheiser? What's going to become of him?'

'I didn't see him,' the phoce said.

Fergesson said, 'How did you fix that changer? How did you *really* do that? It looked like – you healed it. It looked like instead of replacing that broken spring you made the spring whole again. How did you do that? Is that one of those extra-sensory powers or whatever they are?'

'I repaired it,' the phoce said in a stony voice.

To Stuart, Fergesson said, 'He won't say. But I saw him. He was concentrating on it in some peculiar way. Maybe you were right, McConchie; maybe it was a mistake to hire him. Still, it's the results that count. Listen, Hoppy, I don't want you messing around with trances out in public anywhere along this street now that you're working for me; that was okay before, but not now. Have your trances in the privacy of your own home, is that clear?' He once more picked up his stack of tags. 'That's all. Both you guys, go down and do some work instead of standing around.'

The phoce at once spun his cart around and wheeled off,

toward the stairs. Stuart, his hands in his pockets, slowly followed.

When he got downstairs and back to the TV set and the people standing around it he heard the announcer say excitedly that the first three stages of the rocket appeared to have fired successfully.

That's good news, Stuart thought. A bright chapter in the history of the human race. He felt a little better, now, and he parked himself by the counter, where he could obtain a good view of the screen.

Why would I eat a dead rat? he asked himself. It must be a terrible world, the next reincarnation, to live like that. Not even to cook it but just to snatch it up and gobble it down. Maybe, he thought, even fur and all; fur and tail, everything. He shuddered.

How can I watch history being made? he wondered angrily. When I have to think about things like dead rats – I want to fully meditate on this great spectacle unfolding before my very eyes, and instead – I have to have garbage like that put into my mind by that sadistic, that radiation-drug freak that Fergesson had to go and hire. Sheoot!

He thought of Hoppy, then, no longer bound to his cart no longer an armless, legless cripple, but somehow floating. Somehow master of them all, of – as Hoppy had said – the world. And that thought was even worse than the one about the rat.

I'll bet there's plenty he saw, Stuart said to himself, that he isn't going to say, that he's deliberately keeping back. He just tells us enough to make us squirm and then he shuts up. If he can go into a trance and see the next reincarnation then he can see *everything* because what else is there? But I don't believe in that Eastern stuff anyhow, he said to himself. I mean, that isn't Christian.

But he believed what Hoppy had said; he believed because he had seen with his own eyes. There really was a trance. That much was true.

Hoppy had seen *something*. And it was a dreadful something; there was no doubt of that.

What else does he see? Stuart wondered. I wish I could make the little bastard say. What else has that warped, wicked mind perceived about me and about the rest of us, all of us?

I wish, he thought, I could look, too. Because it seemed to Stuart very important, and he ceased looking at the TV screen. He forgot about Walter and Lydia Dangerfield and history in the making; he thought only about Hoppy and the incident at the café. He wished he could stop thinking about it but he could not.

He thought on and on.

Four

The far-off popping noise made Mr Austurias turn his head to see what was coming along the road. Standing on the hillside at the edge of the grove of live oaks, he shielded his eyes and saw on the road below the small phocomobile of Hoppy Harrington; in the center of his cart the phocomelus guided himself along, picking a way past the potholes. But the popping noise had not been made by the phocomobile, which ran from an electric battery.

A truck, Mr Austurias realized. One of Orion Stroud's converted old wood-burners; he saw it now, and it moved at great speed, bearing down on Hoppy's phocomobile. The phocomelus did not seem to hear the big vehicle behind him.

The road belonged to Orion Stroud; he had purchased it from the county the year before, and it was up to him to maintain it and also to allow traffic to move along it other than his own trucks. He was not permitted to charge a toll. And yet, despite the agreement, the wood-burning truck clearly meant to sweep the phocomobile from its path; it headed straight without slowing.

God, Mr Austurias thought. He involuntarily raised his hand, as if warding off the truck. Now it was almost upon the cart, and still Hoppy paid no heed.

'Hoppy!' Mr Austurias yelled, and his voice echoed in the afternoon quiet of the woods, his voice and the popping of the truck's engine.

The phocomelus glanced up, did not see him, continued

on with the truck now so close that— Mr Austurias shut his eyes. When he opened them again he saw the phocomobile off onto the shoulder of the road; the truck roared on, and Hoppy was safe: he had gotten out of the way at the last moment.

Grinning after the truck, Hoppy waved an extensor. It had not bothered him, not frightened him in the least, although he must have known that the truck intended to grind him flat. Hoppy turned, waved at Mr Austurias, who he could not see but who he knew to be there.

His hands trembled, the hands of the grade school teacher; he bent, picked up his empty basket, stepped up the hillside toward the first old oak tree with its damp shadows beneath. Mr Austurias was out picking mushrooms. He turned his back on the road and went up, into the gloom, knowing that Hoppy was safe, and so he could forget him and what he had just now seen; his attention returned swiftly to the image of great orange *Cantharellus cibarius*, the chanterelle mushrooms.

Yes, the color glowed, a circle in the midst of the black humus, the pulpy, spirited flower very low, almost buried in the rotting leaves. Mr Austurias could taste it already; it was big and fresh, this chanterelle; the recent rains had called it out. Bending, he broke its stalk far down, so as to get all there was for his basket. One more and he had his evening meal. Crouching, he looked in every direction, not moving.

Another, less bright, perhaps older . . . he rose, started softly toward it, as if it might escape or he might somehow lose it. Nothing tasted as good as the chanterelle to him, not even the fine shaggy manes. He knew the locations of many stands of chanterelles here and there in West Marin County, on the oak-covered hillsides, in the woods. In all, he gathered eight varieties of forest and pasture mushrooms; he had been almost that many years learning where to expect them, and it was well worth it. Most people feared mushrooms, especially since the Emergency; they feared the new, mutant ones above all, because there the books could not help them.

For instance, Mr Austurias thought, the one he now broke . . . wasn't the color a little off? Turning it over he inspected the veins. Perhaps a pseudo-chanterelle, not seen before in this region, toxic or even fatal, a mutation. He sniffed it, catching the scent of mould.

Should I be afraid to eat this fellow? he asked himself. If the phocomelus can calmly face his danger, I should be able to face mine.

He put the chanterelle in his basket and walked on.

From below, from the road, he heard a strange sound, a grating, rough noise; pausing, he listened. The noise came again, and Mr Austurias strode quickly back the way he had come until he emerged from the oaks and once more stood above the road.

The phocomobile was still pulled off onto the shoulder; it had not gone on, and in it sat the armless, legless handyman, bent over. What was he doing? A convulsion jerked Hoppy about, lifting his head, and Mr Austurias saw to his amazement that the phocomelus was crying.

Fear, Mr Austurias realized. The phocomelus had been terrified by the truck but had not shown it, had by enormous effort hidden it until the truck was out of sight – until, the phocomelus had imagined, everyone was out of sight and he was alone, free to express his emotions.

If you're that frightened, Mr Austurias thought, then why did you wait so long to pull out of the truck's way?

Below him, the phocomelus' thin body shook, swayed back and forth; the bony, hawk-like features bulged with grief. I wonder what Doctor Stockstill, our local medical man, would make of this, Mr Austurias thought. After all, he used to be a psychiatrist, before the Emergency. He always has all sorts of theories about Hoppy, about what makes him plunk along.

Touching the two mushrooms in his basket, Mr Austurias thought, We're very close, all the time, to death. But then was it so much better before? Cancer-producing insecticides, smog that poisoned whole cities, freeways and airline crashes . . . it hadn't been so safe then; it hadn't been an easy life. One had to hop aside both then and now.

We must make the best of things, enjoy ourselves if possible, he said to himself. Again he thought of the savory frying pan of chanterelles, flavored with actual butter and garlic and ginger and his home-made beef broth . . . what a dinner it would be; who could he invite to share it with him? Someone he liked a lot, or someone important. If he could only find one more growing— I could invite George Keller, he thought. George, the school superintendent, my boss. Or even one of the school board members; even Orion Stroud, that big, round fat man, himself.

And, then, too, he could invite George's wife, Bonny Keller, the prettiest woman in West Marin; perhaps the prettiest woman in the county. There, he thought, is a person who has managed to survive in this present society of . . . both of the Kellers, in fact, had done well since E Day. If anything, they were better off than before.

Glancing up at the sun, Mr Austurias computed the time. Possibly it was getting close to four o'clock; time for him to hurry back to town to listen to the satellite as it passed over. Must not miss that, he told himself as he began to walk. Not for a million silver dollars, as the expression used to go. *Of Human Bondage* – forty parts had been read already, and it was getting really interesting. Everyone was attending this particular reading; no doubt of it: the man in the satellite had picked a terrific one this time to read. I wonder if he knows? Mr Austurias asked himself. No way for me to tell him; just listen, can't reply from down here in West Marin. Too bad. It might mean a lot to him, to know.

Walt Dangerfield must be terribly lonely up there alone in the satellite, Mr Austurias said to himself. Circling the Earth, day after day. Awful damn tragedy when his wife died; you can tell the difference – he's never been the same again. If only we could pull him down . . . but then, if we did, we wouldn't have him up there talking to us. No, Mr Austurias concluded. It wouldn't be a good idea to reach him, because that way he'd be sure never to go back up; he must be half-crazy to get out of the thing by now, after all these years.

Gripping his basket of mushrooms, he hurried in the direction of Point Reyes Station, where the one radio could be found, their one contact with Walt Dangerfield in the satellite, and through him the outside world.

'The compulsive,' Doctor Stockstill said, 'lives in a world in which everything is decaying. This is a great insight. Imagine it.'

'Then we must all be compulsives,' Bonny Keller said, 'because that's what's going on around us . . . isn't it?' She smiled at him, and he could not help returning it.

'You can laugh,' he said, 'but there's need for psychiatry, maybe more so even than before.'

'There's no need for it at all,' Bonny contradicted flatly. 'I'm not so sure there was any need for it even then, but at the time I certainly thought so. I was devoted to it, as you well know.'

At the front of the large room, tinkering with the radio, June Raub said, 'Quiet please. We're about to receive him.'

Our authority-figure speaks, Doctor Stockstill thought to

himself, and we do what it tells us. And to think that before the Emergency she was nothing more than a typist at the local Bank of America.

Frowning, Bonny started to answer Mrs Raub, and then she abruptly leaned close to Doctor Stockstill and said, 'Let's go outside; George is coming with Edie. Come on.' She took hold of his arm and propelled him past the chairs of seated people, toward the door. Doctor Stockstill found himself being led outdoors, onto the front porch.

'That June Raub,' Bonny said. 'She's so goddamn bossy.' She peered up and down the road which led past the Foresters' Hall. 'I don't see my husband and daughter; I don't even see our good teacher. Austurias, of course, is out in the woods gathering poisonous toadstools to do us all in, and god knows what Hoppy is up to at the moment. Some peculiar puttering-about.' She pondered, standing there in the dim late-afternoon twilight, looking especially attractive to Doctor Stockstill; she wore a wool sweater and a long, heavy, hand-made skirt, and her hair was tied back in a fierce knot of red. What a fine woman, he said to himself. Too bad she's spoken for. And then he thought, with a trace of involuntary maliciousness, spoken for a number of times over.

'Here comes my dear husband,' Bonny said. 'He's managed to break himself off from his school business. And here's Edie.'

Along the road walked the tall, slender figure of the grammar school principal; beside him, holding his hand, came the diminutive edition of Bonny, the little red-haired child with the bright, intelligent, oddly dark eyes. They approached, and George smiled in greeting.

'Has it started?' he called.

'Not yet,' Bonny said.

The child, Edie, said, 'That's good because Bill hates to miss it. He gets very upset.'

'Who's "Bill"?' Doctor Stockstill asked her.

'My brother,' Edie said calmly, with the total poise of a seven-year-old.

I didn't realize that the Kellers had two children, Stockstill thought to himself, puzzled. And anyhow he did not see another child; he saw only Edie. 'Where is Bill?' he asked her.

'With me,' Edie said. 'Like he always is. Don't you know Bill?'

Bonny said, 'Imaginary playmate.' She sighed wearily.

'No he is not imaginary,' her daughter said.

'Okay,' Bonny said irritably. 'He's real. Meet Bill,' she said to Doctor Stockstill. 'My daughter's brother.'

After a pause, her face set with concentration, Edie said, 'Bill is glad to meet you at last, Doctor Stockstill. He says hello.'

Stockstill laughed. 'Tell him I'm glad to meet him, too.'

'Here comes Austurias,' George Keller said, pointing.

'With his dinner,' Bonny said in a grouchy voice. 'Why doesn't he teach us to find them? Isn't he our teacher? What's a teacher for? I must say, George, sometimes I wonder about a man who—'

'If he taught us,' Stockstill said, 'we'd eat all the mushrooms up.' He knew her question was merely rhetorical anyhow; although they did not like it, they all respected Mr Austurias' retention of secret lore – it was his right to keep his mycological wisdom to himself. Each of them had some sort of equivalent fund to draw from. Otherwise, he reflected, they would not now be alive: they would have joined the great majority; the silent dead beneath their feet, the millions who could either be considered the lucky ones or the unlucky ones, depending on one's point of view. Sometimes it seemed to him that pessimism was called for, and on those days he thought of the dead as lucky. But for him pessimism was a passing mood; he certainly did not feel it now, as he stood in the shadows with Bonny Keller, only a foot or so from her, near enough to reach out easily and touch her . . . but that would not do. She would pop him on the nose, he realized. A good hard blow – and then George would hear, too, as if being hit by Bonny was not enough.

Aloud, he chuckled. Bonny eyed him with suspicion.

'Sorry,' he said. 'I was just wool-gathering.'

Mr Austurias came striding up to them, his face flushed with exertion. 'Let's get inside,' he puffed. 'So we don't miss Dangerfield's reading.'

'You know how it comes out,' Stockstill said. 'You know Mildred comes back and reenters his life again and makes him miserable; you know the book as well as I do – we all do.' He was amused by the teacher's concern.

'I'm not going to listen tonight,' Bonny said. 'I can't stand to be shushed by June Raub.'

With a glance at her, Stockstill said, 'Well, you can be community leader next month.'

'I think June needs a little psychoanalysis,' Bonny said to him. 'She's so aggressive, so masculine; it's not natural. Why don't you draw her aside and give her a couple of hours' worth?'

Stockstill said, 'Sending another patient to me, Bonny? I still recall the last one.' It was not hard to recall, because it had been the day the bomb had been dropped on the Bay Area. Years ago, he thought to himself. In another incarnation, as Hoppy would put it.

'You would have done him good,' Bonny said, 'if you had been able to treat him, but you just didn't have the time.'

'Thanks for sticking up for me,' he said, with a smile.

Mr Austurias said, 'By the way, Doctor, I observed some odd behavior on the part of our little phocomelus, today. I wanted to ask your opinion about him, when there's the opportunity. He perplexes me, I must admit . . . and I'm curious about him. The ability to survive against all odds – Hoppy certainly has that. It's encouraging, if you see what I mean, for the rest of us. If he can make it—' The school teacher broke off. 'But we must get inside.'

To Bonny, Stockstill said, 'Someone told me that Dangerfield mentioned your old buddy the other day.'

'Mentioned Bruno?' Bonny at once became alert. 'Is he still alive, is that it? I was sure he was.'

'No, that's not what Dangerfield said. He said something caustic about the first great accident. You recall. 1972.'

'Yes,' she said tightly. 'I recall.'

'Dangerfield, according to whoever told me—' Actually, he recalled perfectly well who had told him Dangerfield's *bon mot*; it had been June Raub, but he did not wish to antagonize Bonny any further. 'What he said was this. We're *all* living in Bruno's accident, now. We're all the spirit of '72. Of course, that's not so original; we've heard that said before. No doubt I've failed to capture the way Dangerfield said it . . . it's his style, of course, how he says things. No one can give things the twist he gives them.'

At the door of the Foresters' Hall, Mr Austurias had halted, had turned and was listening to them. Now he returned. 'Bonny,' he said, 'did you know Bruno Bluthgeld before the Emergency?'

'Yes,' she said. 'I worked at Livermore for a while.'

'He's dead now, of course,' Mr Austurias said.

'I've always thought he was alive somewhere,' Bonny said remotely. 'He was or is a great man, and the accident in '72 was not his fault; people who know nothing about it hold him responsible.'

Without a word, Mr Austurias turned his back on her, walked off up the steps of the Hall and disappeared inside.

'One thing about you,' Stockstill said to her, 'you can't be accused of concealing your opinions.'

'Someone has to tell people where to head in,' Bonny said. 'He's read in the newspapers all about Bruno. The newspapers. That's one thing that's better off, now; the newspapers are gone, unless you count that dumb little *News & Views*, which I don't. I will say this about Dangerfield, he isn't a liar.'

Together, she and Stockstill followed after Mr Austurias, with George and Edie following, into the mostly-filled Foresters' Hall, to listen to Dangerfield broadcasting down to them from the satellite.

As he sat listening to the static and the familiar voice, Mr Austurias thought to himself about Bruno Bluthgeld and how the physicist was possibly alive. Perhaps Bonny was right. She had known the man, and, from what he had overheard of her conversation with Stockstill (a risky act, these days, overhearing, but he could not resist it) she had sent Bluthgeld to the psychiatrist for treatment . . . which bore out one of his own very deeply held convictions: that Doctor Bruno Bluthgeld had been mentally disturbed during his last few years before the Emergency – had been palpably, dangerously insane, both in his private life and, what was more important, in his public life.

But there had really been no question of that. The public, in its own fashion, had been conscious that something fundamental was wrong with the man; in his public statements there had been an obsessiveness, a morbidity, a tormented expression that had drenched his face, convoluted his manner of speech. And Bluthgeld had talked about the enemy, with its infiltrating tactics, its systematic contamination of institutions at home, of schools and organizations – of the domestic life itself. Bluthgeld had seen the enemy everywhere, in books and in movies, in people, in political organizations that urged views contrary to his own. Of course, he had done it, put forth his views, in a learned way; he was not an ignorant man spouting and ranting in a backward Southern town. No, Bluthgeld had done it in a lofty, scholarly, educated, deeply-worked-out manner. And yet in the final analysis it was no more sane, no more rational or sober, than had been the drunken ramblings of the boozer and woman-chaser, Joe McCarthy, or of any of the others of them.

As a matter of fact, in his student days Mr Austurias had once met Joe McCarthy, and had found him likeable. But there had been nothing likeable about Bruno Bluthgeld, and Mr Austurias had met him too – had more than met him. He and Bluthgeld had both been at University of California at the same time; both had been on the staff, although of course Bluthgeld had been a full professor, chairman of his department, and Austurias had been only an instructor. But they had met and argued, had clashed both in private – in the corridors after class – and in public. And, in the end, Bluthgeld had engineered Mr Austurias' dismissal.

It had not been difficult, because Mr Austurias had sponsored all manner of little radical student groups devoted to peace with the Soviet Union and China, and such like causes, and in addition he had spoken out against bomb testing, which Doctor Bluthgeld advocated even after the catastrophe of 1972. He had in fact denounced the test of '72 and called it an example of psychotic thinking at top levels . . . a remark directed at Bluthgeld and no doubt so interpreted by him.

He who pokes at the serpent, Mr Austurias thought to

himself, runs the risk of being bitten . . . his dismissal had not surprised him but it had confirmed him more deeply in his views. And probably, if he thought of it at all, Doctor Bluthgeld had become more entrenched, too. But most likely Bluthgeld had never thought of the incident again; Austurias had been an obscure young instructor, and the University had not missed him – it had gone on as before, as no doubt had Bluthgeld.

I must talk to Bonny Keller about the man, he said to himself. I must find out all she knows, and it is never hard to get her to talk, so there will be no problem. And I wonder what Stockstill has to offer on the topic, he wondered. Surely if he saw Bluthgeld even once he would be in a position to confirm my own diagnosis, that of paranoid schizophrenia.

From the radio speaker, Walt Dangerfield's voice droned on in the reading from *Of Human Bondage*, and Mr Austurias began to pay attention, drawn, as always, by the powerful narrative. The problems which seemed vital to us, he thought, back in the old days . . . inability to escape from an unhappy human relationship. Now we prize *any* human relationship. We have learned a great deal.

Seated not far from the school teacher, Bonny Keller thought to herself, Another one looking for Bruno. Another one blaming him, making him the scapegoat for all that's happened. As if *one man* could bring about a world war and the deaths of millions, even if he wanted to.

You won't find him through me, she said to herself. I could help you a lot, but I won't, Mr Austurias. So go back to your little pile of coverless books; go back to your hunting mushrooms. Forget about Bruno Bluthgeld, or rather Mr Tree, as he calls himself now. As he has called himself since the day,

Five

Overcoat over his arm, Bruno Bluthgeld walked up Oxford Street, through the campus of the University of California, bent over and not looking about him; he knew the route well and he did not care to see the students, the young people. He was not interested in the passing cars, or in the buildings, so many of them new. He did not see the city of Berkeley because he was not interested in it. He was thinking, and it seemed to him very clearly now that he understood what it was that was making him sick. He did not doubt that he was sick; he felt deeply sick – it was only a question of locating the source of contamination.

It was, he thought, coming to him from the outside, this illness, the terrible infection that had sent him at last to Doctor Stockstill. Had the psychiatrist, on the basis of today's first visit, any valid theory? Bruno Bluthgeld doubted it.

And then, as he walked, he noticed that all the cross streets to the left leaned, as if the city was sinking on that side, as if gradually it was keeling over. Bluthgeld felt amused, because he recognized the distortion; it was his astigmatism, which became acute when he was under stress. Yes, he felt as if he were walking along a tilted sidewalk, raised on one side so that everything had a tendency to slide; he felt himself sliding very gradually, and he had trouble placing one foot before the other. He had a tendency to veer, to totter to the left, too, along with the other things.

Sense-data so vital, he thought. Not merely what you

perceive but how. He chuckled as he walked. Easy to lose your balance when you have an acute astigmatic condition, he said to himself. How pervasively the sense of balance enters into our awareness of the universe around us . . . hearing is derived from the sense of balance; it's an unrecognized basic sense underlying the others. Perhaps I have picked up a mild labyrinthitis, a virus infection of the middle ear. Should have it looked into.

And yes, now it – the distortion in his sense of balance – had begun affecting his hearing, as he had anticipated. It was fascinating, how the eye and the ear joined to produce a Gestalt; first his eyesight, then his balance, now he heard things askew.

He heard, as he walked, a dull, deep echo which rose from his own footsteps, from his shoes striking the pavement; not the sharp brisk noise that a woman's shoe might make, but a shadowy, low sound, a rumble, almost as if it rose from a pit or cave.

It was not a pleasant sound; it hurt his head, sending up reverberations that were acutely painful. He slowed, altered his pace, watched his shoes strike the pavement so as to anticipate the sound.

I know what this is due to, he said to himself. He had experienced it in the past, this echoing of normal noises in the labyrinths of his ear-passages. Like the distortion in vision it had a simple physiological basis, although for years it had puzzled and frightened him. It was due – simply – to tense posture, skeletal tension, specifically at the base of the neck. In fact, by turning his head from side to side, he could test his theory out; he heard the neck-vertebrae give a little crack, a short, sharp sound that set up immediately the most immensely painful reverberations in his ear-channels.

I must be dreadfully worried today, Bruno Bluthgeld said

to himself. For now an even graver alteration in his sense-perceptions was setting in, and one unfamiliar to him. A dull, smoky cast was beginning to settle over all the environment around him, making the buildings and cars seem like inert, gloomy mounds, without color or motion.

And where were the people? He seemed to be plodding along totally by himself in his listing, difficult journey up Oxford Street to where he had parked his Cadillac. Had they (odd thought) all gone indoors? As if, he thought, to get out of the rain . . . this rain of fine, sooty particles that seemed to fill the air, to impede his breathing, his sight, his progress.

He stopped. And, standing there at the intersection, seeing down the side street where it descended into a kind of darkness, and then off to the right where it rose and snapped off, as if twisted and broken, he saw to his amazement – and this he could not explain immediately in terms of some specific physiological impairment of function – that cracks had opened up. The buildings to his left had split. Jagged breaks in them, as if the hardest of substances, the cement itself which underlay the city, making up the streets and buildings, the very foundations around him, were coming apart.

Good Christ, he thought. What is it? He peered into the sooty fog; now the sky was gone, obscured entirely by the rain of dark.

And then he saw, picking about in the gloom, among the split sections of concrete, in the debris, little shriveled shapes: people, the pedestrians who had been there before and then vanished – they were back now, but all of them dwarfed, and gaping at him sightlessly, not speaking but simply poking about in an aimless manner.

What is it? he asked himself again, this time speaking aloud: he heard his voice dully rebounding. It's all broken; the town is broken up into pieces. What has hit it? What has happened to it? He began to walk from the pavement, finding his way among the strewn, severed parts of Berkeley. It isn't me, he realized; some great terrible catastrophe has happened. The noise, now, boomed in his ears, and the soot stirred, moved by the noise. A car horn sounded, stuck on, but very far off and faint.

Standing in the front of Modern TV, watching the television coverage of Walter and Mrs Dangerfield's flight, Stuart McConchie saw to his surprise the screen go blank.

'Lost their picture,' Lightheiser said, disgustedly. The group of people stirred with indignation. Lightheiser chewed on his toothpick.

'It'll come back on,' Stuart said, bending to switch to another channel; it was, after all, being covered by all networks.

All channels were blank. And there was no sound, either. He switched it once more. Still nothing.

Up from the basement came one of the repairmen, running toward the front of the store yelling, 'Red alert!'

'What's that?' Lightheiser said wonderingly, and his face became old and unhealthy-looking; seeing it, Stuart McConchie knew without the words or the thoughts ever occurring in his mind. He did not have to think; he knew, and he ran out of the store onto the street, he ran onto the empty sidewalk and stood, and the group of people at the TV set, seeing him and the repairman running, began to run, too, in different directions, some of them across the street, out into traffic, some of them in circles, some of them away in a straight line, as if each of them saw something different, as if it was not the same thing happening to any two of them.

Stuart and Lightheiser ran up the sidewalk to where the gray-green metal sidewalk doors were which opened onto the underground storage basement that once, a long time ago, a drugstore had used for its stock but which now was empty. Stuart tore at the metal doors, and so did Lightheiser, and both of them yelled that it wouldn't open; there was no way to open it except from below. At the entrance of the men's clothing store a clerk appeared, saw them; Lightheiser shouted at him, yelled for him to run downstairs and open up the sidewalk. 'Open the sidewalk!' Lightheiser yelled, and so did Stuart, and now so did several people all standing or squatting at the sidewalk doors, waiting for the sidewalk to open. So the clerk turned and ran back into the clothing store. A moment later a clanking noise sounded under Stuart's feet.

'Get back,' a heavy-set elderly man said. 'Get off the doors.' The people saw down into cold gloom, a cave under the sidewalk, an empty cavity. They all jumped down into it, falling to the bottom; they lay pressed against damp concrete, rolling themselves up into balls or flattening themselves out – they squirmed and pressed down into crumbly soil with the dead sowbugs and the smell of decay.

'Close it from above,' a man was saying. There did not seem to be any women, or if there were they were silent; his head pressed into a corner of the concrete, Stuart listened but heard only men, heard them as they grabbed at the doors above, trying to shut them. More people came down now, falling and tumbling and yelling, as if dumped from above.

'How long, oh Lord?' a man was saying.

Stuart said, 'Now.' He knew it was now; he knew that the bombs were going off – he felt them. It seemed to occur inside him. Blam, blam, blam, blam, went the bombs, or perhaps it was things sent up by the Army to help, to stop the bombs; perhaps it was defense. Let me down, Stuart thought. Low as I can be. Let me into the ground. He pressed down, rolled his body to make a depression. People lay now on top of him, choking coats and sleeves, and he was glad; he did not mind – he did not want emptiness around him; he wanted solidness on every side. He did not need to breathe. His eyes were shut; they, and the other openings of his body, his mouth and ears and nose, all had shut; he had walled himself in, waiting.

Blam, blam, blam.

The ground jumped.

We'll get by, Stuart said. Down here, safe in the earth. Safe inside where it's safe; it'll pass by overhead. The wind.

The wind, above on the surface, passed by at huge speed; he knew it moved up there, the air itself, driven along altogether, as a body.

In the nose cone of Dutchman IV, Walt Dangerfield, while still experiencing the pressure of many gravities on his body, heard in his earphones the voices from below, from the control bunker.

'Third stage successful, Walt. You're in orbit. We'll fire off the final stage at 15:45 instead of 15:44, they tell me.'

Orbital velocity, Dangerfield said to himself, straining to see his wife. She had lost consciousness; he looked away from her at once, concentrating on his oxygen supply, knowing she was all right but not wanting to witness her suffering. Okay, he thought, we're okay. In orbit, waiting for the final thrust. It wasn't so bad.

The voice in his earphones said, 'A perfect sequence so far, Walt. The President is standing by. You have eight minutes six seconds before the initial corrections for the fourth-stage firing. If in correcting minor—'

Static erased the voice; he no longer heard it.

If in correcting minor but vital errors in attitude, Walter Dangerfield said to himself, there is a lack of complete success, we will be brought back down, as they did before in the robot-runs. And later on we will try it again. There is no danger; reentry is an old story. He waited.

The voice in his earphones came on again. '*Walter, we are under attack down here.*'

'What?' he said. 'What did you say?'

'God save us,' the voice said. It was a man already dead; the voice had no feeling, it was empty and then it was silent. Gone.

'From whom?' Walt Dangerfield said into his microphone. He thought of pickets and rioters, he thought of bricks, angry mobs. Attacked by nuts or something, is that it?

He struggled up, disconnected himself from the straps, saw through the port the world below. Clouds, and the ocean, the globe itself. Here and there on it matches were lit; he saw the puffs, the flares. Fright overcame him, as he sailed silently through space, looking down at the pinches of burning scattered about; he knew what they were.

It's death, he thought. Death lighting up spots, burning up the world's life, second by second.

He continued to watch.

There was, Doctor Stockstill knew, a community shelter under one of the big banks, but he could not remember which one. Taking his secretary by the hand he ran from the building and across Center Street, searching for the black and white sign that he had noticed a thousand times, that had become part of the perpetual background of his daily business existence on the public street. The sign had merged into the unchanging, and now he needed it; he wanted it to step forward so that he could notice it as he had at the beginning: as a real sign, meaning something vital, something by which to preserve his life.

It was his secretary, tugging at his arm, who pointed the

way to him; she yelled in his ear over and over again and he saw – he turned in that direction and together they crossed the street, running out into the dead, stalled traffic and among the pedestrians, and then they were struggling and fighting to get into the shelter, which was the basement of the building.

As he burrowed down, lower and lower, into the basement shelter and the mass of people pressed together in it, he thought about the patient whom he had just seen; he thought about Mr Tree and in his mind a voice said with clarity, you did this. See what you did, you've killed us all.

His secretary had become separated from him and he was alone with people he did not know, breathing into their faces and being breathed on. And all the time he heard a wailing, the noise of women and probably their small children, shoppers who had come in here from the department stores, midday mothers. Are the doors shut? he wondered. Has it begun? It has; the moment has. He closed his eyes and began to pray out loud, noisily, trying to hear the sound. But the sound was lost.

'Stop that racket,' someone, a woman, said in his ear, so close that his ear hurt. He opened his eyes; the woman, middle-aged, glared at him, as if this was all that mattered, as if nothing was happening except his noisy praying. Her attention was directed on stopping him, and in surprise he stopped.

Is that what you care about? he wondered, awed by her, by the narrowness of her attention, by its mad constrictedness. 'Sure,' he said to her. 'You damn fool,' he said, but she did not hear him. 'Was I bothering you?' he went on, unheeded; she was now glaring at someone else who had bumped or shoved her. 'Sorry,' he said. 'Sorry, you stupid old crow, you—' He cursed at the woman, cursing instead of praying and feeling more relief by that; he got more out of that.

And then, in the middle of his cursing, he had a weird,

vivid notion. The war had begun and they were being bombed and would probably die, but it was Washington that was dropping the bombs on them, not the Chinese or the Russians; something had gone wrong with an automatic defense system out in space, and it was acting out its cycle this way – and no one could halt it, either. It was war and death, yes, but it was error; it lacked intent. He did not feel any hostility from the forces overhead. They were not vengeful or motivated; they were empty, hollow, completely cold. It was as if his car had run over him: it was real but meaningless. It was not policy, it was breakdown and failure, chance.

So at this moment, he felt himself devoid of retaliatory hatred for the enemy because he could not imagine – did not actually believe in or even understand – the concept. It was as if the previous patient, Mr Tree or Doctor Bluthgeld or whoever he had been, had taken in, absorbed all that, left none of it for anyone else. Bluthgeld had made Stockstill over into a different person, one who could not think that way even now. Bluthgeld, by being insane, had made the concept of *the enemy* unbelievable.

'We'll fight back, we'll fight back, we'll fight back,' a man near Doctor Stockstill was chanting. Stockstill looked at him in astonishment, wondering who he would fight back against. Things were falling on them; did the man intend to fall back upward into the sky in some kind of revenge? Would he reverse the natural forces at work, as if rolling a film-sequence backward? It was a peculiar, nonsensical idea. It was as if the man had been gripped by his unconscious. He was no longer living a rational, ego-directed existence; he had surrendered to some archetype.

The impersonal, Doctor Stockstill thought, has attacked us. That is what it is; attacked us from inside and out. The end of the cooperation, where we applied ourselves together. Now it's atoms only. Discrete, without any windows. Colliding but not making any sound, just a general hum.

He put his fingers in his ears, trying not to hear the noises from around him. The noises appeared – absurdly – to be below him, rising instead of descending. He wanted to laugh.

Jim Fergesson, when the attack began, had just gone downstairs into the repair department of Modern TV. Facing Hoppy Harrington he saw the expression on the phocomelus' face when the red alert was announced over the FM radio and the conalrad system went at once into effect. He saw on the lean, bony face a grin like that of greed, as if in hearing and understanding, Hoppy was filled with joy, the joy of life itself. He had become lit up for an instant, had thrown off everything that inhibited him or held him to the surface of the earth, every force that made him slow. His eyes burst into light and his lips twitched; he seemed to be sticking out his tongue, as if mocking Fergesson.

To him Fergesson said, 'You dirty little freak.'

The phoce yelled, 'It's the end!' The look on his face was already gone. Perhaps he had not even heard what Fergesson had said; he seemed to be in a state of self-absorption. He shivered, and the artificial manual extensors emanating from his cart danced and flicked like whips.

'Now listen,' Fergesson said. 'We're below street-level.' He caught hold of the repairman, Bob Rubenstein. 'You moronic jackass, stay where you are. I'll go upstairs and get those people down here. You clear as much space as you can; make space for them.' He let go of the repairman and ran to the stairs.

As he started up the steps two at a time, clutching the handrail and using it as a fulcrum, something happened to his legs. The bottom part of him fell off and he pitched backward, rolled back and down, and onto him rained tons of white plaster. His head hit the concrete floor and he knew that the building had been hit, taken away, and the people were gone. He was hurt, too, cut into two pieces, and only Hoppy and Bob Rubenstein would survive and maybe not even they.

He tried to speak but could not.

Still at the repair bench Hoppy felt the concussion and saw the doorway fill up with pieces of the ceiling and the wood of the steps turned into flying fragments and among the fragments of wood something soft, bits of flesh; if the pieces were Fergesson – he was dead. The building shook and boomed, as if doors were shutting. We're shut in, Hoppy realized. The overhead light popped, and now he saw nothing. Blackness. Bob Rubenstein was screeching.

The phoce wheeled his cart backward, into the black cavity of the basement, going by the touch of his extensors. He felt his way among the stock inventory, the big television sets in their cardboard cartons; he got as deep as possible, slowly and carefully burrowed in all the way to the back as far from the entrance as he could. Nothing fell on him. Fergesson had been right. This was safe, here, below the street level. Upstairs they were all rags of flesh mixed with the white, dry powder that had been the building, but here it was different.

Just not time, he thought. They told us and then it began; it's still going on. He could feel the wind moving over the surface upstairs; it moved unimpeded, because everything which had stood was now down. We must not go up even later, because of radiation, he realized. That was the mistake those Japs made; they came right up and smiled.

How long will I live down here? he wondered. A month? No water, unless a pipe breaks. No air after a while, unless molecules filtering through the debris. Still, better than trying to come out. I will not come out, he reiterated. I know better; I'm not dumb like the others.

Now he heard nothing. No concussion, no rain of falling pieces in the darkness around him: small objects jarred loose from stacks and from shelves. Just silence. He did not hear Bob Rubenstein. Matches. From his pocket he got matches, lit one; he saw that TV cartons had toppled to enclose him. He was alone, in a space of his own.

Oh boy, he said to himself with exultation. Am I lucky; this space was just made for me. I'll stay and stay; I can go days and then be alive, I know I was *intended* to be alive. Fergesson was intended to die right off the bat. It's God's will. God knows what to do; He watches out, there is no chance about this. All this, a great cleansing of the world. Room must be made, new space for people, for instance myself.

He put out the match and the darkness returned; he did not mind it. Waiting, in the middle of his cart, he thought, this is my chance, it was made for me deliberately. It'll be different when I emerge. Destiny at work from the start, back before I was born. Now I understand it all, my being so different from the others; I see the reason.

How much time has passed? he wondered presently. He had begun to become impatient. An hour? I can't stand to wait, he realized. I mean, I have to wait, but I wish it would hurry up. He listened for the possible sound of people overhead, rescue teams from the Army beginning to dig people out, but not yet; nothing so far.

I hope it isn't too long, he said to himself. There's lots to do; I have work ahead of me.

When I get out of here I have to get started and organize, because that's what will be needed: organization and direction; everyone will be milling around. Maybe I can plan now.

In the darkness he planned. All manner of inspirations came to him; he was not wasting his time, not being idle just because he had to be stationary. His head wildly rang with original notions; he could hardly wait, thinking about them and how they would work when tried out. Most of them had to do with ways of survival. No one would be dependent on big society; it would all be small towns and individuality, like Ayn Rand talked about in her books. It would be the end of conformity and the mass mind and junk; no more factory-produced junk, like the cartons of color 3-D television sets which had fallen on all sides of him.

His heart pounded with excitement and impatience; he could hardly stand waiting – it was like a million years already. And still they hadn't found him yet, even though they were busy looking. He knew that; he could feel them at work, getting nearer.

'Hurry!' he exclaimed aloud, lashing his manual extensors; the tips scratched against the TV cartons, making a dull sound. In his impatience he began to beat on the cartons. The drumming filled the darkness, as if there were many living things imprisoned, an entire nest of people, not just Hoppy Harrington alone.

In her hillside home in West Marin County, Bonny Keller realized that the classical music on the stereo set in the living room had gone off. She emerged from the bedroom, wiping the water color paint from her hands and wondering if the same tube as before had – as George put it – cut out.

And then through the window she saw against the sky to the south a stout trunk of smoke, as dense and brown as a living stump. She gaped at it, and then the window burst; it pulverized and she crashed back and slid across the floor along with the powdery fragments of it. Every object in the house tumbled, fell and shattered and then skidded with her, as if the house had tilted on end.

The San Andreas Fault, she knew. Terrible earthquake, like

back eighty years ago; all we've built . . . all ruined. Spinning, she banged into the far wall of the house, only now it was level and the floor had raised up; she saw lamps and tables and chairs raining down and smashing, and it was amazing to her how flimsy everything was. She could not understand how things she had owned for years could break so easily; only the wall itself, now beneath her, remained as something hard.

My house, she thought. Gone. Everything that's mine, that means something to me. Oh, it isn't fair.

Her head ached as she lay panting; she smoothed herself, saw her hands white and covered with fine powder and trembling – blood streaked her wrist, from some cut she could not make out. On my head, she thought. She rubbed her forehead, and bits of material fell from her hair. Now – she could not understand it – the floor was flat again, the wall was upright as it had always been. Back to normal. But the objects; they were all broken. That remained. The garbage house, she thought. It'll take weeks, months. We'll never build back. It's the end of our life, our happiness.

Standing, she walked about; she kicked the pieces of a chair aside. She kicked through the trash, toward the door. The air swirled with particles and she inhaled them; she choked on them, hating them. Glass everywhere, all her lovely plate glass windows gone. Empty square holes with a few shards which still broke loose and dropped even as she watched. She found a door – it had been bent open. Shoving it, putting her weight against it, she made it move aside so that she could go unsteadily out of the house to stand a few yards away, surveying what had happened.

Her headache had become worse. Am I blinded? she wondered; it was hard to keep her eyes open. Did I see a light? She had a memory of one click of light, like a camera shutter opening so suddenly, so swiftly, that her optic nerves had not responded – she had not really *seen* it. And yet, her eyes were hurt; she felt the injury there. Her body, all of her, seemed damaged, and no wonder. But the ground. She did not see any fissure. And the house stood; only the windows and the household goods had been destroyed. The structure, the empty container, remained with nothing left in it.

Walking slowly along, she thought, I better go get help. I need medical help. And then, as she stumbled and half fell, she looked around her, up into the air, and saw once again the column of brown smoke from the south. Did San Francisco catch fire already? she asked herself.

It's burning, she decided. It's a calamity. The city got it, not just West Marin, here. Not just a few rural people up here, but all the city people; there must be thousands dead. They'll have to declare a national emergency and get the Red Cross and Army; we'll remember this to the day we die. Walking, she began to cry, holding her hands to her face, not seeing where she was going, not caring. She did not cry for herself or her ruined house now; she cried for the city to the south. She cried for all the people and things in it and what had happened to them.

I'll never see it again, she knew. There is no more San Francisco; it is over. The end had come about, today. Crying, she wandered on in the general direction of town; already she could hear people's voices, rising up from the flatland below. Going by the sound she moved that way.

A car drew up beside her. The door opened; a man reached out for her. She did not even know if he lived around here or if he was passing through. Anyhow, she hugged him.

'All right,' the man said, squeezing her around the waist.

Sobbing, she struggled closer to him, pressing herself against the car seat and drawing him over her.

Later, she once more found herself walking, this time down

a narrow road with oak trees, the gnarled old live oaks which she loved so much, on both sides of her. The sky overhead was bleak and gray, swept by heavy clouds which drifted in monotonous procession toward the north. This must be Bear Valley Ranch Road, she said to herself. Her feet hurt and when she stopped she discovered that she was barefoot; somewhere along the way she had lost her shoes.

She still wore the paint-splattered jeans which she had had on when the quake had happened, when the radio had gone off. Or had it really been a quake after all? The man in the car, frightened and babbling like a baby, had said something else, but it had been too garbled, too full of panic, for her to understand.

I want to go home, she said to herself. I want to be back in my own home and I want my shoes. I'll bet that man took them; I'll bet they're back in his car. And I'll never see them again.

She plodded on, wincing at the pain, wishing she could find somebody, wondering about the sky overhead and becoming more lonely with each passing moment.

Six

Driving his Volkswagen bus away, Andrew Gill caught one last sight of the woman in the paint-spattered jeans and sweater whom he had just let off; he watched her as she trudged barefoot along the road and then he lost her as his bus passed a bend. He did not know her name but it seemed to him that she was about the prettiest woman he had ever seen, with her red hair and small, delicately-formed feet. And, he thought to himself in a daze, he and she had just now made love, in the back of his VW bus.

It was, to him, a pageant of figments, the woman and the great explosions from the south that had torn up the countryside and raised the sky of gray overhead. He knew that it was war of some sort or at least a bad event of some modern kind entirely new to the world and to his experience.

He had, that morning, driven from his shop in Petaluma to West Marin to deliver to the pharmacy at Point Reyes Station a load of imported English briar pipes. His business was fine liquors – especially wines – and tobaccos, everything for the serious smoker including little nickel-plated devices for cleaning pipes and tamping the tobacco down. Now as he drove he wondered how his shop was; had the event encompassed the Petaluma area?

I had better get the hell back there and see how it is, he said to himself, and then he thought once again of the small red-haired woman in the jeans who had hopped into his bus – or allowed him to draw her into it; he no longer was certain which had happened – and it seemed to him that he ought to drive after her and make sure she was all right. Does she live around here? he asked himself. And how do I find her again? Already he wanted to find her again; he had never met or seen anyone like her. And did she do it because of shock? he wondered. Was she in her right mind at the time? Had she ever done such a thing before . . . and, more important, would she ever do it again?

However, he kept on going, not turning back; his hands felt numb, as if they were lifeless. He was exhausted. I know there's going to be other bombs or explosions, he said to himself. They landed one on the Bay Area and they'll keep shooting them off at us. In the sky overhead he saw now flashes of light in quick succession and then, after a time, a distant rumble seized his bus and made it buck and quake. Bombs going off up there, he decided. Maybe our defenses. But there will be more getting through.

Then, too, there was the radiation.

Drifting, overhead, now, the clouds of what he knew to be deadly radiation passed on north, and did not seem to be low enough yet to affect life on the surface, his life and that of the bushes and trees along the road. Maybe we'll wither and die in another few days, he thought. Maybe it's only a question of time. Is it worth hiding? Should I head north, try to escape? But the clouds were moving north. I better stay here, he said to himself, and try to find some local shelter. I think I read somewhere once that this is a protected spot; the winds blow on past West Marin and go inland, toward Sacramento.

And still he saw no one. Only the girl – the only person he had seen since the first great bomb and the realization of what it meant. No cars. No people on foot. They'll be showing up from down below pretty soon, he reasoned. By the thousands. And dying as they go. Refugees. Maybe I should get ready to help. But all he had in his VW truck were pipes and cans of tobacco and bottles of California wine from small vintners; he had no medical supplies and no know-how. And anyhow he was over fifty years old and he had a chronic heart problem called paroxysmal tachycardia. It was a wonder, in fact, that he had not had an attack of it back there when he was making love with the girl.

My wife and the two kids, he thought. Maybe they're dead. I just have to get back to Petaluma. A phone call? Absurd. The phones are certainly out. And still he drove on, pointlessly, not knowing where to go or what to do. Not knowing how much danger he was in, if the attack by the enemy was over or if this was just the start. I could be wiped out any second, he realized.

But he felt safe in the familiar VW bus, which he had owned for six years now. It had not been changed by what had happened; it was sturdy and reliable, whereas – he felt – the world, the rest of things, all had undergone a permanent, dreadful metamorphosis.

He did not wish to look.

What if Barbara and the boys are dead? he asked himself. Oddly, the idea carried with it the breath of release. A new life, as witness me meeting that girl. The old is all over; won't tobacco and wines be very valuable now? Don't I in actual fact have a fortune here in this bus? I don't have to go back to Petaluma ever; I can disappear, and Barbara will never be able to find me. He felt buoyed up, cheerful, now.

But that would mean – God forbid – he would have to abandon his shop, and that was a horrible notion, overlain with the sense of peril and isolation. I can't give that up, he decided. That represents twenty years of gradually building up a good customer relationship, of genuinely finding out people's wants and serving them.

However, he thought, those people are possibly dead now,

along with my family. I have to face it: *everything* has changed, not merely the things I don't care for.

Driving slowly along, he tried to cogitate over each possibility, but the more he cogitated the more confused and uneasy he became. I don't think any of us will survive, he decided. We probably all have radiation exposure; my relationship with that girl is the last notable event in my life, and the same for her – she is no doubt doomed too.

Christ, he thought bitterly. Some numbskull in the Pentagon is responsible for this; we should have had two or three hours warning, and instead we got – five minutes. At the most!

He felt no animosity toward the enemy now; he felt only a sense of shame, a sense of betrayal. Those military saps in Washington are probably safe and sound down in their concrete bunkers, like Adolf Hitler at the end, he decided. And we're left up here to die. It embarrassed him; it was awful.

Suddenly he noticed that on the seat beside him lay two empty shoes, two worn slippers. The girl's. He sighed, feeling weary. Some memento, he thought with gloom.

And then he thought in excitement, It's not a memento; it's a sign – for me to stay here in West Marin, to begin all over again here. If I stay here I'll run into her again; I know I will. It's just a question of being patient. That's why she left her shoes; she already knew it, that I'm just beginning my life here, that after what's happened I won't – can't – leave. The hell with my shop, with my wife and children, in Petaluma.

As he drove along he began to whistle with relief and glee.

There was no doubt in the mind of Bruno Bluthgeld now; he saw the unceasing stream of cars all going one way, going north toward the highway that emptied into the countryside. Berkeley had become a sieve, out of which at every hole leaked the people pressing upward from beneath, the people from Oakland and San Leandro and San Jose; they were all passing through along the streets that had become one-way streets, now. It's not me, Doctor Bluthgeld said to himself as he stood on the sidewalk, unable to cross the street to get to his own car. And yet, he realized, even though it is real, even though it is the end of everything, the destruction of the cities and the people on every side, I am responsible.

He thought, In some way I made it happen.

I must make amends, he told himself. He clasped his hands together, tense with concern. It must un-happen, he realized. I must shut it back off.

What has happened is this, he decided. They were developing their arrangements to injure me but they hadn't counted on my ability, which in me seems to lie partly in the subconscious. I have only a dubious control over it; it emanates from suprapersonal levels, what Jung would call the collective unconscious. They didn't take into account the almost limitless potency of my reactive psychic energy, and now it's flowed back out at them in response to their arrangements. I didn't will it to; it simply followed a psychic law of stimulus and response, but I must take moral responsibility for it anyhow, because it is I, the greater I, the Self, which transcends the conscious ego. I must wrestle with it, now that it's done its work contra the others. Surely it has done enough; isn't, in fact, the damage too great?

But no, it was not too great, in the pure physical sense, the pure realm of action and reaction. A law of conservation of energy, a parity, was involved; his collective unconscious had responded commensurate to the harm intended by the others. Now, however, it was time to atone for it; that was, logically, the next step. It had expended itself . . . or had it? He felt doubt and a deep confusion; had the reactive process, his metabiological defense system, completed its cycle of response, *or was there more?*

He sniffed the atmosphere, trying to anticipate. The sky, an admixture of particles: debris light enough to be carried. What lay behind it, concealed as in a womb? The womb, he thought, of pure essence within me, as I stand here debating. I wonder if these people driving by in these cars, these men and women with their blank faces – I wonder if they know *who I am*. Are they aware that I am the omphalos, the center, of all this cataclysmic disruption? He watched the passing people, and presently he knew the answer; they were quite aware of him, that he was the source of this all, but they were afraid to attempt any injury in his direction. They had learned their lesson.

Raising his hand toward them he called, 'Don't worry; there won't be any more. I promise.'

Did they understand and believe him? He felt their thoughts directed at him, their panic, their pain, and also their hatred toward him now held in abeyance by the tremendous demonstration of what he could accomplish. I know how you feel, he thought back, or perhaps said aloud – he could not tell which. You have learned a hard, bitter lesson. And so have I. I must watch myself more carefully; in the future I must guard my powers with a greater awe, a greater reverence at the trust placed in my hands.

Where should I go now? he questioned himself. Away from here, so that this will gradually die down of its own accord? For their sakes; it would be a good idea, a kind, humane, equitable solution.

Can I leave? he asked himself. Of course. Because the forces at work were, to at least some extent, disposable; he could summon them, once he was aware of them, as he was now. What had been wrong before had simply been his ignorance of them. Perhaps, through intense psychoanalysis, he would have gotten to them in time, and this great disturbance might have been avoided. But too late to worry about that now. He began to walk back the way he had come. I can pass over this traffic and absent myself from this region, he assured himself. To prove it, he stepped from the curb, out into the solid stream of cars; other people were doing so, too, other individuals on foot, many of them carrying household goods, books, lamps, even a bird in a cage or a cat. He joined them, waving to them to indicate that they should cross with him, follow him because he could pass on through at will.

The traffic had almost halted. It appeared to be due to cars forcing their way in from a side street ahead, but he knew better; that was only the apparent cause – the genuine cause was his desire to cross. An opening between two cars lay directly ahead, and Doctor Bluthgeld led the group of people on foot across to the far side.

Where do I want to go? he asked himself, ignoring the thanks of the people around him; they were all trying to tell him how much they owed him. Out into the country, away from the city? I am dangerous to the city, he realized. I should go fifty or sixty miles to the east, perhaps all the way to the Sierras, to some remote spot. West Marin; I could go back up there. Bonny is up there. I could stay with her and George. I think that would be far enough away, but if it is not I will continue on – I must absent myself from these people, who do not deserve to be punished any further. If necessary, I will continue on forever; I will never stop in one place.

Of course, he realized, I can't get to West Marin by car; none of these cars are moving or are ever going to move again. The congestion is too great. And the Richardson Bridge is certainly gone. I will have to walk; it will take days, but eventually I will make it there. I will go up to the Black Point Road, up toward Vallejo, and follow the route across the sloughs. The land is flat; I can cut directly across the fields if necessary.

In any case it's a penance for what I've done. This will be a voluntary pilgrimage, a way of healing the soul.

He walked, and as he did so he concentrated on the damage about him; he viewed it with the idea of healing it, of restoring the city, if at all possible, to its pure state. When he came to a building that had collapsed he paused and said, *Let this building be restored*. When he saw injured people he said, *Let these people be adjudged innocent and so forgiven*. Each time, he made a motion with his hand which he had devised; it indicated his determination to see that things such as this did not recur. Perhaps they have learned a permanent lesson, he thought. They may leave me alone, now.

But, it occurred to him, perhaps they would go in the opposite direction; they would, after they had dragged themselves from the ruins of their houses, develop an even greater determination to destroy him. This might in the long run increase, rather than dispel, their animosity.

He felt frightened, thinking about their vengeance. Maybe I should go into hiding, he thought. Keep the name 'Mr Tree,' or use some other fictive name for purposes of concealment. Right now they are wary of me . . . but I'm afraid it will not last.

And yet, even knowing that, he still continued to make his special sign to them as he walked along. He still bent his efforts to achieving a restoration for them. His own emotions contained no hostility; he was free of that. It was only they who harbored any hate.

★

At the edge of the Bay, Doctor Bluthgeld emerged from the traffic to see the white, shattered, glass-like city of San Francisco lying everywhere on the far side of the water. Nothing stood. Overhead, smoke and yellow fire manifested themselves in a way that he could not believe. It was as if the city had become a stick of stove wood, incinerated without leaving a trace. And yet there were people coming out of it. He saw, on the water, bobbing chunks; the people had floated every kind of object out, and were clinging to them, trying to push across to Marin County.

Doctor Bluthgeld stood there, unable to go on, his pilgrimage forgotten. First he had to cure them, and then if possible cure the city itself. He forgot his own needs. He concentrated on the city, using both hands, making new gestures which he had never hit on before he tried everything, and after a long time he saw the smoke begin to clear. That gave him hope. But the people bobbing across, escaping, began to diminish in number; he saw fewer and fewer until the bay was empty of them, and only naked debris remained.

So he concentrated then on saving the people themselves; he thought of the escape routes north, where the people should go and what they would need to find. Water, first of all, and then rations. He thought of the Army bringing in supplies, and the Red Cross; he thought of small towns in the country making their possessions available. Finally, what he willed began reluctantly to come to pass, and he remained where he was a long time, getting it to be. Things improved. The people found treatment for burns; he saw to that. He saw, too, to the healing of their great fear; that was important. He saw to the first glimmerings of their getting themselves established once more, in at least a rudimentary way.

But curiously, at the same time that he devoted himself to improving their condition, he noticed to his surprise and shock that his own had deteriorated. He had lost everything in the service of the general welfare, because now his clothes were in rags, like sacks. His toes poked through his shoes. On his face a ragged beard hung down; a mustache had grown over his mouth, and his hair fell all the way over his ears and brushed his torn collar, and his teeth – even his teeth – were gone. He felt old and sick and empty, but nonetheless it was worth it. How long had he stood here, doing this job? The streams of cars had long since ceased. Only damaged, abandoned wrecks of autos lay along the freeway to his right. Had it been weeks? Possibly months. He felt hungry, and his legs trembled with the cold. So once more he began to walk.

I gave them everything I had, he told himself, and thinking that he felt a little resentment, more than a trace of anger. What did I get back? I need a haircut and a meal and medical attention; I need a few things myself. Where can I get them? Now, he thought, I'm too tired to walk to Marin County; I'll have to stay here, on this side of the Bay, for a while, until I can rest up and get my strength back. His resentment grew as he walked slowly along.

But anyhow he had done his job. He saw, not far ahead, a first aid station with rows of dingy tents; he saw women with armbands and knew they were nurses. He saw men with metal helmets carrying guns. Law and order, he realized. Because of my efforts it's been reestablished, here and there. They owe me a lot, but of course they don't acknowledge it. I'll let it pass, he decided.

When he reached the first dingy tent, one of the men with guns stopped him. Another man, carrying a clipboard, approached. Where are you from? The man with the clipboard asked.

'From Berkeley,' he answered.

'Name.'

'Mr Jack Tree.'

They wrote that down, then tore off a card and handed it to him. It had a number on it, and the two men explained that he should keep the number because without it he could not obtain food rations. Then he was told that if he tried – or had tried – to collect rations at another relief station he would be shot. The two men then walked off, leaving him standing there with his numbered card in his hand.

Should I tell them that I did all this? he wondered. That I'm solely responsible, and eternally damned for my dreadful sin in bringing this about? No, he decided, because if I do they'll take my card back; I won't get any food ration. And he was terribly, terribly hungry.

Now one of the nurses approached him and in a matter of fact voice said, 'Any vomiting, dizziness, change of color of the stool?'

'No,' he said.

'Any superficial burns which have failed to heal?'

He shook his head no.

'Go over there,' the nurse said, pointing, 'and get rid of your clothing. They'll delouse you and shave your head, and you can get your shots there. We're out of the typhoid serum so don't ask for that.'

To his bewilderment he saw a man with an electric razor powered by a gasoline generator shaving the heads of men and women both; the people waited patiently in line. A sanitary measure? he wondered.

I thought I had fixed that, he thought. Or did I forget about disease. Evidently I did. He began to walk in that direction, bewildered by his failure to have taken everything into account. I must have left out a variety of vital things, he realized as he joined the line of people waiting to have their heads shaved.

*

In the ruins of a cement basement of a house on Cedar Street in the Berkeley hills, Stuart McConchie spied something fat and gray that hopped from one split block and behind the next. He picked up his broom handle – one end came to a cracked, elongated point – and wriggled forward.

The man with him in the basement, a sallow, lean man named Ken, who was dying of radiation exposure, said, 'You're not going to eat that.'

'Sure I am,' Stuart said, wriggling through the dust which had settled into the open, exposed basement until he lay against the split block of cement. The rat, aware of him, squeaked with fear. It had come up from the Berkeley sewer and now it wanted to get back. But he was between it and the sewer; or rather, he thought, between her and the sewer. It was no doubt a big female. The males were skinnier.

The rat scurried in fright, and Stuart drove the sharp end of the stick into it. Again it squeaked, long and sufferingly. On the end of the stick it was still alive; it kept on squeaking. So he held it against the ground, held the stick down, and crushed its head with his foot.

'At least,' the dying man with him said, 'you can cook it.'

'No,' Stuart said, and, seating himself, got out the pocket knife which he had found – it had been in the pants pocket of a dead school boy – and began skinning the rat. While the dying man watched with disapproval, Stuart ate the dead, raw rat.

'I'm surprised you don't eat me,' the man said, afterward.

'It's no worse than eating raw shrimp,' Stuart said. He felt much better now; it was his first food in days.

'Why don't you go looking for one of those relief stations that helicopter was talking about when it flew by yesterday?' the dying man said. 'It said – or I understood it to say – that there's a station over near the Hillside Grammar School. That's only a few blocks from here; you could get that far.'

'No,' Stuart said.

'Why not?'

The answer, although he did not want to say it, was simply that he was afraid to venture out of the basement onto the street. He did not know why, except that there were things moving in the settling ash which he could not identify; he believed they were Americans but possibly they were Chinese or Russians. Their voices sounded strange and echoey, even in daytime. And the helicopter, too; he was not certain about that. It could have been an enemy trick to induce people to come out and be shot. In any case he still heard gunfire from the flat part of the city; the dim sounds started before the sun rose and occurred intermittently until nightfall.

'You can't stay here forever,' Ken said. 'It isn't rational.' He lay wrapped up in the blankets which had belonged to one of the beds in the house; the bed had been hurled from the house as the house disintegrated, and Stuart and the dying man had found it in the backyard. Its neatly tucked-in covers had been still on it, all in place including its two duck-feather pillows.

What Stuart was thinking was that in five days he had collected thousands of dollars in money from the pockets of dead people he had found in the ruins of houses along Cedar Street – from their pockets and from the houses themselves. Other scavengers had been after food and different objects such as knives and guns, and it made him uneasy that he alone wanted money. He felt, now, that if he stirred forth, if he reached a relief station, he would discover the truth: the money was worthless. And if it was he was a horse's ass for collecting it, and when he showed up at the relief station carrying a pillowcase full of it, everyone would jeer at him and rightly so, because a horse's ass deserved to be jeered at.

And also, no one else seemed to be eating rats. Perhaps there was a superior food available of which he knew nothing; it sounded like him, down here eating something everyone else had discarded. Maybe there were cans of emergency rations being dropped from the air; maybe the cans came down early in the morning while he was still asleep and got all picked up before he had a chance to see them. He had had for several days now a deep and growing dread that he was missing out, that something free was being dispensed – perhaps in broad daylight – to everyone but him. Just my luck, he said to himself, and he felt glum and bitter, and the rat, which he had just eaten, no longer seemed a surfeit, as before.

Hiding, these last few days, down in the ruined cement basement of the house on Cedar Street, Stuart had had a good deal of time to think about himself, and he had realized that it had always been hard for him to make out what other people were doing; it had only been by the greatest effort that he had managed to act as they acted, appear like them. It had nothing to do, either, with his being a Negro because he had the same problem with black people as with white. It was not a social difficulty in the usual sense; it went deeper than that. For instance, Ken, the dying man lying opposite him. Stuart could not understand him; he felt cut off from him. Maybe that was because Ken was dying and he was not. Maybe that set up a barrier; the world was clearly divided into two new camps now: people who were getting weaker with each passing moment, who were perishing, and people like himself, who were going to make it. There was no possibility of communication between them because their worlds were too different.

And yet that was not it only, between himself and Ken; there was still more, the same old problem that the bomb attack had not created but merely brought to the surface. Now the gulf was wider; it was obvious that he did not actually comprehend the meaning of most activities conducted around him . . . he had been brooding, for instance, about the yearly trip to the Department of Motor Vehicles for his auto license renewal. As he lay in the basement it seemed to him more clearly each moment that the other people had gone to the Department of Motor Vehicles office over on Sacramento Street for a *good reason*, but he had gone because they had gone; he had, like a littler kid, merely tagged along. And now there was no one present to tag after; now he was alone. And therefore he could not think up any action to follow, he could not make any decision or follow any plan for the life of him.

So he simply waited, and as he waited, wondered about the 'copter which flew overhead now and then and about the vague shapes in the street, and more than anything else if he was a horse's ass or not.

And then, all at once, he thought of something; he remembered what Hoppy Harrington had seen in his vision at Fred's Fine Foods. Hoppy had seen him, Stuart McConchie, eating rats, but in the excitement and fear of all that had happened since, Stuart had forgotten. This now was what the phoce had seen; this was the vision – not the afterlife at all!

God damn that little crippled freak, Stuart thought to himself as he lay picking his teeth with a piece of wire. He was a fraud; he put something over on us.

Amazing how gullible people are, he said to himself. We believed him, maybe because he's so peculiarly built anyhow . . . it seemed more credible with him being like he is – or was. He's probably dead now, buried down in the service department. Well, that's one good thing this war has done: wiped out all the freaks. But then, he realized, it's also brewed up a whole new batch of them; there'll be freaks strutting around for the next million years. It'll be Bluthgeld's paradise;

in fact he's probably quite happy right now – because this was really bomb testing.

Ken stirred and murmured, 'Could you be induced to crawl across the street? There's that corpse there and it might have cigarettes on it.'

Cigarettes, hell, Stuart thought. It probably has a walletful of money. He followed the dying man's gaze and saw, sure enough, the corpse of a woman lying among the rubble on the far side. His pulse raced, because he could see a bulging handbag still clutched.

In a weary voice Ken said, 'Leave the money, Stuart. It's an obsession with you, a symbol of God knows what.' As Stuart crawled out from the basement Ken raised his voice to call, 'A symbol of the opulent society.' He coughed, retched. 'And that's gone now,' he managed to add.

Up yours, Stuart thought as he crawled on across the street to the purse lying there. Sure enough, when he opened it he found a wad of bills, ones and fives and even a twenty. There was also a U-No candy bar in the purse, and he got that, too. But as he crawled back to the basement it occurred to him that the candy bar might be radioactive, so he tossed it away.

'The cigarettes?' Ken asked, when he returned.

'None.' Stuart opened the pillow case, which was buried up to its throat in the dry ash which had filled the basement; he stuffed the bills in with the others and tied the pillow case shut again.

'How about a game of chess?' Ken propped himself up weakly, opened the wooden box of chessmen which he and Stuart had found in the wreckage of the house. Already, he had managed to teach Stuart the rudiments of the game; before the war Stuart had never played.

'Naw,' Stuart said. He was watching, far off in the gray sky, the moving shape of some plane or rocket ship, a cylinder. God, he thought, could it be a bomb? Dismally, he watched it sink lower and lower; he did not even lie down, did not seek to hide as he had done that first time, in the initial few minutes on which so much – their being alive now – had depended. 'What's that?' he asked.

The dying man scrutinized it. 'It's a balloon.'

Not believing him, Stuart said, 'It's the Chinese!'

'It really is a balloon, a little one. What they used to call a blimp, I think. I haven't seen one since I was a boy.'

'Could the Chinese float across the Pacific in balloons?' Stuart said, imagining thousands of such small, gray cigar-shaped balloons, each with a platoon of Mongolian-type Chinese peasant soldiers, armed with Czech automatic rifles, clutching handholds, clinging to every fold. 'It's just what you'd expect them to think up from the beginning; they reduce the world to their level, back a couple centuries. Instead of catching up with us—' He broke off, because now he saw that the balloon had on its side a sign in English:

HAMILTON AIR FORCE BASE

The dying man said drily, 'It's one of ours.'

'I wonder where they got it,' Stuart said.

'Ingenious,' the dying man said, 'isn't it? I suppose all the gasoline and kerosene are gone by now. Used right up. We'll be seeing a lot of strange transportation from now on. Or rather you will.'

'Stop feeling sorry for yourself,' Stuart said.

'I don't feel sorry for myself or anyone,' the dying man said as he carefully laid out the chess pieces. 'This is a nice set,' he said. 'Made in Mexico, I notice. Hand-carved, no doubt . . . but very fragile.'

'Explain to me again how the bishop moves,' Stuart said.

Overhead, the Hamilton Air Force Base balloon loomed

larger as it drifted closer. The two men in the basement bent over their chess board, paying no attention to it. Possibly it was taking pictures. Or possibly it was on a strategic mission; it might have a walkie-talkie aboard and was in contact with the Sixth Army units south of San Francisco. Who knew? Who cared? The balloon drifted by as the dying man advanced his king's pawn two spaces to open the game.

'The game begins,' the dying man said. And then he added in a low voice, 'For you, anyhow, Stuart. A strange, unfamiliar, new game ahead . . . you can even bet your pillowcase of money, if you want.'

Grunting, Stuart pondered his own men and decided to move a rook's pawn as his opening gambit – and knew, as soon as he had touched it, that it was an idiotic move.

'Can I take it back?' he asked hopefully.

'When you touch a piece you must move it,' Ken said, bringing out one of his knights.

'I don't think that's fair; I mean, I'm just learning,' Stuart said. He glared at the dying man, but the sallow face was adamant. 'Okay,' he said resignedly, this time moving his king's pawn, as Ken had done. I'll watch his moves and do what he does, he decided. That way I'll be safer.

From the balloon, now directly overhead, bits of white paper scattered, drifted and fluttered down. Stuart and the dying man paused in their game. One of the bits of paper fell near them in the basement and Ken reached and picked it up. He read it, passed it to Stuart.

'Burlingame!' Stuart said, reading it. It was an appeal for volunteers, for the Army. 'They want us to hike from here to *Burlingame* and be inducted? That's fifty or sixty miles, all the way down this side of the Bay and around. They're nuts!'

'They are,' Ken said. 'They won't get a soul.'

'Why hell, I can't even make it down to LeConte Street to

the relief station,' Stuart said. He felt indignant and he glared at the Hamilton Field balloon as it drifted on. They're not going to get me to join up, he said to himself. Fork that.

'It says,' Ken said, reading the proclamation, 'that if you reach Burlingame they guarantee you water, food, cigarettes, anti-plague shots, treatment for radiation burns. How about that? But no girls.'

'Can you get interested in sex?' He was amazed. 'Christ, I haven't felt the slightest urge since the first bomb fell; it's like the thing dropped off in fear, fell right off.'

'That's because the diencephalic center of the brain suppresses the sex instinct in the face of danger,' Ken said. 'But it'll return.'

'No,' Stuart said, 'because any child born would be a freak; there shouldn't be any intercourse for say around ten years. They ought to make it a law. I can't stand the idea of the world populated by freaks because I have had personal experience; one worked at Modern TV sales with me, or rather in the service department. One was enough. I mean, they ought to hang that Bluthgeld up by his balls for what he did.'

'What Bluthgeld did in the '70s' Ken said, 'is insignificant when compared to this.' He indicated the ruins of the basement around them.

'I'll grant you that,' Stuart said, 'but it was the start.'

Overhead, now, the balloon was drifting back the way it had come. Perhaps it had run out of little messages and was returning to Hamilton Field, over on the other side of the Bay or wherever it was.

Gazing up at it, Stuart said, 'Talk to us some more.'

'It can't,' Ken said. 'That's all it had to say; it's a very simple creature. Are you going to play, or should I move your pieces? Either is satisfactory to me.'

With great caution, Stuart moved a bishop – and again

knew at once that it had been the wrong move; he could tell by the dying man's face.

In the corner of the basement, among the cement blocks, something agile and frightened plopped to safety, scurried and twittered with anxiety as it spied them. Stuart's attention wandered from the board to the rat, and he looked about for his broom handle.

'Play!' Ken said angrily.

'Okay, okay,' Stuart said, feeling grumpy about it. He made a random move, his attention still on the rat.

Seven

In front of the pharmacy in Point Reyes Station, at nine in the morning. Eldon Blaine waited. Under his arm he held tightly his worn briefcase tied together with string. Meanwhile, inside the building, the pharmacist removed chains and struggled with the metal doors; Eldon listened to the sound and felt impatience.

'Just a minute,' the pharmacist called, his voice muffled. As he at last got the doors open he apologized, 'This was formerly the back end of a truck. You have to use both hands and feet to make it work. Come on in, mister.' He held the high door aside, and Eldon saw into the dark interior of the pharmacy, with its unlit electric light bulb which hung from the ceiling by an ancient cord.

'What I'm here for,' Eldon said rapidly, 'is a wide-spectrum antibiotic, the kind used in clearing up a respiratory infection.' He made his need sound casual; he did not tell the pharmacist how many towns in Northern California he had visited in the last few days, walking and hitching rides, nor did he mention how sick his daughter was. It would only jack up the price asked, he knew. And anyhow he did not see much actual stock, here. Probably the man did not have it.

Eyeing him, the pharmacist said, 'I don't see anything with you; what do you have in exchange, assuming I have what you're after?' In a nervous manner he smoothed his thinning gray hair back; he was an elderly, small man, and it was obvious that he suspected Eldon of being a napper. Probably he suspected everyone.

Eldon said, 'Where I come from I'm known as the glasses man.' Unzipping his briefcase, he showed the pharmacist the rows of intact and nearly-intact lenses, frames, and lenses in frames, scavenged from all over the Bay Area, especially from the great deposits near Oakland. 'I can compensate almost any eye defect,' he said. 'I've got a fine variety, here. What are you, near- or far-sighted or astigmatic? I can fix you up in ten minutes, by changing around a lens or two.'

'Far-sighted,' the pharmacist said slowly, 'but I don't think I have what *you* want.' He looked at the rows of glasses longingly.

With anger, Eldon said, 'Then why didn't you say so right off, so I can go on? I want to make Petaluma today; there's a lot of drugstores there – all I have to do is find a hay truck going that way.'

'Couldn't you trade me a pair of glasses for something else?' the pharmacist asked plaintively, following after him as he started away. 'I got a valuable heart medicine, quinidine gluconate; you could most likely trade it for what you want. Nobody else in Marin County has quinidine gluconate but me.'

'Is there a doctor around here?' Eldon said, pausing at the edge of the weed-infested county road with its several stores and houses.

'Yes,' the pharmacist said, with a nod of pride. 'Doctor Stockstill, he migrated here several years ago. But he doesn't have any drugs. Just me.'

Briefcase under his arm, Eldon Blaine walked on along the county road, listening hopefully for the pop-popping noise of the wood-burning truck motor rising out of the stillness of the early-morning California countryside. But the sound faded. The truck, alas, was going the other way.

This region, directly north of San Francisco, had once been owned by a few wealthy dairy ranchers; cows had cropped in these fields, but that was gone now, along with the meat-animals, the steer and sheep. As everyone knew, an acre of land could function better as a source of grains or vegetables. Around him now he saw closely-planted rows of corn, an early-ripening hybrid, and between the rows, great hairy squash plants on which odd yellow squash like bowling balls grew. This was an unusual eastern squash which could be eaten skin and seeds and all; once it had been disdained in California valleys . . . but that was changed, now.

Ahead, a little group of children ran across the little-used road on their way to school; Eldon Blaine saw their tattered books and lunch pails, heard their voices, thought to himself how calming this was, other children well and busy, unlike his own child. If Gwen died, others would replace her. He accepted that unemotionally. One learned how. One had to.

The school, off to the right in the saddle of two hills: most of it the remains of a single-story modern building, put up no doubt just before the war by ambitious, public-spirited citizens who had bonded themselves into a decade of indebtedness without guessing that they would not live to make payment. Thus they had, without intending it, gotten their grammar school free.

Its windows made him laugh. Salvaged from every variety of old rural building, the windows were first tiny, then huge, with ornate boards holding them in place. Of course the original windows had been blown instantly out. Glass, he thought. So rare these days . . . if you own glass in any form you are rich. He gripped his briefcase tighter as he walked.

Several of the children, seeing a strange man, stopped to peer at him with anxiety augmented by curiosity. He grinned at them, wondering to himself what they were studying and what teachers they had. An ancient, senile old lady, drawn out of retirement, to sit once more behind a desk? A local man who happened to hold a college degree? Or most likely some of the mothers themselves, banded together, using a precious armload of books from the local library.

A voice from behind him called; it was a woman, and as he turned he heard the squeak-squeak of a bicycle. 'Are you the glasses man?' she called again, severe and yet attractive, with dark hair, wearing a man's cotton shirt and jeans, pedaling along the road after him, bouncing up and down with each rut. 'Please stop. I was talking to Fred Quinn our druggist just now and he said you were by.' She reached him, stopped her bicycle, panting for breath. 'There hasn't been a glasses man by here in months; why don't you come oftener?'

Eldon Blaine said, 'I'm not here selling; I'm here trying to pick up some antibiotics.' He felt irritated. 'I have to get to Petaluma,' he said, and then he realized that he was gazing at her bike with envy; he knew it showed on his face.

'We can get them for you,' the woman said. She was older than he had first thought; her face was lined and a little dark, and he guessed that she was almost forty. 'I'm on the Planning Committee for everyone, here in West Marin; I know we can scare up what you need, if you'll just come back with me and wait. Give us two hours. We need several pairs . . . I'm not going to let you go.' Her voice was firm, not coaxing.

'You're not Mrs Raub, are you?' Eldon Blaine asked.

'Yes,' she said. 'You recognized me – how?'

He said, 'I'm from the Bolinas area; we know all about what you're doing up here. I wish we had someone like you on our Committee.' He felt a little afraid of her. Mrs Raub always got her own way, he had heard. She and Larry Raub had organized West Marin after the Cooling-off; before, in the old days, she had not amounted to anything and the Emergency had given her her chance, as it had many people, to show what she was really made of.

As they walked back together, Mrs Raub said, 'Who are the antibiotics for? Not yourself; you look perfectly healthy to me.'

'My little girl is dying,' he said.

She did not waste sympathetic words; there were none left in the world, anymore – she merely nodded. 'Infectious hepatitis?' she asked. 'How's your water supply? Do you have a chlorinator? If not—'

'No, it's like strep throat,' he said.

'We heard from the satellite last night that some German drug firms are in operation again, and so if we're lucky we'll be seeing German drugs back on the market, at least on the East Coast.'

'You get the satellite?' Excitedly, he said, 'Our radio went dead, and our handy is down somewhere near South San Francisco scavenging for refrigeration parts and won't be back probably for another month. Tell me; what's he reading now? The last time we picked him up, it was so darn long ago – he was on Pascal's *Provincial Letters*.'

Mrs Raub said, 'Dangerfield is now reading *Of Human Bondage*.'

'Isn't that about that fellow who couldn't shake off that girl he met?' Eldon said. 'I think I remember it from the previous time he read it, several years ago. She kept coming back into his life. Didn't she finally ruin his life, in the end?'

'I don't know; I'm afraid we didn't pick it up the previous time.'

'That Dangerfield is really a great disc jockey,' Eldon said, 'the best I've ever heard even *before* the Emergency, I mean, we never miss him; we generally get a turnout of two hundred people every night at our fire station. I think one of us could fix that damn radio, but our Committee ruled that we had to let it alone and wait until the handy's back. If he ever is . . . the last one disappeared on a scavenging trip.'

Mrs Raub said, 'Now perhaps your community understands the need of standby equipment, which I've always said is essential.'

'Could – we send a representative up to listen with your group and report back to us?'

'Of course,' Mrs Raub said. 'But—'

'It wouldn't be the same,' he agreed. 'It's not—' He gestured. What was it about Dangerfield, sitting up there above them in the satellite as it passed over them each day? Contact with the world . . . Dangerfield looked down and saw everything, the rebuilding, all the changes both good and bad; he monitored every broadcast, recording and preserving and then playing back, so that through him they were joined.

In his mind, the familiar voice now gone so long from their community – he could summon it still, hear the rich low chuckle, the earnest tones, the intimacy, and never anything phony. No slogans, no Fourth-of-July expostulations, none of the stuff that had gotten them all where they were now.

Once he had heard Dangerfield say, 'Want to know the real reason I wasn't in the war? Why they carefully shot me off into space a little bit in advance? They knew better than to give me a gun . . . I would have shot an officer.' And he had chuckled, making it a joke; but it was true, what he said, everything he told them was true, even when it was made funny. Dangerfield hadn't been politically reliable, and yet now he sat up above them passing over their heads year in, year out. And he was a man they believed.

Set on the side of a ridge, the Raub house overlooked West Marin County, with its vegetable fields and irrigation ditches, an occasional goat staked out, and of course the horses; standing at the living room window, Eldon Blaine saw below him, near a farmhouse, a great Percheron which no doubt pulled a plow . . . pulled, too, an engineless automobile along the road to Sonoma County when it was time to pick up supplies.

He saw now a horse-car moving along the county road; it would have picked him up if Mrs Raub hadn't found him first, and he would have soon reached Petaluma.

Down the hillside below him pedaled Mrs Raub on her way to find him his antibiotics; to his amazement she had left him alone in her house, free to nap everything in sight, and now he turned to see what there was. Chairs, books, in the kitchen, food and even a bottle of wine, clothes in all the closets – he roamed about the house, savoring everything; it was almost like before the war, except that of course the useless electrical appliances had been thrown out long ago.

Through the back windows of the house he saw the green wooden side of a large water-storage tank. The Raubs, he realized, had their own supply of water. Going outside he saw a clear, untainted stream.

At the stream a kind of contraption lurked, like a cart on wheels. He stared at it; extensions from it were busily filling buckets with water. In the center of it sat a man with no arms or legs. The man nodded his head as if conducting music, and the machinery around him responded. It was a phocomelus, Eldon realized, mounted on his phocomobile, his combination cart and manual grippers which served as mechanical substitutes for his missing limbs. What was he doing, stealing the Raubs' water?

'Hey,' Eldon said.

At once the phocomelus turned his head; his eyes blazed at Eldon in alarm, and then something whacked into Eldon's middle – he was thrown back, and as he wobbled and struggled to regain his balance he discovered that his arms were pinned at his sides. A wire mesh had whipped out at him from the phocomobile, had fastened in place. The phocomelus' means of defense.

'Who are you?' the phocomelus said, stammering in his wary eagerness to know. 'You don't live around here; I don't know you.'

'I'm from Bolinas,' Eldon said. The metal mesh crushed in until he gasped. 'I'm the glasses man. Mrs Raub, she told me to wait here.'

Now the mesh seemed to ease. 'I can't take chances,' the phocomelus said. 'I won't let you go until June Raub comes back.' The buckets once more began dipping in the water; they filled methodically until the tank lashed to the phocomobile was slopping over.

'Are you supposed to be doing that?' Eldon asked. 'Taking water from the Raubs' stream?'

'I've got a right,' the phocomelus said. 'I give back more than I take, to everybody around here.'

'Let me go,' Eldon said. 'I'm just trying to get medicine for my kid; she's dying.'

' "My kid, she's dying," ' the phocomelus mimicked, picking up the quality of his voice with startling accuracy. He rolled away from the stream, now, closer to Eldon. The 'mobile gleamed; all its parts were new-looking and shiny. It was one of the best-made mechanical constructions that Eldon Blaine had ever seen.

'Let me go,' Eldon said, 'and I'll give you a pair of glasses free. Any pair I have.'

'My eyes are perfect,' the phocomelus said. 'Everything about me is perfect. Parts are missing, but I don't need them; I can do better without them. I can get down this hill faster than you, for instance.'

'Who built your 'mobile?' Eldon asked. Surely in seven years it would have become tarnished and partly broken, like everything else.

'I built it,' the phocomelus said.

'How can you build your own 'mobile? That's a contradiction.'

'I used to be body-wired. Now I'm brain-wired; I did that myself, too. I'm the handy, up here. Those old extensors the Government built before the war – they weren't even as good as the flesh things, like you have.' The phocomelus grimaced. He had a thin, flexible face, with a sharp nose and extremely white teeth, a face ideal for the emotion which he now showed Eldon Blaine.

'Dangerfield says that the handies are the most valuable people in the world,' Eldon said. 'He declared Worldwide Handyman Week, one time we were listening, and he named different handies who were especially well-known. What's your name? Maybe he mentioned you.'

'Hoppy Harrington,' the phocomelus said. 'But I know he didn't mention me because I keep myself in the background, still; it isn't time for me to make my name in the world, as I'm going to be doing. I let the local people see a little of what I can do, but they're supposed to be quiet about it.'

'Sure they'd be quiet,' Eldon said. 'They don't want to lose you. We're missing our handy, right now, and we really feel it. Could you take on the Bolinas area for a little while, do you think? We've got plenty to trade you. In the Emergency hardly anybody got over the mountain to invade us, so we're relatively untouched.'

'I've been down there to Bolinas,' Hoppy Harrington said. 'In fact I've traveled all around, even as far inland as Sacramento. Nobody has seen what I've seen; I can cover *fifty miles a day* in my 'mobile.' His lean face twitched and then he stammered, 'I wouldn't go back to Bolinas because there are sea monsters in the ocean, there.'

'Who says so?' Eldon demanded. 'That's just superstition – tell me who said that about our community.'

'I think it was Dangerfleld.'

'No, he couldn't,' Eldon said. 'He can be relied on, he wouldn't peddle such trash as that. I never once heard him tell a superstition on any of his programs. Maybe he was kidding; I bet he was kidding and you took him seriously.'

'The hydrogen bombs woke up the sea monsters,' Hoppy said, 'from their slumber in the depths.' He nodded earnestly.

'You come and see our community,' Eldon said. 'We're orderly and advanced, a lot more so than any city. We even have streetlights going again, four of them for an hour in the evening. I'm surprised a handy would believe such superstition.'

The phocomelus looked chagrined. 'You never can be sure,' he murmured. 'I guess maybe it wasn't Dangerfield I heard it from.'

Below them, on the ascending road, a horse moved; the sound of its hoofs reached them and they both turned. A big fleshy man with a red face came riding up and up, toward them, peering at them. As he rode he called, 'Glasses man! Is that you?'

'Yes,' Eldon said, as the horse veered into the grass-extinguished driveway of the Raub house. 'You have the antibiotics, mister?'

'June Raub will bring them,' the big florid man said, reining his horse to a stop. 'Glasses man, let's see what you have. I'm near-sighted but I also have an acute astigmatism in my left eye; can you help me?' He approached on foot, still peering.

'I can't fit you,' Eldon said, 'because Hoppy Harrington has me tied up.'

'For God's sake, Hoppy,' the big florid man said with agitation. 'Let the glasses man go so he can fit me; I've been waiting months and I don't mean to wait any longer.'

'Okay, Leroy,' Hoppy Harrington said sullenly. And, from around Eldon, the metal mesh uncoiled and then slithered back across the ground to the waiting phocomelus in the center of his shiny, intricate 'mobile.

As the satellite passed over the Chicago area its wing-like extended sensors picked up a flea signal, and in his earphones Walter Dangerfield heard the faint, distant, hollowed-out voice from below.

'. . . and please play "Waltzing Matilda," a lot of us like that. And play "The Woodpecker Song." And—' The flea signal faded out, and he heard only static. It had definitely not been a laser beam, he thought to himself archly.

Into his microphone, Dangerfield said, 'Well, friends, we have a request here for "Waltzing Matilda."' He reached to snap a switch at the controls of a tape transport. 'The great bass-baritone Peter Dawson – which is also the name of a very good brand of Scotch – in "Waltzing Matilda."' From well-worn memory he selected the correct reel of tape, and in a moment it was on the transport, turning.

As the music played, Walt Dangerfield tuned his receiving equipment, hoping once more to pick up the same flea signal. However, instead he found himself party to a two-way transmission between military units involved in police action somewhere in upstate Illinois. Their brisk chatter interested him, and he listened until the end of the music.

'Lots of luck to you boys in uniform,' he said into the microphone, then. 'Catch those boodle-burners and bless you all.' He chuckled, because if ever a human being had immunity from retaliation, it was he. No one on Earth could reach him – it had been attempted six times since the Emergency, with no success. 'Catch those bad guys . . . or should I say catch those *good* guys. Say, who are the good guys, these days?' His receiving equipment had picked up, in the last few weeks, a number of complaints about Army brutality. 'Now let me tell you something, boys,' he said smoothly. 'Watch out for those squirrel rifles; that's all.' He began hunting through the satellite's tape library for the recording of 'The Woodpecker Song.' 'That's all, brother,' he said, and put on the tape.

Below him the world was in darkness, its night side turned his way; yet already he could see the rim of day appearing on the edge, and soon he would be passing into that once more. Lights here and there glowed like holes poked in the surface of the planet which he had left seven years ago – left for another purpose, another goal entirely. A much more noble one.

His was not the sole satellite still circling Earth, but it was the sole one with life aboard. Everyone else had long since perished. But they had not been outfitted as he and Lydia had been, for a decade of life on another world. He was lucky; besides food and water and air he had a million miles of video and audio tape to keep him amused. And now, with it, he kept *them* amused, the remnants of the civilization which had shot him up here in the first place. They had botched the job of getting him to Mars – fortunately for them. Their failure had paid them vital dividends ever since.

'Hoode hoode hoo,' Walt Dangerfield chanted into his

microphone, using the transmitter which should have carried his voice back from millions of miles, not merely a couple hundred. 'Things you can do with the timer out of an old RCA washer-dryer combination. This item arrives from a handy in the Geneva area; thanks to you, Georg Schilper – I know everyone will be pleased to hear you give this timely tip in your own words.' He played into his transmitter the tape recording of the handyman himself speaking; the entire Great Lakes region of the United States would now know Georg Schilper's bit of lore, and would no doubt wisely apply it at once. The world hungered for the knowledge tucked away in pockets here and there, knowledge which – without Dangerfield – would be confined to its point of origin, perhaps forever.

After the tape of Georg Schilper he put on his canned reading from *Of Human Bondage* and rose stiffly from his seat.

There was a pain in his chest which worried him; it had appeared one day, located beneath his breastbone, and now for the hundredth time he got down one of the microfilms of medical information and began scanning the section dealing with the heart. Does it feel like the heel of a hand squeezing my breath out of me? he asked himself. Someone pushing down with all his weight? It was difficult to recall what 'weight' felt like in the first place. Or does it merely burn . . . and if so, when? Before meals or after?

Last week he had made contact with a hospital in Tokyo, had described his symptoms. The doctors were not sure what to tell him. What you need, they had said, is an electrocardiogram, but how could he give himself a test like that up here? How could anyone, anymore? The Japanese doctors were living in the past, or else there had been more of a revival in Japan than he realized; than anyone realized.

Amazing, he thought suddenly, that I've survived so long.

It did not seem long, though, because his time-sense had become faulty. And he was a busy man; at this moment, six of his tape recorders monitored six much-used frequencies, and before the reading from the Maugham book had ended he would be obliged to play them back. They might contain nothing or they might contain hours of meaningful talk. One never knew. If only, he thought, I had been able to make use of the high-speed transmission . . . but the proper decoders were no longer in existence, below. Hours could have been compressed into seconds, and he could have given each area in turn a complete account. As it was, he had to dole it out in small clusters, with much repetition. Sometimes it took months to read through a single novel, this way.

But at least he had been able to lower the frequency on which the satellite's transmitter broadcast to a band which the people below could receive on a common AM radio. That had been his one big achievement; that, by itself, had made him into what he was.

The reading of the Maugham book ended, then automatically restarted itself; it droned from the start once more for the next area below. Walt Dangerfield ignored it and continued to consult his medical reference microfilms. I think it's only spasms of the pyloric valve, he decided. If I had phenobarbital here . . . but it had been used up several years ago; his wife, in her last great suicidal depression, had consumed it all – consumed it and then taken her life anyhow. It had been the abrupt silence of the Soviet space station, oddly enough, that had started her depression; up until then she had believed that they would all be reached and brought safely back down to the surface. The Russians had starved to death, all ten of them, but no one had foreseen it because they had kept up their duty-oriented line of scientific patter right into the last few hours.

'Hoode hoode hoo,' Dangerfield said to himself as he read about the pyloric valve and its spasms. 'Folks,' he murmured. 'I have this funny pain brought on by over-indulgence . . . what I need is four-way relief, don't you agree?' He snapped on his microphone, cutting out the tape-in-progress. 'Remember those old ads?' he asked his darkened, unseen audience below. 'Before the war – let's see, how did they go? Are you building more H-bombs but enjoying it less?' He chuckled. 'Has thermonuclear war got you down? New York, can you pick me up, yet? I want every one of you within the reach of my voice, all sixty-five of you, to quick light up a match so I'll know you're there.'

In his earphones a loud signal came in. 'Dangerfield, this is the New York Port Authority; can you give us any idea of the weather?'

'Oh,' Dangerfield said, 'we've got *fine* weather coming. You can put out to sea in those little boats and catch those little radioactive fish; nothing to worry about.'

Another voice, fainter, came in now. 'Mr Dangerfield could you possibly please play some of those opera arias you have? We'd especially appreciate "Thy Tiny Hand Is Frozen" from *La Boheme*.'

'Heck, I can *sing* that,' Dangerfield said, reaching for the tape as he hummed tenorishly into the microphone.

Returning to Bolinas that night, Eldon Blaine fed the first of the antibiotics to his child and then quickly drew his wife aside. 'Listen, they have a top-notch handy up in West Marin which they've been keeping quiet about, and only twenty miles from here. I think we should send a delegation up there to nap him and bring him down here.' He added, 'He's a phoce and you should see the 'mobile he built himself; none of the handies we've had could do anything half that good.'

Putting his wool jacket back on he went to the door of their room. 'I'm going to ask the Committee to vote on it.'

'But our ordinance against funny people,' Patricia protested. 'And Mrs Wallace is Chairman of the Committee this month; you know how she feels, she'd never let any more phoces come here and settle. I mean, we have four as it is and she's always complaining about them.'

'That ordinance refers only to funny people who could become a financial burden to the community,' Eldon said. 'I ought to know; I helped draft it. Hoppy Harrington is no burden; he's an asset – the ordinance doesn't cover him, and I'm going to stand up to Mrs Wallace and fight it out. I knew I can get official permission; I've got it all worked out how we'll do the napping. They invited us to come up to their area and listen to the satellite, and we'll do that; we'll show up but not just to listen to Dangerfield. While they're involved in that we'll nap Hoppy; we'll put his phocomobile out of action and haul him down here, and they'll never know what happened. Finders keepers, losers weepers. And our police force will protect us.'

Patricia said, 'I'm scared of phoces. They have peculiar powers, not natural ones; everybody knows it. He probably built his 'mobile by means of magic.'

Laughing with derision, Eldon Blaine said, 'So much the better. Maybe that's what we need: magic spells, a community magician. I'm all for it.'

'I'm going to see how Gwen is,' Patricia said, starting toward the screened-off portion of the room where their child lay on her cot. 'I won't have any part of this; I think it's dreadful, what you're doing.'

Eldon Blaine stepped from the room, out into night darkness. In a moment he was striding down the path toward the Wallaces' house.

*

As the citizens of West Marin County one by one entered the Foresters' Hall and seated themselves, June Raub adjusted the variable condenser of the twelve-volt car radio and noticed that once again Hoppy Harrington had not shown up to hear the satellite. What was it he had said? '*I don't like to listen to sick people.*' A strange thing to say, she thought to herself.

From the speaker of the radio static issued and then first faint beepings from the satellite. In a few more minutes they would be picking it up clearly . . . unless the wet-cell battery powering the radio chose to give out again, as it had briefly the other day.

The rows of seated people listened attentively as the initial words from Dangerfield began to emerge from the static '. . . lice-type typhus is said to be breaking out in Washington up to the Canadian border,' Dangerfield was saying. 'So stay away from there, my friends. If this report is true it's a very bad sign indeed. Also, a report from Portland, Oregon, more on the cheerful side. Two ships have arrived from the Orient. That's welcome news, isn't it? Two big freighters, just plain packed with manufactured articles from little factories in Japan and China, according to what I hear.'

The listening roomful of people stirred with excitement.

'And here's a household tip from a food consultant in Hawaii,' Dangerfield said, but now his voice faded out; once more the listening people heard only static. June Raub turned up the volume, but it did no good. Disappointment showed clearly on all the faces in the room.

If Hoppy were here, she thought, he could tune it so much better than I can. Feeling nervous, she looked to her husband for support.

'Weather conditions,' he said, from where he sat in the first row of chairs. 'We just have to be patient.'

But several people were glaring at her with hostility, as if it was her fault that the satellite had faded out. She made a gesture of helplessness.

The door of the Foresters' Hall opened and three men awkwardly entered. Two were strangers to her and the third was the glasses man. Ill-at-ease, they searched for seats, while everyone in the room turned to watch.

'Who are you fellows?' Mr Spaulding, who operated the feed barn, said to them. 'Did anyone say you could come in here?'

June Raub said, 'I invited this delegation from Bolinas to make the trip up here and listen with us; their radio set is not working.'

'Shhh,' several people said, because once again the voice from the satellite could be heard.

'. . . anyhow,' Dangerfield was saying, 'I get the pain mostly when I've been asleep and before I eat. It seems to go away when I eat, and that makes me suspect it's an ulcer, not my heart. So if any doctors are listening and they have access to a transmitter, maybe they can give me a buzz and let me know their opinion. I can give them more information, if it'll help them.'

Astonished, June Raub listened as the man in the satellite went on to describe in greater and greater detail his medical complaint. Was this what Hoppy meant? she asked herself. Dangerfield had turned into a hypochondriac and no one had noticed the transition, except for Hoppy whose senses were extra acute. She shivered. That poor man up there, doomed to go around and around the Earth until at last, as with the Russians, his food or air gave out and he died.

And what will we do then? she asked herself. Without Dangerfield . . . how can we keep going?

Eight

Orion Stroud, chairman of the West Marin school board, turned up the Coleman gasoline lantern so that the utility school room in the white glare became clearly lit, and all four members of the board could make out the new teacher.

'I'll put a few questions to him,' Stroud said to the others. 'First, this is Mr Barnes and he comes from Oregon. He tells me he's a specialist in science and natural edibles. Right, Mr Barnes?'

The new teacher, a short, young-looking man wearing khaki trousers and workshirt, nervously cleared his throat and said, 'Yes, I am familiar with chemicals and plants and animal-life, especially whatever is found out in the woods such as berries and mushrooms.'

'We've recently had bad luck with mushrooms,' said Mrs Tallman, the elderly lady who had been a member of the board even in the old days before the Emergency. 'It's been our tendency to leave them alone; we've lost several people either because they were greedy or careless or just plain ignorant.'

Stroud said, 'But Mr Barnes here isn't ignorant. He went to the University at Davis, and they taught him how to tell a good mushroom from the poisonous ones. He doesn't guess or pretend; right, Mr Barnes?' He looked to the new teacher for confirmation.

'There are species which are nutritious and about which

you can't go wrong,' Mr Barnes said, nodding. 'I've looked through the pastures and woods in your area, and I've seen some fine examples; you can supplement your diet without taking any chances. I even know the Latin names.'

The board stirred and murmured. That had impressed them, Stroud realized, that about the Latin names.

'Why did you leave Oregon?' George Keller, the principal, asked bluntly.

The new teacher faced him and said, 'Politics.'

'Yours or theirs?'

'Theirs,' Barnes said. 'I have no politics. I teach children how to make ink and soap and how to cut the tails from lambs even if the lambs are almost grown. And I've got my own books.' He picked up a book from the small stack beside him, showing the board in what good shape they were. 'I'll tell you something else: you have the means here in this part of California to make paper. Did you know that?'

Mrs Tallman said, 'We knew it, Mr Barnes, but we don't know quite how. It has to do with bark of trees, doesn't it?'

On the new teacher's face appeared a mysterious expression, one of concealment. Stroud knew that Mrs Tallman was correct, but the teacher did not want to let her know; he wanted to keep the knowledge to himself because the West Marin trustees had not yet hired him. His knowledge was not yet available – he gave nothing free. And that of course was proper: Stroud recognized that, respected Barnes for it. Only a fool gave something away for nothing.

For the first time the newest member of the board, Miss Costigan, spoke up. 'I – know a little about mushrooms myself, Mr Barnes. What's the first thing you look for to be sure it isn't the deadly amanita?' She eyed the new teacher intently, obviously determined to pin the man down to concrete facts.

'The death cup,' Mr Barnes answered. 'At the base of the stripe; the volva. The amanitas have it, most other kinds don't. And the universal veil. And generally the deadly amanita has white spores . . . and of course white gills.' He smiled at Miss Costigan, who smiled back.

Mrs Tallman was scrutinizing the new teacher's stack of books. 'I see you have Carl Jung's *Psychological Types*. Is one of your sciences psychology? How nice, to acquire a teacher for our school who can tell edible mushrooms and also is an authority on Freud and Jung.'

'There's no value in such stuff,' Stroud said, with irritation. 'We need useful science, not academic hot air.' He felt personally let down; Mr Barnes had not told him about that, about his interest in mere theory. 'Psychology doesn't dig any septic tanks.'

'I think we're ready to vote on Mr Barnes,' Miss Costigan said. 'I for one am in favor of accepting him, at least on a provisional basis. Does anyone feel otherwise?'

Mrs Tallman said to Mr Barnes, 'We killed our last teacher, you know. That's why we need another. That's why we sent Mr Stroud out looking up and down the Coast until he found you.'

With a wooden expression, Mr Barnes nodded. 'I know. That does not deter me.'

'His name was Mr Austurias and he was very good with mushrooms, too,' Mrs Tallman said, 'although actually he gathered them for his own use alone. He did not teach us anything about them, and we appreciated his reasons; it was not for that that we decided to kill him. We killed him because he lied to us. You see, his real reason for coming here had nothing to do with teaching. He was looking for some man named Jack Tree, who it turned out, lived in this area. Our Mrs Keller, a respected member of this community and the wife of George Keller here, our principal, is a dear friend of Mr Tree, and she brought the news of the situation to us and of course we acted legally and officially, through our chief of police, Mr Earl Colvig.'

'I see,' Mr Barnes said stonily, listening without interrupting.

Speaking up, Orion Stroud said, 'The jury which sentenced and executed him was composed of myself, Cas Stone, who's the largest landowner in West Marin, Mrs Tallman and Mrs June Raub. I say "executed," but you understand that the act – when he was shot, the shooting itself – was done by Earl. That's Earl's job, after the West Marin Official Jury has made its decision.' He eyed the new teacher.

'It sounds,' Mr Barnes said, 'Very formal and law-abiding to me. Just what I'd be interested in. And—' He smiled at them all, 'I'll share *my* knowledge of mushrooms with you; I won't keep it to myself, as your late Mr Austurias did.'

They all nodded; they appreciated that. The tension in the room relaxed, the people murmured. A cigarette – one of Andrew Gill's special deluxe Gold Labels – was lit up; its good, rich smell wafted to them all, cheering them and making them feel more friendly to the new teacher and to one another.

Seeing the cigarette, Mr Barnes got a strange expression on his face and he said in a husky voice, 'You've got *tobacco* up here? After seven years?' He clearly could not believe it.

Smiling in amusement, Mrs Tallman said, 'We don't have any tobacco, Mr Barnes, because of course no one does. But we do have a tobacco expert. He fashions these special deluxe Gold Labels for us out of choice, aged vegetable and herbal materials the nature of which remain – and justly so – his individual secret.'

'How much do they cost?' Mr Barnes asked.

'In terms of State of California boodle money,' Orion

Stroud said, 'about a hundred dollars apiece. In terms of pre-war silver, a nickel apiece.'

'I have a nickel,' Mr Barnes said, reaching shakily into his coat pocket; he fished about, brought up a nickel and held it toward the smoker, who was George Keller, leaning back in his chair with his legs crossed to make himself comfortable.

'Sorry,' George said, 'I don't want to sell. You better go directly to Mr Gill; you can find him during the day at his shop: It's here in Point Reyes Station but of course he gets all around; he has a horse-drawn VW minibus.'

'I'll make a note of that,' Mr Barnes said. He put his nickel away, very carefully.

'Do you intend to board the ferry?' the Oakland official asked. 'If not, I wish you'd move your car, because it's blocking the gate.'

'Sure,' Stuart McConchie said. He got back into his car, flicked the reins that made Edward Prince of Wales, his horse, begin pulling. Edward pulled, and the engineless 1975 Pontiac passed back through the gate and out onto the pier.

The Bay, choppy and blue, lay on both sides, and Stuart watched through the windshield as a gull swooped to seize some edible from the pilings. Fishing lines, too . . . men catching their evening meals. Several of the men wore the remains of Army uniforms. Veterans who perhaps lived beneath the pier. Stuart drove on.

If only he could afford to telephone San Francisco. But the underwater cable was out again, and the lines had to go all the way down to San Jose and up the other side, along the peninsula, and by the time the call reached San Francisco it would cost him five dollars in silver money. So, except for a rich person, that was out of the question; he had to wait the two hours until the ferry left . . . but could he stand to wait that long?

He was after something important.

He had heard a rumor that a huge Soviet guided missile had been found, one which had failed to go off; it lay buried in the ground near Belmont, and a farmer had discovered it while plowing. The farmer was selling it off in the form of individual parts, of which there were thousands in the guidance system alone. The farmer wanted a penny a part, your choice. And Stuart, in his line of work, needed many such parts. But so did lots of other people. So it was first come, first serve; unless he got across the Bay to Belmont fairly soon, it would he too late – there would be no electronic parts left for him and his business.

He sold (another man made them) small electronic traps. Vermin had mutated and now could avoid or repel the ordinary passive trap, no matter how complicated. The cats in particular had become different, and Mr Hardy built a superior cat trap, even better than his rat and dog traps.

It was theorized by some that in the years since the war cats had developed a language. At night people heard them mewing to one another in the darkness, a stilted, brisk series of gruff sounds unlike any of the old noises. And the cats ganged together in little packs and – this much at least was certain – collected food for the times ahead. It was these caches of food, cleverly stored and hidden, which had first alarmed people, much more so than the new noises. But in any case the cats, as well as the rats and dogs, were dangerous. They killed and ate small children almost at will – or at least so one heard. And of course wherever possible, they themselves were caught and eaten in return. Dogs, in particular, if stuffed with rice, were considered delicious; the little local Berkeley newspaper which came out once a week, the Berkeley *Tribune*, had recipes for dog soup, dog stew, even dog pudding.

Meditating about dog pudding made Stuart realize how

hungry he was. It seemed to him that he had not stopped being hungry since the first bomb fell; his last really adequate meal had been the lunch at Fred's Fine Foods that day he had run into the phoce doing his phony vision-act. And where, he wondered suddenly, was that little phoce now? He hadn't thought of him in years.

Now, of course, one saw many phoces, and almost all of them on their 'mobiles, exactly as Hoppy had been, placed dead center, each in his own little universe, like an armless, legless god. The sight still repelled Stuart, but there were so many repellent sights these days . . . it was one of many and certainly not the worst. What he objected to the most, he had decided, was the sight of symbiotics ambling along the street: several people fused together at some part of their anatomy, sharing common organs. It was a sort of Bluthgeld elaboration of the old Siamese twins . . . but these were not limited to two. He had seen as many as six joined. And the fusions had occurred – not in the womb – but shortly afterward. It saved the lives of imperfects, those born lacking vital organs, requiring a symbiotic relationship in order to survive. One pancreas now served several people . . . it was a biological triumph. But in Stuart's view, the imperfects should simply have been allowed to die.

On the surface of the Bay to his right a legless veteran propelled himself out onto the water aboard a raft, rowing himself toward a pile of debris that was undoubtedly a sunken ship. On the hulk a number of fishing lines could be seen; they belonged to the veteran and he was in the process of checking them. Watching the raft go, Stuart wondered if it could reach the San Francisco side. He could offer the man fifty cents for a one-way trip; why not? Stuart got out of his car and walked to the edge of the water.

'Hey,' he yelled. 'Come here.' From his pocket he got a

penny; he tossed it down onto the pier and the veteran saw it, heard it. At once he spun the raft about and came paddling rapidly back, straining to make speed, his face streaked with perspiration. He grinned up at Stuart, cupping his ear.

'Fish?' he called. 'I don't have one yet today, but maybe later. Or how about a small shark? Guaranteed safe.' He held up the battered Geiger counter which he had connected to his waist by a length of rope – in case it fell from the raft or someone tried to steal it, Stuart realized.

'No,' Stuart said, squatting down at the edge of the pier. 'I want to get over to San Francisco; 'I'll pay you a quarter for one way.'

'But I got to leave my lines to do that,' the veteran said, his smile fading. 'I got to collect them all or somebody'd steal them while I was gone.'

'Thirty-five cents,' Stuart said.

In the end they agreed, at a price of forty cents. Stuart locked the legs of Edward Prince of Wales together so no one could steal him, and presently he was out on the Bay, bobbing up and down aboard the veteran's raft, being rowed to San Francisco.

'What field are you in?' the veteran asked him. 'You're not a tax collector, are you?' He eyed him calmly.

'Naw,' Stuart said. 'I'm a small trap man.'

'Listen, my friend,' the veteran said, 'I got a pet rat lives under the pilings with me. He's smart; he can play the flute. I'm not putting you under an illusion, it's true. I made a little wooden flute and he plays it, through his nose . . . it's practically an Asiatic nose-flute like they have in India. Well, I did have him, but the other day he got run over. I saw the whole thing happen; I couldn't go get him or nothing. He ran across the pier to get something, maybe a piece of cloth . . . he has this bed I made for him but he gets – I mean he got – cold all the time because when they mutated, this particular line, they lost their hair.'

'I've seen those,' Stuart said, thinking how well the hairless brown rat evaded even Mr Hardy's electronic vermin trap. 'Actually I believe what you said,' he said. 'I know rats pretty well. But they're nothing compared to those little striped gray-brown tabby cats . . . I'll bet you had to make the flute, he couldn't construct it himself.'

'True,' the veteran said. 'But he was an artist. You ought to have heard him play; I used to get a crowd at night, after we finished with the fishing. I tried to teach him the Bach Chaconne in D.'

'I caught one of those tabby cats once,' Stuart said, 'that I kept for a month until it escaped. It could make little sharp-pointed things out of tin can lids. It bent them or something; I never did see how it did it, but they were wicked.'

The veteran, rowing, said, 'What's it like south of San Francisco these days? I can't come up on land.' He indicated the lower part of his body. 'I stay on the raft. There's a little trap door, when I have to go to the bathroom. What I need is to find a dead phoce sometime and get his cart. They call them phocomobiles.'

'I knew the first phoce,' Stuart said, 'before the war. He was brilliant; he could repair anything.' He lit up an imitation-tobacco cigarette; the veteran gaped at it longingly. 'South of San Francisco it's just farmland now. Nobody ever rebuilt there, and it was mostly those little tract houses so they left hardly any decent basements. They grow peas and corn and beans down there. What I'm going to see is a big rocket a farmer just found; I need relays and tubes and other electronic gear for Mr Hardy's traps.' He paused. 'You ought to have a Hardy trap.'

'Why? I live on fish, and why should I hate rats? I like them.'

'I like them, too,' Stuart said, 'but you have to be practical; you may have to look to the future. Someday America may be taken over by rats if we aren't vigilant. We owe it to our country to catch and kill rats, especially the wiser ones that would be natural leaders.'

The veteran glared at him. 'Sales talk, that's all.'

'I'm sincere.'

'That's what I have against salesmen; they believe their own lies. You know that the best rats can *ever* do, in a million years of evolution, is maybe be useful as servants to us human beings. They could carry messages maybe and do a little manual work. But dangerous—' He shook his head. 'How much does one of your traps sell for?'

'Ten dollars silver. No State boodle accepted; Mr Hardy is an old man and you know how old people are, he doesn't consider boodle to be real money.' Stuart laughed.

'Let me tell you about a rat I once saw that did a heroic deed,' the veteran began, but Stuart cut him off.

'I have my own opinions,' Stuart said. 'There's no use arguing about it.'

They were both silent, then. Stuart enjoyed the sight of the Bay on all sides; the veteran rowed. It was a nice day, and as they bobbed along towards San Francisco, Stuart thought of the electronic parts he might be bringing back to Mr Hardy and the factory on San Pablo Avenue, near the ruins of what had once been the west end of the University of California.

'What kind of cigarette is that?' the veteran asked presently.

'This?' Stuart examined the butt; he was almost ready to put it out and stick it away in the metal box in his pocket. The box was full of butts, which would be opened and made into new cigarettes by Tom Frandi, the local cigarette man in

South Berkeley. 'This,' he said, 'is imported. From Marin County. It's a special deluxe Gold Label made by—' He paused for effect. 'I guess I don't have to tell you.'

'By Andrew Gill,' the veteran said. 'Say I'd like to buy a whole one from you; I'll pay you a dime.'

'They're worth fifteen cents apiece,' Stuart said. 'They have to come all the way around Black Point and Sear's Point and along the Lucas Valley Road, from beyond Nicasio somewhere.'

'I had one of those Andrew Gill special deluxe Gold Labels one time,' the veteran said. 'It fell out of the pocket of some man who was getting on the ferry; I fished it out of the water and dried it.'

All of a sudden Stuart handed him the butt.

'For God's sake,' the veteran said, not looking directly at him. He rowed more rapidly, his lips moving, his eyelids blinking.

'I got more,' Stuart said.

The veteran said, 'I'll tell you what else you got; you got real humanity, mister, and that's rare today. Very rare.'

Stuart nodded. He felt the truth of the veteran's words.

Knocking at the door of the small wooden cabin, Bonny said, 'Jack? Are you in there?' She tried the door, found it unlocked. To Mr Barnes she said, 'He's probably out with his flock somewhere. This is lambing season and he's been having trouble; they're so many sports born and a lot of them won't pass through the birth canal without help.'

'How many sheep does he have?' Barnes asked.

'Three hundred. They're out in the canyons around here, wild, so an accurate count is impossible. You're not afraid of rams, are you?'

'No,' Barnes said.

'We'll walk, then,' Bonny said.

'And he's the man the former teacher tried to kill,' Barnes murmured, as they crossed a sheep-nibbled field toward a low ridge overgrown with fir and shrubbery. Many of the shrubs, he noticed, had been nibbled; bare branches showed, indicating that a good number of Mr Tree's sheep were in the vicinity.

'Yes,' the woman said, striding along, hands in her pockets. She added quickly, 'But I have no idea why. Jack is – just a sheep rancher. I know it's illegal to raise sheep on ground that could be plowed . . . but as you can see, very little of his land could be plowed; most of it is canyon. Maybe Mr Austurias was jealous.'

Mr Barnes thought to himself, I don't believe her. However, he was not particularly interested. He meant to avoid his predecessor's mistake, in any case, whoever or whatever Mr Tree was, he sounded, to Barnes, like something that had become part of the environment, no longer fully peripatetic and human. His notion of Mr Tree made him uncomfortable; it was not a reassuring image that he held in his mind.

'I'm sorry Mr Gill couldn't come with us,' Barnes said. He still had not met the famous tobacco expert, of whom he had heard even before coming to West Marin. 'Did you tell me you have a music group? You play some sort of instruments?' It had sounded interesting, because he, at one time, had played the cello.

'We play recorders,' Bonny said. 'Andrew Gill and Jack Tree. And I play the piano; we play early composers, such as Henry Purcell and Johann Pachelbel. Doctor Stockstill now and then joins us, but—' She paused, frowning. 'He's so busy; he has so many towns to visit. He's just too exhausted in the evenings.'

'Can anyone join your group?' Barnes inquired hopefully.

'What do you play? I warn you: we're severely classical. It's not just an amateur get-together; George and Jack and I played in the old days, before the Emergency. We began – nine years ago. Gill joined us after the Emergency.' She smiled, and Barnes saw what lovely teeth she had. So many people, suffering from vitamin deficiencies and radiation sickness in recent times . . . they had lost teeth, developed soft gums. He hid his own teeth as best he could; they were no longer good.

'I once played the cello,' he said, knowing that it was worthless as a former skill because there were – very simply – no cellos anywhere around now. Had he played a metal instrument . . .

'What a shame,' Bonny said.

'There are no stringed instruments in this area?' He believed that if necessary he could learn, say, the viola; he would be glad to, he thought, if by doing so he could join their group.

'None,' Bonny said.

Ahead, a sheep appeared, a black-faced Suffolk; it regarded them, then bucked, turned and fled. A ewe, Barnes saw, a big handsome one, with much meat on it and superb wool. He wondered if it had ever been sheared.

His mouth watered. He had not tasted lamb in years.

To Bonny he said, 'Does he slaughter, or is it for wool only?'

'For wool,' she answered. 'He has a phobia about slaughtering; he won't do it no matter what he's offered. People sneak up and steal from his flock, of course . . . if you want lamb that's the only way you'll get it, so I advise you now; his flock is well-protected.' She pointed, and Barnes saw on a hilltop a dog standing watching them. At once he recognized it as an extreme mutation, a useful one; its face was intelligent, in a new way.

'I won't go near his sheep,' Barnes said. 'It won't bother us now, will it? It recognizes you?'

Bonny said, 'That's why I came with you, because of the dog. Jack has only the one. But it's sufficient.'

Now the dog trotted toward them.

Once, Barnes conjectured, its folk had been the familiar gray or black German shepherd; he identified the ears, the muzzle. But now – he waited rigidly as it approached. In his pocket he of course carried a knife; it had protected him many times, but surely this – it would not have done the job, here. He stayed close to the woman, who walked on unconcernedly.

'Hi,' she said to the dog.

Halting before them, the dog opened its mouth and groaned. It was a hideous sound, and Barnes shivered; it sounded like a human spastic, a damaged person trying to work a vocal apparatus which had failed. Out of the groaning he detected – or thought he detected – a word or so, but he could not be sure. Bonny, however, seemed to understand.

'Nice Terry,' she said to the dog. 'Thank you, nice Terry.' The dog wagged its tail. To Barnes she said, 'We'll find him a quarter mile along the trail.' She strode on.

'What did the dog say?' he asked, when they were out of earshot of the animal.

Bonny laughed. It irritated him, and he scowled. 'Oh,' she said, 'my God, it evolves a million years up the ladder – one of the greatest miracles in the evolution of life – and you can't understand what it said.' She wiped her eyes. 'I'm sorry, but it's too damn funny. I'm glad you didn't ask me where it could hear.'

'I'm not impressed,' he said, defensively. 'I'm just not very much impressed. You've been stuck here in this small rural area and it seems like a lot to you, but I've been up and down the Coast and I've seen things that would make you—' He broke off. 'That's nothing, that dog. Nothing by comparison, although intrinsically I suppose it's a major feat.'

Bonny took hold of his arm, still laughing. 'Yes, you're from the great outside. You've seen all there is; you're right. What have you seen, Barnes? You know, my husband is your boss, and Orion Stroud is his boss. Why did you come here? Is this so remote? So rustic? I think this is a fine place to live; we have a stable community here. But as you say, we have few wonders. We don't have the miracles and freaks, as you have in the big cities where the radiation was stronger. Of course, we have Hoppy.'

'Hell,' Barnes said, 'phoces are a dime a dozen; you see them everywhere, now.'

'But you took a job here,' Bonny said, eyeing him.

'I told you. I got into political trouble with little two-bit local authorities who considered themselves kings in their own little kingdom.'

Thoughtfully, Bonny said, 'Mr Austurias was interested in political matters. And in psychology, as you are.' She continued to survey him, as they walked along. 'He was not good-looking, and you are. He had a little round head like an apple. And his legs wobbled when he ran; he never should have run.' She became sober, now. 'He did cook a delightful mushroom stew, shaggy manes and chanterelles – he knew them all. Will you invite me over for a mushroom dinner? It's been too long . . . we did try hunting on our own, but as Mrs Tallman said, it didn't work out; we got promptly sick.'

'You're invited,' he said.

'Do you find me attractive?' she asked him.

Startled, he mumbled, 'Sure, I certainly do.' He held onto her arm tightly, as if she were leading him. 'Why do you ask?' he said, with caution and a growing deeper emotion whose nature he could not fathom; it was new to him. It resembled excitement and yet it had a cold, rational quality to it, so perhaps it was not an emotion at all; perhaps it was an awareness, a form of acute intuition, about himself and the landscape, about all things visible about him – it seemed to take in every aspect of reality, and most especially it had to do with her.

In a split second he grasped the fact – without having any data to go on – that Bonny Keller had been having an affair with someone, possibly Gill the tobacco man or even this Mr Tree or Orion Stroud; in any case the affair was over or leastwise nearly over and she was searching for another to replace it. She searched in an instinctive, practical way, rather than in some starry-eyed romantic school-girl fashion. So no doubt she had had a good many affairs; she seemed expert in this, in the sounding people out to see how they would fit.

And me, he thought; I wonder if I would fit. Isn't it dangerous? My God, her husband, as she said, is my boss, the school principal.

But then perhaps he was imagining it, because it really did not appear very likely that this attractive woman who was a leader in the community and who scarcely knew him would select him like this . . . but she had not selected him; she was merely in the process of exploring. He was being tried, but as yet he had not, succeeded. His pride began to swim up as an authentic emotion coloring the cold, rational insight of a moment before. Its distorting power made itself felt instantly; all at once he wanted to be successful, to be selected, whatever the risk. And he did not have any love or sexual desire toward her; it was far too early for that. All that was involved was his pride, his desire not to be passed over.

It's weird, he thought to himself; he was amazed at himself, at how simple he was. His mind worked like some low order of life, something on the order of a starfish; it had one or two responses and that was all.

'Listen,' he said, 'where is this man Tree?' He walked on ahead of her now, peering to see, concentrating on the ridge ahead with its trees and flowers. He saw a mushroom in a dark hollow and at once started toward it. 'Look,' he said. 'Chicken-of-the-forest, they call it. Very delectable. You don't see it very often, either.'

Coming over to see, Bonny Keller bent down. He caught a glimpse of her bare, pale knees as she seated herself on the grass by the mushroom. 'Are you going to pick it?' she asked. 'And carry it off like a trophy?'

'I'll carry it off,' he said, 'but not like a trophy. More like a thing to pop into the frying pan with a bit of beef fat.'

Her dark, attractive eyes fixed themselves on him somberly; she sat brushing her hair back, looking as if she were going to speak. But she did not. At last he became uncomfortable; apparently she was waiting for him, and it occurred to him – chillingly – that he was not merely supposed to say something; he was supposed to *do* something.

They stared at each other, and Bonny, too, now looked frightened, as if she felt as he did. Neither of them did anything, however; each sat waiting for the other to make a move. He had the sudden hunch that if he reached toward her she would either slap him or run off . . . and there would be unsavory consequences. She might – good lord; they had killed their last teacher. The thought came to him now with enormous force; *could it have been this?* Could she have been having a love affair with him and he started to tell her husband or some damn thing? Is this as dangerous as that? Because if it is, my pride can go to hell; I want to get away.

Bonny said, 'Here's Jack Tree.'

Over the ridge came the dog, the mutation with the alleged

ability to speak, and slightly behind it came a haggard-faced man, bent, with round, stooped shoulders. He wore a seedy coat, a city man's coat, and dirty, blue-gray trousers. In no way did he look like a farmer; he looked, Mr Barnes thought, like a middle-aged insurance clerk who had been lost in the forest for a month or so. The man had a black-smeared chin which contrasted in an unpleasant manner with his unnaturally white skin. Immediately Mr Barnes experienced dislike. But, was it because of Mr Tree's physical appearance? God knew he had seen maimed, burned, damaged and blighted humans and creatures in profusion, during the last years . . . no, his reaction to Mr Tree was based on the man's peculiar shambling walk. It was the walk – not of a well man – but of a violently sick man. A man sick in a sense that Barnes had never experienced before.

'Hi,' Bonny said, rising to her feet.

The dog frisked up, acting in a most natural manner now.

'I'm Barnes, the new school teacher,' Barnes said, rising, too, and extending his hand.

'I'm Tree,' the sick man said, also extending his hand. When Barnes took it he found it unaccountably moist; it was difficult if not impossible for him to hold onto it – he let it drop at once.

Bonny said, 'Jack, Mr Barnes here is an authority on removing lambs' tails after they're grown and the danger of tetanus is not so great.'

'I see,' Tree said, nodding. But he seemed only to be going through the motions; he did not seem really to care or even to understand. Reaching down he thumped the dog. 'Barnes,' he said to the dog distinctly, as if he were teaching the dog the name.

The dog groaned. '. . . brnnnnz . . .' It barked, eying its master with gleaming hopefulness.

'Right,' Mr Tree said, smiling. He displayed almost no teeth at all, just empty gums. Worse even than me, Barnes thought. The man must have been down below, near San Francisco, when the big bomb fell; that's one possibility, or it could simply be diet, as in my case. Anyhow, he avoided looking; he walked away, hands in his pockets.

'You've got a lot of land here,' he said over his shoulder. 'Through what legal agency did you acquire title? The County of Marin?'

'There's no title,' Mr Tree said. 'I just have use. The West Marin Citizens' Council and the Planning Committee allow me, through Bonny's good offices.'

'That dog fascinates me,' Barnes said, turning. 'It really talks; it said my name clearly.'

'Say "good day" to Mr Barnes,' Mr Tree said to the dog.

The dog woofed, then groaned, 'Gddday, Mrbarn-zzzzz.' It woofed again, this time eying him for his reaction.

To himself, Barnes sighed. 'Really terrific,' he said to the dog. It whined and skipped about with joy.

At that, Mr Barnes felt some sympathy for it. Yes, it was a remarkable feat. Yet – the dog repelled him as did Tree himself; both of them had an isolated, warped quality, as if by being out here in the forest alone they had been cut off from normal reality. They had not gone wild; they had not reverted to anything resembling barbarism. They were just plain unnatural. He simply did not like them.

But he did like Bonny and he wondered how the hell she had gotten mixed up with a freak like Mr Tree. Did owning a lot of sheep make the man a great power in this small community; was it that? Or – was there something more, something which might explain the former – dead – teacher's action in trying to kill Mr Tree?

His curiosity was aroused; it was the same instinct, perhaps, that came into play when he spotted a new variety of mushroom and felt the intense need to catalogue it, to learn exactly which species it was. Not very flattering to Mr Tree, he thought caustically, comparing him to a fungus. But it was true; he did feel that way, about both him and his weird dog.

Mr Tree said to Bonny, 'Your little girl isn't along today.'

'No,' Bonny said. 'Edie isn't well'

'Anything serious?' Mr Tree said in his hoarse voice. He looked concerned.

'A pain in her stomach, that's all. She gets it every now and then; has as far back as I can remember. It's swollen and hard. Possibly it's appendicitis, but surgery is so dangerous these days—' Bonny broke off, then turned to Barnes. 'My little girl, you haven't met her . . . she loves this dog. Terry. They're good friends, they talk back and forth by the hour when we're out here.'

Mr Tree said, 'She and her brother.'

'Listen,' Bonny said, 'I've gotten sick and tired of that. I told Edie to quit that. In fact, that's why I like her to come out here and play with Terry; she should have actual playmates and not become so introverted and delusional. Don't you agree, Mr Barnes; you're a teacher – a child should relate to actuality, not fantasy, isn't that right?'

'These days,' Barnes said thoughtfully, 'I can understand a child withdrawing into fantasy . . . it's hard to blame him. Perhaps we all ought to be doing that.' He smiled, but Bonny did not smile back, nor did Mr Tree.

Not for a moment had Bruno Bluthgeld taken his eyes off the new young teacher – if this actually was the truth; if this short young man dressed in khaki trousers and workshirt really was a teacher, as Bonny had said.

Is he after me, too? Bluthgeld asked himself. Like the last

one? I suppose so. And Bonny brought him here . . . does that mean that even she, after all, is on their side? Against me?

He could not believe that. Not after all these years. And it had been Bonny who had discovered Mr Austurias' actual purpose in coming to West Marin. Bonny had saved him from Mr Austurias and he was grateful; he would not now be alive except for her, and he could never forget that, so perhaps this Mr Barnes was exactly what he claimed to be and there was nothing to worry about. Bluthgeld breathed a little more relaxedly now; he calmed himself and looked forward to showing Barnes his new-born Suffolk lambs.

But sooner or later, he said to himself, someone will track me here and kill me. It's only a matter of time; they all detest me and they will never give up. The world is still seeking the man responsible for all that happened and I can't blame them. They are right in doing so. After all, I carry on my shoulders the responsibility for the death of millions, the loss of three-fourths of the world, and neither they nor I can forget that. Only God has the power to forgive and forget such a monstrous crime against humanity.

He thought, I would not have killed Mr Austurias; I would have let him destroy me. But Bonny and the others – the decision was theirs. It was not mine, because I can no longer make decisions. I am no longer allowed to by God; it would not be proper. My job is to wait here, tending my sheep, wait for *him who is to come*, the man appointed to deal out final justice. The world's avenger.

When will he come? Bluthgeld asked himself. Soon? I've waited years now. I'm tired . . . I hope it won't be too much longer.

Mr Barnes was saying, 'What did you do, Mr Tree, before you became a sheep rancher?'

'I was an atomic scientist,' Bluthgeld said.

Nine

When Stuart McConchie returned to the East Bay from his trip to the peninsula south of San Francisco he found that someone – no doubt a group of veterans living under the pier – had killed and eaten his horse, Edward Prince of Wales. All that remained was the skeleton, legs and head, a heap worthless to him or to anyone else. He stood by it, pondering. Well, it had been a costly trip. And he had arrived too late anyhow; the farmer, at a penny apiece, had already disposed of the electronic parts of his Soviet missile.

Mr Hardy would supply another horse, no doubt, but he had been fond of Edward Prince of Wales. And it was wrong to kill a horse for food because they were so vitally needed for other purposes; they were the mainstay of transportation, now that most of the wood had been consumed by the wood-burning cars and by people in cellars using it in the winter to keep warm, and horses were needed in the job of reconstruction – they were the main source of power, in the absence of electricity. The stupidity of killing Edward maddened him; it was, he thought, like barbarism, the thing they all feared. It was anarchy, and right in the middle of the city; right in downtown Oakland, in broad day. It was what he would expect the Red Chinese to do.

Now, on foot, he walked slowly toward San Pablo Avenue. The sun had begun to sink into the lavish, extensive sunset which they had become accustomed to seeing in the years since the Emergency. He scarcely noticed it. Maybe I ought to go into some other business, he said to himself. Small animal traps – it's a living, but there's no advancement possible in it. I mean, where can you rise to in a business like that?

The loss of his horse had depressed him; he gazed down at the broken, grass-infested sidewalk as he picked his way along, past the rubble which once had been factories. From a burrow in a vacant lot something with eager eyes noted his passing; something, he surmised gloomily, that ought to be hanging by its hind legs minus its skin.

This, he thought, explains why Hoppy might legitimately have imagined he was seeing the afterlife. These ruins, the smoky, flickering pallor of the sky . . . the eager eyes still following him as the creature calculated whether it could safely attack him. Bending, he picked up a sharp hunk of concrete and chucked it at the burrow – a dense layer of organic and inorganic material packed tightly, glued in place by some sort of white slime. The creature had emulsified some of the debris lying around, had reformed it into a usable paste. Must be a brilliant animal, he thought. But he did not care. The world could do without the brilliant and deranged life forms exposed to the light of day in the past years.

I've evolved, too, he said, turning one last time to face the creature, in case it might scuttle after him from behind. My wits are much clearer than they formerly were; I'm a match for you any time, so give up.

Evidently the creature agreed; it did not even come forth from its burrow.

I've evolved, he thought, but sentimental. For he genuinely missed the horse. Damn those criminal veterans, he said to himself. They probably swarmed all over Edward the moment we pushed off in the raft. I wish I could get out of town; I wish I could emigrate to the open country where there's none of this brutal cruelty and hoodlumism. That's what that psychiatrist did, after the Emergency. Stockstill got right out of the East Bay; I saw him go. He was smart. He did not try to return to his old rut, he did not merely pick up where he left off, as I did.

I mean, he thought, I'm no better off now than I was before the goddam Emergency; I sold TV sets then and now I sell electronic vermin traps. What is the difference? One's as bad as the other. I'm going downhill, in fact.

To cheer himself he got out one of his remaining special deluxe Gold Label Andrew Gill cigarettes and lit up.

A whole day wasted, he realized, on this wild-goose chase to the far side of the Bay. In two hours it would be dark and he would be going to sleep, down in the cat-pelt-lined basement room which Mr Hardy rented him for a dollar in silver a month. Of course, he could light his fat lamp; he could burn it for a little while, read a book or part of a book – most of his library consisted of merely sections of books, the remaining portions having been destroyed or lost. Or he could visit old Mr and Mrs Hardy and sit in on the evening transmission from the satellite.

After all, he had personally radioed a request to Dangerfield just the other day, from the transmitter out on the mudflats in West Richmond. He had asked for 'Good Rockin' Tonight,' an old-fashioned favorite which he remembered from his childhood. It was not known if Dangerfield had that tune on his miles of tapes, however, so perhaps he was waiting in vain.

As he walked along he sang to himself,

> Oh I heard the news:
> There's good rockin' tonight.
> Oh I heard the *news*!
> There's good rockin' tonight!
> Tonight I'll be a mighty fine man.
> I'll hold my baby as tight as I can.

It brought tears to his eyes to remember one of the old songs, from the world the way it was. All gone now, he said to himself. Bluthgelded out of existence, as they say . . . and what do we have instead, a rat that can play the noseflute, and not even that because the rat got run over.

There was another old favorite, the tune about the man who had the knife; he tried to recall how it had gone. Something about the shark having teeth or pretty teeth. It was too vague; he could not recollect it. His mother had played a record of it for him; a man, with a gravelly voice, had sung it and it was beautiful.

I'll bet the rat couldn't play that, he said to himself. Not in a million years. I mean, that's practically sacred music. Out of our past, our sacred past that no brilliant animal and no funny person can share. The past belongs only to us genuine human beings. I wish (the idea stirred him) that I could do like Hoppy used to do; I wish I could go into a trance, but not see ahead like he did – I want to go *back*.

If Hoppy's alive now, can he do that? Has he tried it? I wonder where he is, that preview; that's what he was, a preview. The first phoce. I'll bet he did escape with his life. He probably went over to the Chinese when they made that landing up north.

I'd go back, he decided, to that first time I met Jim Fergesson, when I was looking for a job and it was still tough for a Negro to find a job in which he met the public. That was the thing about Fergesson; he didn't have any prejudice. I remember that day; I had a job selling aluminum pans door-to-door and then I got the job with the Britannica people but that was also door-to-door. My god, Stuart realized, my first genuine job was with Jim Fergesson, because you can't count that door-to-door stuff.

While he was thinking about Jim Fergesson – who was

now dead and gone all these years since the bomb fell – he arrived on San Pablo Avenue with its little shops open here and there, little shacks which sold everything from coat hangers to hay. One of them, not far off, was HARDY'S HOMEOSTATIC VERMIN TRAPS, and he headed in that direction.

As he entered, Mr Hardy glanced up from his assembly table in the rear; he worked under the white light of an arc lamp, and all around him lay heaps of electronic parts which he had scavenged from every corner of Northern California. Many had come from the ruins out in Livermore; Mr Hardy had connections with State officials and they had permitted him to dig there in the restricted deposits.

In former times Dean Hardy had been an engineer for an AM radio station in downtown Oakland; he was a slender, quiet-spoken, elderly man who wore a green sweater and necktie even now – and a tie was unique, in these times. His hair was gray and curly, and he reminded Stuart of a beardless Santa Claus: he had a droll, dour expression and a roguish sense of humor. Physically, he was small; he weighed only a hundred and twenty pounds. But he had a near-violent temper and Stuart respected him. Hardy was nearly sixty, and in many respects he had become a father-figure to Stuart. Stuart's actual father, dead since the '70's, had been an insurance underwriter, also a quiet man who wore a tie and sweater, but he had not had Hardy's ferocity, his outbursts; or if he had, Stuart had never witnessed them or had repressed the memory of them.

And, too, Dean Hardy resembled Jim Fergesson.

That more than any other factor had drawn Stuart to him, three years ago. He was conscious of it; he did not deny it or want to deny it. He missed Jim Fergesson and he was drawn to anyone who resembled him.

To Mr Hardy he said, 'They ate my horse.' He seated himself on a chair at the front of the shop.

At once Ella Hardy, his employer's wife, appeared from the living quarters in the rear; she had been fixing dinner. 'You *left* him?'

'Yes,' he admitted. She, a formidable woman, glared at him with accusing indignation. 'I thought he was safe out on the City of Oakland public ferry pier; there's an official there who—'

'It happens all the time.' Hardy said wearily. 'The bastards. It must have been those war vets who hole up down there. Somebody ought to drop a cyanide bomb under that pier; they're down there by the hundreds. What about the car? You had to leave it, I guess.'

'I'm sorry,' Stuart said.

Mrs Hardy said caustically, 'Edward was worth eighty-five silver US dollars. That's a week's profit gone.'

'I'll pay it back,' Stuart said, rigidly.

'Forget it,' Hardy said. 'We have more horses at our store out in Orinda. What about the parts from the rocket?'

'No luck,' Stuart said. 'All gone when I got there. Except for this.' He held up a handful of transistors. 'The farmer didn't notice these; I picked them up for nothing. I don't know if they're any good, though.' Carrying them over to the assembly table he laid them down. 'Not much for an all-day trip.' He felt more glum than ever.

Without a word, Ella Hardy returned to the kitchen; the curtain closed after her.

'You want to have some dinner with us?' Hardy said, shutting off his light and removing his glasses.

'I dunno,' Stuart said. 'I feel strange. It upset me to come back and find Edward eaten.' He roamed about the shop. Our relationship, he thought, is different with animals now. It's much closer; there isn't the great gap between us and them that there was. 'Over on the other side of the Bay I saw something I've never seen before,' he said. A flying animal like a bat but not a bat. More like a weasel, very skinny and long, with a big head. They call them *tommies* because they're always gliding up against windows and looking in, like peeping toms.'

Hardy said, 'It's a squirrel. I've seen them.' He leaned back in his chair, loosened his necktie. 'They evolved from the squirrels in Golden Gate Park.' He yawned. 'I once had a scheme for them . . . they could be useful – in theory, at least – as message carriers. They can glide or fly or whatever they do for amounts up to a mile. But they're too feral. I gave it up after catching one.' He held up his right hand. 'Look at the scar, there on my thumb. That's from a tom.'

'This man I talked to said they taste good. Like old-time chicken. They sell them at stalls in downtown San Francisco; you see old ladies selling them cooked for a quarter apiece, still hot, very fresh.'

'Don't try one,' Hardy said. 'Many of them are toxic. It has to do with their diet.'

'Hardy,' Stuart said suddenly, 'I want to get out of the city and out into the country.'

His employer regarded him.

'It's too brutal here,' Stuart said.

'It's brutal everywhere.'

'Not so much if you get away from town, really far away, say fifty to a hundred miles.'

'But then it's hard to make a living.'

'Do you sell any traps in the country?' Stuart asked.

'No,' Hardy said.

'Why not?'

'Vermin live in towns, where there's ruins. You know that.

Stuart, you're a woolgatherer. The country is sterile; you'd miss the flow of ideas that you have here in the city. Nothing happens; they just farm and listen to the satellite. Anyhow, you're apt to run into the old race prejudice against Negroes, out in the country; they've reverted to the old patterns.' Once more he put on his glasses, turned his arc light back on and resumed the assembling of the trap before him. 'It's one of the greatest myths that ever existed, the superiority of the country. I know you'd be back here in a week.'

'I'd like to take a line of traps say out around Napa,' Stuart persisted. 'Maybe up to the St Helena Valley. Maybe I could trade them for wine; they grow grapes up there, I understand, like they used to.'

'But it doesn't taste the same,' Hardy said. 'The ground is altered. The wine is—' He gestured. 'You'd have to taste it, I can't tell you, but it's really awful. Foul.'

They were both silent, then.

'They drink it, though,' Stuart said. 'I've seen it here in town, brought in on those old wood-burning trucks.'

'Of course, because people will drink anything they can get their hands on now. So do you, so do I.' Mr Hardy raised his head and regarded Stuart. 'You know who has liquor? I mean the genuine thing; you can't tell if it's pre-war that he's dug up or new that he's made.'

'Nobody in the Bay Area.'

Hardy said, 'Andrew Gill, the tobacco expert.'

'I don't believe it.' He sucked in his breath, fully alert, now.

'Oh, he doesn't produce much of it. I've only seen one bottle, a fifth of brandy. I had one single drink from it.' Hardy smiled at him crookedly, his lips twitching. 'You would have liked it.'

'How much does he want for it?' He tried to sound casual.

'More than you have to pay.'

'And – it tastes like the real thing? The *pre-war*?'

Hardy laughed and returned to his trap-assembling. 'That's right.'

I wonder what sort of a man Andrew Gill is, Stuart said to himself. Big, maybe, with a beard, a vest . . . walking with a silver-headed cane; a giant of a man with wavy, snow-white hair, imported monocle – I can picture him. He probably drives a Jaguar, converted of course now to wood, but still a great, powerful Mark XVI Saloon.

Seeing the expression on Stuart's face, Hardy leaned toward him. 'I can tell you what else he sells.'

'English briar pipes?'

'Yes, that, too.' Hardy lowered his voice. 'Girly photos. In artistic poses – you know.'

'Aw, Christ,' Stuart said, his imagination boggling; it was too much. 'I don't believe it.'

'God's truth. Genuine pre-war girly calendars, from as far back as 1950. They're worth a fortune, of course. I've heard of a thousand silver dollars changing hands over a 1962 *Playboy* calendar; that's supposed to have happened somewhere back East, in Nevada, somewhere like that.' Now Hardy had become pensive; he gazed off into space, his vermin trap forgotten.

'Where I worked when the bomb fell,' Stuart said, 'at Modern TV, we had a lot of girly calendars downstairs in the service department. They were all incinerated, naturally.' At least so he had always assumed.

Hardy nodded in a resigned way.

'Suppose a person were poking around in the ruins somewhere,' Stuart said. 'And he came onto an entire warehouse full of girly calendars. Can you imagine that?' His mind raced. 'How much could he get? Millions? He could trade them for real estate; he could acquire a whole county!'

'Right,' Hardy said, nodding.

'I mean, he'd be rich forever. They make a few in the Orient, in Japan, but they're no good.'

'I've seen them,' Hardy agreed. 'They're crude. The knowledge of how to do it has declined, passed into oblivion; it's an art that has died out. Maybe forever.'

'Don't you think it's partly because there aren't the girls any more who look like that?' Stuart said. 'Everybody's scrawny now and have no teeth; the girls most of them now have burn-scars from radiation, and with no teeth what kind of a girly calendar does that make?'

Shrewdly, Hardy said, 'I think the girls exist. I don't know where; maybe in Sweden or Norway, maybe in out-of-the-way places like the Solomon Islands. I'm convinced of it from what people coming in by ship say. Not in the US or Europe or Russia or China, any of the places that were hit – I agree with you there.'

'Could we find them?' Stuart said. 'And go into the business?'

After considering for a little while Hardy said, 'There's no film. There're no chemicals to process it. Most good cameras have been destroyed or have disappeared. There's no way you could get your calendars printed in quantity. If you did print them—'

'But if someone could find a girl with no burns and good teeth, the way they had before the war—'

'I'll tell you,' Hardy said, 'what would be a good business. I've thought about it many times.' He faced Stuart meditatively. 'Sewing machine needles. You could name your own price; you could have anything.'

Gesturing, Stuart got up and paced about the shop. 'Listen, I've got my eye on the big time; I don't want to mess around with selling any more – I'm fed up with it. I sold aluminum pots and pans and encyclopedias and TV sets and now these vermin traps. There good traps and people want them, but I just feel there must be something else for me.'

Hardy grunted, frowning.

'I don't mean to insult you,' Stuart said, 'but I want to grow. I *have* to; you either grow or you go stale, you die on the vine. The war set me back years, it set us all back. I'm just where I was ten years ago, and that's not good enough.'

Scratching his nose, Hardy said, 'What did you have in mind?'

'Maybe I could find a mutant potato that would feed everybody in the world.'

'Just one potato?'

'I mean a type of potato. Maybe I could become a plant breeder, like Luther Burbank. There must be millions of freak plants growing around out in the country, like there're all those freak animals and funny people here in the city.'

Hardy said, 'Maybe you could locate an intelligent bean.'

'I'm not joking about this,' Stuart said quietly.

They faced each other, neither speaking.

'It's a service to humanity,' Hardy said at last, 'to make homeostatic vermin traps that destroy mutated cats and dogs and rats and squirrels. I think you're acting infantile. Maybe your horse being eaten while you were over in South San Francisco—'

Entering the room, Ella Hardy said, 'Dinner is ready, and I'd like to serve it while it's hot. It's baked cod-head and rice and it took me three hours standing in line down at Eastshore Freeway to get the cod-head.'

The two men rose to their feet. 'You'll eat with us?' Hardy asked Stuart.

At the thought of the baked fish head, Stuart's mouth watered. He could not say no and he nodded, following after

Mrs Hardy toward the little combination living room and kitchen in the rear of the building. It had been a month since he had tasted fish; there were almost none left in the Bay any longer – most of the schools had been wiped out and had never returned. And those that were caught were often radioactive. But it did not matter; people had become able to eat them anyhow. People could eat almost anything; their lives depended on it.

The little Keller girl sat shivering on the examination table, and Doctor Stockstill, surveying her thin, pale body, thought of a joke which he had seen on television years ago, long before the war. A Spanish ventriloquist, speaking through a chicken . . . the chicken had produced an egg.

'My son,' the chicken said, meaning the egg.

'Are you sure?' the ventriloquist asked. 'It's not your daughter?'

And the chicken, with dignity, answered, 'I know my business.'

This child was Bonny Keller's daughter, but Doctor Stockstill thought, it isn't George Keller's daughter; I am certain of that . . . I know my business. Who had Bonny been having an affair with, seven years ago? The child must have been conceived very close to the day the war began. But she had not been conceived before the bomb fell; that was clear. Perhaps it was on that very day, he ruminated. Just like Bonny, to rush out while the bomb was falling, while the world was coming to an end, to have a brief, frenzied spasm of love with someone, perhaps some man she did not even know, the first man she happened onto . . . and now this.

The child smiled at him and he smiled back. Superficially, Edie Keller appeared normal; she did not seem to be a funny child. How he wished, God damn it, that he had an x-ray machine. Because—

He said aloud, 'Tell me more about your brother.'

'Well,' Edie Keller said in her frail, soft voice, 'I talk to my brother all the time and sometimes he answers but more often he's asleep. He sleeps almost all the time.'

'Is he asleep now?'

For a moment the child was silent. 'No, he's awake.'

Rising to his feet and coming over to her, Doctor Stockstill said, 'I want you to show me exactly where he is.'

The child pointed to her right side, low down; near, he thought, the appendix. The pain was there. That had brought the child in; Bonny and George had become worried. They knew about the brother, but they assumed him to be imaginary, a pretend playmate which kept their little daughter company. He himself had assumed so at first; the chart did not mention a brother, and yet Edie talked about him. Bill was exactly the same age as she. Born, Edie had informed the doctor, at the same time as she, of course.

'Why of course?' he had asked, as he began examining her – he had sent the parents into the other room because the child seemed reticent in front of them.

Edie had answered in her calm, solemn way, 'Because he's my twin brother. How else could he be inside me?' And, like the Spanish ventriloquist's chicken, she spoke with authority, with confidence; she, too, knew her business.

In the years since the war Doctor Stockstill had examined many hundreds of funny people, many strange and exotic variants on the human life form which flourished now under a much more tolerant – although smokily veiled – sky. He could not be shocked. And yet, this – a child whose brother lived inside her body, down in the inguinal region. For seven years Bill Keller had dwelt inside there, and Doctor Stockstill, listening to the girl, believed her; he knew that it was possible. It was not the first case of this kind. If he had his x-ray machine he would be able to see the tiny, wizened shape, probably no larger than a baby rabbit. In fact, with his hands he could feel the outline . . . he touched her side, carefully noting the firm cyst-like sack within. The head in a normal position, the body entirely within the abdominal cavity, limbs and all. Someday the girl would die and they would open her body, perform an autopsy; they would find a little wrinkled male figure, perhaps with a snowy white beard and blind eyes . . . her brother, still no larger than a baby rabbit.

Meanwhile, Bill slept mostly, but now and then he and his sister talked. What did Bill have to say? What possibly could he know?

To the question, Edie had an answer. 'Well, he doesn't know very much. He doesn't see anything but he thinks. And I tell him what's going on so he doesn't miss out.'

'What are his interests?' Stockstill asked. He had completed his examination; with the meager instruments and tests available to him he could do no more. He had verified the child's account and that was something, but he could not see the embryo or consider removing it; the latter was out of the question, desirable as it was.

Edie considered and said, 'Well, he uh, likes to hear about food.'

'Food!' Stockstill said, fascinated.

'Yes. He doesn't eat, you know. He likes me to tell him over and over again what I had for dinner, because he does get it after a while . . . I think he does anyhow. Wouldn't he have to, to live?'

'Yes,' Stockstill agreed.

'He gets it from me,' Edie said as she put her blouse back on, buttoning it slowly. 'And he wants to know what's in it.

He especially likes it if I have apples or oranges. And – he likes to hear stories. He always wants to hear about places. Faraway, especially, like New York. My mother tells me about New York so I told him; he wants to go there someday and see what it's like.'

'But he can't see.'

'I can, though,' Edie pointed out. 'It's almost as good.'

'You take good care of him, don't you?' Stockstill said, deeply touched. To the girl, it was normal; she had lived like this all her life – she did not know of any other existence. There is nothing, he realized once more, which is 'outside' nature; that is a logical impossibility. In a way there are no freaks, no abnormalities, except in the statistical sense. This is an unusual situation, but it's not something to horrify us; actually it ought to make us happy. Life per se is good, and this is one form which life takes. There's no special pain here, no cruelty or suffering. In fact there is solicitude and tenderness.

'I'm afraid,' the girl said suddenly, 'that he might die someday.'

'I don't think he will,' Stockstill said. 'What's more likely to happen is that he'll get larger. And that might pose a problem; it might be hard for your body to accommodate him.'

'What would happen, then?' Edie regarded him with large, dark eyes. 'Would he get born, then?'

'No,' Stockstill said. 'He's not located that way; he would have to be removed surgically. But – he wouldn't live. The only way he can live is as he's living now, inside you.' Parasitically, he thought, not saying the word aloud. 'We'll worry about that when the time comes,' he said, patting the child on the head. 'If it ever does.'

'My mother and father don't know,' Edie said.

'I realize that,' Stockstill said.

'I told them about him,' Edie said. 'But—' She laughed.

'Don't worry. Just go on and do what you'd ordinarily do. It'll all take care of itself.'

Edie said, 'I'm glad I have a brother; he keeps me from being lonely. Even when he's asleep I can feel him there, I know he's there. It's like having a baby inside me; I can't wheel him around in a baby carriage or anything like that, or dress him, but talking to him is a lot of fun. For instance, I get to tell him about Mildred.'

'Mildred!' He was puzzled.

'You know.' The child smiled at his ignorance. 'The girl that keeps coming back to Philip. And spoils his life. We listen every night. The satellite.'

'Of course.' It was Dangerfield's reading of the Maugham book. Eerie, Doctor Stockstill thought, this parasite swelling within her body, in unchanging moisture and darkness, fed by her blood, hearing from her in some unfathomable fashion a second-hand account of a famous novel . . . it makes Bill Keller part of our culture. He leads his grotesque social existence, too. God knows what he makes of the story. Does he have fantasies about it, about our life? Does he *dream* about us?

Bending, Doctor Stockstill kissed the girl on the forehead. 'Okay,' he said, leading her toward the door. 'You can go, now. I'll talk to your mother and father for a minute; there're some very old genuine pre-war magazines out in the waiting room that you can read, if you're careful with them.'

'And then we can go home and have dinner,' Edie said happily, opening the door to the waiting room. George and Bonny rose to their feet, their faces taut with anxiety.

'Come in,' Stockstill said to them. He shut the door after them. 'No cancer,' he said, speaking to Bonny in particular, whom he knew so well. 'It's a growth, of course; no doubt of that. How large it may get I can't say. But I'd say, don't worry about it. Perhaps by the time it's large enough to cause trouble our surgery will be advanced enough to deal with it.'

The Kellers sighed with relief; they trembled visibly.

'You could take her to the UC Hospital in San Francisco,' Stockstill said. 'They are performing minor surgery there . . . but frankly, if I were you I'd let it drop.' Much better for you not to know, he realized. It would be hard on you to have to face it . . . especially you, Bonny. Because of the circumstances involving the conception; it would be so easy to start feeling guilt. 'She's a healthy child and enjoys life,' he said. 'Leave it at that. She's had it since birth.'

'Has she?' Bonny said. 'I didn't realize. I guess I'm not a good mother; I'm so wrapped up in community activities—'

'Doctor Stockstill,' George Keller broke in, 'let me ask you this. Is Edie a – special child?'

' "Special"?' Stockstill regarded him cautiously.

'I think you know what I mean.'

'You mean, is she a funny person?'

George blanched, but his intense, grim expression remained; he waited for an answer. Stockstill could see that; the man would not be put off by a few phrases.

Stockstill said, 'I presume that's what you mean. Why do you ask? Does she seem to be funny in some fashion? Does she look funny?'

'She doesn't look funny,' Bonny said, in a flurry of concern; she held tightly onto her husband's arm, clinging to him. 'Christ, that's obvious; she's perfectly normal-looking. Go to hell, George. What's the matter with you? How can you be morbid about your own child; are you bored or something, is that it?'

'There are funny people who don't show it,' George Keller said. 'After all, I see many children; I see all our children. I've developed an ability to tell. A hunch, which usually is proved correct. We're required, we in the schools, as you know, to turn any funny children over to the State of California for special training. Now—'

'I'm going home,' Bonny said. She turned and walked to the door of the waiting room. 'Good-bye, Doctor.'

Stockstill said, 'Wait, Bonny.'

'I don't like this conversation,' Bonny said. 'It's ill. You're both ill. Doctor, if you intimate in any fashion that she's funny I won't ever speak to you again. Or you either, George. I mean it.'

After a pause, Stockstill said, 'You're wasting your words, Bonny. I am not intimating, because there's nothing to intimate. She has a benign tumor in the abdominal cavity; that's all.' He felt angry. He felt, in fact, the desire to confront her with the truth. She deserved it.

But, he thought, after she has felt guilt, after she's blamed herself for going out and having an affair with some man and producing an abnormal birth, then she will turn her attention to Edie; she will hate her. She will take it out on the child. It always goes like that. The child is a reproach to the parents, in some dim fashion, for what they did back in the old days or in the first moments of the war when everyone ran his own crazy way, did his private, personal harm as he realized what was happening. Some of us killed to stay alive, some of us just fled, some of us made fools out of ourselves . . . Bonny went wild, no doubt; she let herself go. And she's that same person now; she would do it again, perhaps has done it again. And she is perfectly aware of that.

Again he wondered who the father was.

Someday I am going to ask her point blank, he decided. Perhaps she doesn't even know; it is all a blur to her, that time in our lives. Those horrible days. Or was it horrible for her?

Maybe it was lovely; she could kick the traces, do what she wanted without fear because she believed, we all did, *that none of us would survive.*

Bonny made the most if it, he realized, as she always does; she makes the most out of life in every contingency. I wish I were the same . . . he felt envious, as he watched her move from the room toward her child. The pretty, trim woman; she was as attractive now as she had been ten years ago – the damage, the impersonal change that had descended on them and their lives, did not seem to have touched her.

The grasshopper who fiddled. That was Bonny. In the darkness of the war, with its destruction, its infinite sporting of life forms, Bonny fiddled on, scraping out her tune of joy and enthusiasm and lack of care; she could not be persuaded, even by reality, to become reasonable. The lucky ones: people like Bonny, who are stronger than the forces of change and decay. That's what she has eluded – the forces of decay which have set in. The roof fell on us, but not on Bonny.

He remembered a cartoon in *Punch*—

Interrupting his thoughts, Bonny said, 'Doctor, have you met the new teacher, Hal Barnes?'

'No,' he said. 'Not yet. I saw him at a distance only.'

'You'd like him. He wants to play the cello, except of course he has no cello.' She laughed merrily, her eyes dancing with pure life. 'Isn't that pathetic?'

'Very,' he agreed.

'Isn't that all of us?' she said. 'Our cellos are gone. And what does that leave? You tell me.'

'Christ,' Stockstill said, 'I don't know; I haven't the foggiest idea.'

Bonny, laughing, said, 'Oh, you're so earnest.'

'She says that to me, too,' George Keller said, with a faint smile. 'My wife sees mankind as a race of dung-beetles laboring away. Naturally, she does not include herself.'

'She shouldn't,' Stockstill said. 'I hope she never does.'

George glanced at him sourly, then shrugged.

She might change, Stockstill thought, if she understood about her daughter. That might do it. It would take something like that, some odd blow unprecedented and unanticipated. She might even kill herself; the joy, the vitality, might switch to its utter opposite.

'Kellers,' he said aloud, 'introduce me to the new teacher one day soon. I'd like to meet an ex-cello player. Maybe we can make him something out of a washtub strung with baling wire. He could play it with—'

'With horsetail,' Bonny said practically. 'The bow we can make; that part is easy. What we need is a big resonating chamber, to produce the low notes. I wonder if we can find an old cedar chest. That might do. It would have to be wood, certainly.'

George said, 'A barrel, cut in half.'

They laughed at that; Edie Keller, joining them, laughed, too, although she had not heard what her father – or rather, Stockstill thought, her mother's husband – had said.

'Maybe we can find something washed up on the beach,' George said. 'I notice that a lot of wooden debris shows up, especially after storms. Wrecks of old Chinese ships, no doubt, from years ago.'

Cheerfully, they departed from Doctor Stockstill's office; he stood watching them go, the little girl between them. The three of them, he thought. Or rather, the four, if the invisible but real presence within the girl was counted.

Deep in thought, he shut the door.

It could be my child, he thought. But it isn't, because seven years ago Bonny was up in West Marin here and I was at my office in Berkeley. But if I had been near her that day—

Who was up here then? he asked himself. When the bombs fell . . . who of us could have been with her that day? He felt a peculiar feeling toward the man, whoever he was. I wonder how he would feel, Stockstill thought, if he knew about his child . . . about his *children*. Maybe someday I'll run into him. I can't bring myself to tell Bonny, but perhaps I will tell him.

Ten

At the Foresters' Hall, the people of West Marin sat discussing the illness of the man in the satellite. Agitated, they interrupted one another in their eagerness to speak. The reading from *Of Human Bondage* had begun, but no one in the room wanted to listen; they were all murmuring grim-faced, all of them alarmed, as June Raub was, to realize what would happen to them if the disc jockey were to die.

'He can't really be that sick,' Cas Stone, the largest landowner in West Marin exclaimed. 'I never told anybody this, but listen; I've got a really good doctor, a specialist in heart diseases, down in San Rafael. I'll get him to a transmitter somewhere and he can tell Dangerfield what's the matter with him. And he can cure him.'

'But he's got no medicines up there,' old Mrs Lully, the most ancient person in the community, said. 'I heard him say once that his departed wife used them all up.'

'I've got quinidine,' the pharmacist spoke up. 'That's probably exactly what he needs. But there's no way to get it up to him.'

Earl Colvig, who headed the West Marin Police, said, 'I understand that the Army people at Cheyenne are going to make another try to reach him later this year.'

'Take your quinidine to Cheyenne,' Cas Stone said to the pharmacist.

'To Cheyenne?' the pharmacist quavered. 'There aren't any through roads over the Sierras any more. I'd never get there.'

In as calm a voice as possible, June Raub said, 'Perhaps he isn't actually ill; perhaps it's only hypochondria, from being isolated and alone up there all these years. Something about the way he detailed each symptom made me suspect that.' However, hardly anyone heard her. The three representatives from Bolinas, she noticed, had gone quietly over beside the radio and were stooping down to listen to the reading. 'Maybe he won't die,' she said, half to herself.

At that, the glasses man glanced up at her. She saw on his face an expression of shock and numbness, as if the realization that the man in the satellite might be sick and would die was too much for him. The illness of his own daughter, she thought, had not affected him so.

A silence fell over the people in the furthest part of the Hall, and June Raub looked to see what had happened.

At the door, a gleaming platform of machinery had rolled into sight. Hoppy Harrington had arrived.

'Hoppy, you know what?' Cas Stone called. 'Dangerfield said he's got something wrong with him, maybe his heart.'

They all became silent, waiting for the phocomelus to speak.

Hoppy rolled past them and up to the radio; he halted his 'mobile, sent one of his manual extensions over to delicately diddle at the tuning knob. The three representatives from Bolinas respectfully stood aside. Static rose, then faded, and the voice of Walt Dangerfield came in clear and strong. The reading was still in progress, and Hoppy, in the center of his machinery, listened intently. He, and the others in the room, continued to listen without speaking until at last the sound faded out as the satellite passed beyond the range of reception. Then, once again, there was only the static.

All of a sudden, in a voice exactly like Dangerfield's, the

phocomelus said, 'Well, my dear friends, what'll we have next to entertain us?'

This time the imitation was so perfect that several people in the room gasped. Others clapped, and Hoppy smiled. 'How about some more of that juggling?' the pharmacist called. 'I like that.'

' "Juggling," ' the phocomelus said, this time exactly in the pharmacist's quavering, prissy voice. ' "I like that." '

'No,' Cas Stone said, 'I want to hear him do Dangerfield; do some more of that, Hoppy. Come on.'

The phocomelus spun his 'mobile around so that he faced the audience. 'Hoode hoode hoo,' he chuckled in the low, easy-going tones which they all knew so well. June Raub caught her breath; it was eerie, the phoce's ability to mimic. It always disconcerted her . . . if she shut her eyes she could imagine that it actually was Dangerfield still talking, still in contact with them. She did so, deliberately pretending to herself. He's not sick, he's not dying, she told herself; listen to him. As if in answer to her own thoughts, the friendly voice was murmuring, 'I've got a little pain here in my chest, but it doesn't amount to a thing; don't worry about it, friends. Upset stomach, most likely. Over-indulgence. And what do we take for that? Does anybody out there remember?'

A man in the audience shouted, 'I remember: alkalize with Alka Seltzer!'

'Hoode hoode hoo,' the warm voice chuckled. 'That's right. Good for you. Now let me give you a tip on how to store gladiola bulbs all through the winter without fear of annoying pests. Simply wrap them in aluminum foil.'

People in the room clapped, and June Raub heard someone close by her say, 'That's exactly what Dangerfield would have said.' It was the glasses man from Bolinas. She opened her eyes and saw the expression on his face. I must have looked like that, she realized, that night when I first heard Hoppy imitating him.

'And now,' Hoppy continued, still in Dangerfield's voice, 'I'll perform a few feats of skill that I've been working on. I think you'll all get a bang out of this, dear friends. Just watch.'

Eldon Blaine, the glasses man from Bolinas, saw the phocomelus place a coin on the floor several feet from his 'mobile. The extensions withdrew, and Hoppy, still murmuring in Dangerfield's voice, concentrated on the coin until all at once, with a clatter, it slid across the floor toward him. The people in the Hall clapped. Flushing with pleasure, the phocomelus nodded to them and then once more set the coin down away from him, this time farther than before.

Magic, Eldon thought. What Pat said; the phoces can do that in compensation for not having been born with arms or legs, it's nature's way of helping them survive. Again the coin slid toward the 'mobile and again the people in the Foresters' Hall applauded.

To Mrs Raub, Eldon said, 'He does this every night?'

'No,' she answered. 'He does various tricks; I've never seen this one before, but of course I'm not always here – I have so much to do, helping to keep our community functioning. It's remarkable, isn't it?'

Action at a distance, Eldon realized. Yes, it is remarkable. *And we must have him*, he said to himself. No doubt of it now. For when Walt Dangerfield dies – and it is becoming obvious that he will, soon – we would have this memory of him, this reconstruction, embodied in this phoce. Like a phonograph record, to be played back forever.

'Does he frighten you?' June Raub asked.

'No,' Eldon said. 'Should he?'

'I don't know,' she said in a thoughful voice.

'Has he ever transmitted to the satellite?' Eldon asked. 'A lot of other handies have. Odd he hasn't, with his ability.'

June Raub said, 'He intended to. Last year he started building a transmitter; he's been working on it off and on, but evidently nothing came of it. He tries all sorts of projects . . . he's always busy. You can see the tower. Come outside a minute and I'll show you.'

He followed her to the door of the Foresters' Hall. Together, they stood outside in the darkness until they were able to see. Yes, there it was, a peculiar, crooked mast, rising up into the night sky but then breaking off abruptly.

'That's his house,' June Raub said. 'It's on his roof. And he did it without any help from us; he can amplify the impulses from his brain into what he calls his servo-assists, and that way he's quite strong, much more so than any unfunny man.' She was silent a moment. 'We all admire him. He's done a lot for us.'

'Yes,' Eldon said.

'You came here to nap him away from us,' June Raub said quietly. 'Didn't you?'

Startled, he protested, 'No, Mrs Raub – honest, we came to listen to the satellite; you know that.'

'It's been tried before,' Mrs Raub said. 'You can't nap him because he won't let you. He doesn't like your community down there; he knows about your ordinance. We have no such discrimination up here and he's grateful for that. He's very sensitive about himself.'

Disconcerted, Eldon Blaine moved away from the woman, back toward the door of the Hall.

'Wait,' Mrs Raub said. 'You don't have to worry: I won't say anything to anyone. I don't blame you for seeing him and wanting him for your own community. You know, he wasn't born here in West Marin. One day, about three years ago, he came rolling into town on his 'mobile, not this one but the older one the Government built before the Emergency. He had rolled all the way up from San Francisco, he told us. He wanted to find a place where he could settle down, and no one had given him that, up until us.'

'Okay,' Eldon murmured. 'I understand.'

'Everything nowadays can be napped,' Mrs Raub said. 'All it takes is sufficient force. I saw your police-cart parked down the road, and I know that the two men with you are on your police force. But Hoppy does what he wants. I think if you tried to coerce him he'd kill you; it wouldn't be much trouble for him and he wouldn't mind.'

After a pause Eldon said, 'I – appreciate your candor.'

Together, silently, they re-entered the Foresters' Hall.

All eyes were on Hoppy Harrington, who was still immersed in his imitation of Dangerfield. '. . . it seems to go away when I eat,' the phocomelus was saying. 'And that makes me think it's an ulcer, not my heart. So if any doctors are listening and they have access to a transmitter—'

A man in the audience interrupted, 'I'm going to get hold of my doctor in San Rafael; I'm not kidding when I say that. We can't have another dead man circling around and around the Earth.' It was the same man who had spoken before; he sounded even more earnest now. 'Or if as Mrs Raub says it's just in his mind, couldn't we get Doc Stockstill to help him?'

Eldon Blaine thought, But Hoppy was not here in the Hall when Dangerfield said those words. How can he mimic something he did not hear?

And then he understood. It was obvious. The phocomelus had a radio receiver at his house; before coming to the Foresters' Hall he had sat by himself in his house, listening to the satellite. That meant there were *two* functioning radios in West Marin, compared to none at all in Bolinas. Eldon felt rage and despair. We have nothing, he realized. And these people here have everything, even an extra, private radio set, for just one person alone.

It's like before the war, he thought blindly. They're living as good as then. *It isn't fair.*

Turning, he plunged back out of the Hall, into the night darkness. No one noticed him; they did not care. They were far too busy arguing about Dangerfield and his health to pay attention to anyone else.

Coming up the road, carrying a kerosene lantern, three figures confronted him: a tall, skinny man, a young woman with dark red hair, and between them a small girl.

'Is the reading over?' the woman asked. 'Are we too late?'

'I don't know,' Eldon said, and continued on past them.

'Oh, we missed it,' the little girl was clamoring. 'I told you we should have hurried!'

'Well, we'll go on inside anyhow,' the man told her, and then their voices faded away as Eldon Blaine, despairing, continued on into the darkness, away from the sounds and presence of other people, of the wealthy West Mariners who had so much.

Hoppy Harrington, doing his imitation of Dangerfield, glanced up to see the Kellers, with their little girl, enter the room and take seats in the rear. About time, he said to himself, glad of a greater audience. But then he felt nervous, because the little girl was scrutinizing him. There was something in the way she looked at him that upset him; it had always been so, about Edie. He did not like it, and he ceased suddenly.

'Go ahead, Hoppy,' Cas Stone called.

'Go on,' other voices chimed in.

'Do that one about Kool Aid,' a woman called. 'Sing that, the little tune the Kool Aid twins sing; you know.'

'Kool-Aid, Kool-Aid, can't wait,' Hoppy sang, but once more he stopped. 'I guess that's enough for tonight,' he said.

The room became silent.

'My brother,' the little Keller girl spoke up, 'he says that Mr Dangerfield is somewhere in this room.'

Hoppy laughed. 'That's right,' he said excitedly.

'Has he done the reading?' Edie Keller asked.

'Oh yeah, the reading's over,' Earl Colvig said, 'but we weren't listening to that; we're listening to Hoppy and watching what he does. He did a lot of funny things tonight, didn't you, Hoppy?'

'Show the little girl that with the coin,' June Raub said. 'I think she'd enjoy that.'

'Yes, do that again,' the pharmacist called from his seat. 'That was good; we'd all like to see that again, I'm sure.' In his eagerness to watch he rose to his feet, forgetting the people behind him.

'My brother,' Edie said quietly, 'wants to hear the reading. That's what he came for. He doesn't care about anything with a coin.'

'Be still,' Bonny said to her.

Brother, Hoppy thought. She doesn't have any brother. He laughed out loud at that, and several people in the audience automatically smiled. 'Your brother?' he said, wheeling his 'mobile toward the child. 'Your *brother*?' He halted the 'mobile directly before her, still laughing. 'I can do the reading,' he said. 'I can be Philip and Mildred and everybody in the book; I can be Dangerfield – sometimes I actually am. I was tonight and that's why your brother thinks Dangerfield's in the room. What it is, it's me.' He looked around at the people. 'Isn't that right, folks? Isn't it actually Hoppy?'

'That's right, Hoppy,' Cas Stone agreed, nodding. The others nodded, too, all of them, or at least most of them.

'Christ sake, Hoppy,' Bonny Keller said severely. 'Calm down or you'll shake yourself right off your cart.' She eyed him in her stern, domineering way and he felt himself recede; he drew back in spite of himself. 'What's been going on here?' Bonny demanded.

Fred Quinn, the pharmacist, said, 'Why, Hoppy's been imitating Walt Dangerfield so well you'd think it was him!'

The others nodded, chiming in with their agreement.

'You have no brother, Edie,' Hoppy said to the little girl. 'Why do you say your brother wants to hear the reading when you have no brother?' He laughed and laughed. The girl remained silent. 'Can I see him?' he asked. 'Can I talk to him? Let me hear him talk and – I'll do an imitation of him.' Now he was laughing so hard that he could barely see; tears filled his eyes and he had to wipe them away with an extensor.

'That'll be quite an imitation,' Cas Stone said.

'Like to hear that,' Earl Colvig said. 'Do that, Hoppy.'

'I'll do it,' Hoppy said, 'as soon as he says something to me.' He sat in the center of his 'mobile, waiting. 'I'm waiting,' he said.

'That's enough,' Bonny Keller said. 'Leave my child alone.' Her cheeks were red with anger.

To Edie, ignoring the child's mother, Hoppy said, 'Where is he? Tell me where – is he nearby?'

'Lean down' Edie said. 'Toward me. And he'll speak to you.' Her face, like her mother's, was grim.

Hoppy leaned toward her, cocking his head on one side, in a mock-serious gesture of attention.

A voice, speaking from inside him, as if it were a part of the interior world, said, 'How did you fix that record changer? How did you *really* do that?'

Hoppy screamed.

Everyone was staring at him, white-faced; they were on their feet now, all of them rigid.

'I heard Jim Fergesson,' Hoppy said.

The girl regarded him calmly. 'Do you want to hear my brother say more, Mr Harrington? Say some more words to him, Bill, he wants you to say more.'

And in Hoppy's interior world, the voice said, 'It looked like you healed it. It looked like instead of replacing that broken spring—'

Hoppy wheeled his cart wildly, spun up the aisle to the far end of the room, wheeled again and sat panting, a long way from the Keller girl; his heart pounded and he stared at her. She returned his stare silently, but now with the faint trace of a smile on her lips.

'You heard my brother, didn't you?' she said.

'Yes,' Hoppy said. 'Yes I did.'

'And you know where he is.'

'Yes.' He nodded. 'Don't do it again. Please. I won't do any more imitations if you don't want me to; okay?' He looked pleadingly at her, but there was no response there, no promise. 'I'm sorry,' he said to her. 'I believe you now.'

'Good lord,' Bonny said softly. She turned toward her husband, as if questioning him. George shook his head but did not answer.

Slowly and steadily the child said, 'You can see him too, if you want, Mr Harrington. Would you like to see what he looks like?'

'No,' he said. 'I don't want to.'

'Did he scare you?' Now the child was openly smiling at him, but her smile was empty and cold. 'He paid you back because you were picking on me. It made him angry, so he did that.'

Coming up beside Hoppy, George Keller said, 'What happened, Hop?'

'Nothing,' he said shortly.

Scared me, he thought. Fooled me, by imitating Jim Fergesson; he took me completely in, I really thought it was Jim again. Edie was conceived the day Jim Fergesson died; I know because Bonny told me once, and I think her brother was conceived simultaneously. But – it's not true; it wasn't Jim. It was – an *imitation*.

'You see,' the child said, 'Bill does imitations, too.'

'Yes.' He nodded, trembling. 'Yes, he does.'

'They're good.' Edie's dark eyes sparkled.

'Yes, very good,' Hoppy said. As good as mine, he thought. Maybe better than mine. I better be careful of him, he thought, of her brother Bill; I better stay away. I really learned my lesson.

It could have been Fergesson, he realized, in there. Reborn, what they call reincarnation; the bomb might have done it somehow in a way I don't understand. Then it's not an imitation and I was right the first time, but how'll I know? He won't tell me; he hates me, I guess because I made fun of his sister Edie. That was a mistake; I shouldn't have done that.

'Hoode hoode hoo,' he said, and a few people turned his way; he got some attention, here and there in the room. 'Well, this is your old pal,' he said. But his heart wasn't in it; his voice shook. He grinned at them, but no one grinned back. 'Maybe we can pick up the reading a little while more,' he said, 'Edie's brother wants to listen to it.' Sending out an extensor, he turned up the volume of the radio, tuned the dial.

You can have what you want, he thought to himself. The reading or anything else. How long have you been in there? Only seven years? It seems more like forever. As if – you've always existed. It had been a terribly old, wizened, white thing that had spoken to him. Something hard and small, floating. Lips overgrown with downy hair that hung trailing, streamers of it, wispy and dry. I bet it was Fergesson, he said to himself; it *felt* like him. He's in there, inside that child.

I wonder. Can he get out?

Edie Keller said to her brother, 'What did you do to scare him like you did? He was really scared.'

From within her the familiar voice said, 'I was someone he used to know, a long time ago. Someone dead.'

'Oh,' she said, 'so that's it. I thought it was something like that.' She was amused. 'Are you going to do any more to him?'

'If I don't like him,' Bill said, 'I may do more to him, a lot of different things, maybe.'

'How did you know about the dead person?'

'Oh,' Bill said, 'because – you know why. Because I'm dead, too.' He chuckled, deep down inside her stomach; she felt him quiver.

'No you're not,' she said. 'You're as alive as I am, so don't say that; it isn't right.' It frightened her.

Bill said, 'I was just pretending; I'm sorry. I wish I could have seen his face. How did it look?'

'Awful,' Edie said, 'when you said that. It turned all inward, like a frog's. But you wouldn't know what a frog looks like either; you don't know what anything looks like, so there's no use trying to tell you.'

'I wish I could come out,' Bill said plaintively. 'I wish I could be born like everybody else. Can't I be born later on?'

'Doctor Stockstill said you couldn't.'

'Then can't he make it so I could be? I thought you said—'

'I was wrong,' Edie said. 'I thought he could cut a little round hole and that would do it, but he said no.'

Her brother, deep within her, was silent then.

'Don't feel bad,' Edie said. 'I'll keep on telling you how things are.' She wanted to console him; she said, 'I'll never do again like I did that time when I was mad at you, when I stopped telling you about what's outside; I promise.'

'Maybe I could *make* Doctor Stockstill let me out,' Bill said.

'Can you do that? You can't.'

'I can if I want.'

'No,' she said. 'You're lying; you can't do anything but sleep and talk to the dead and maybe do imitations like you did. That isn't much; I can practically do that myself, and a lot more.'

There was no response from within.

'Bill,' she said, 'you know what? Well, now two people know about you – Hoppy Harrington does and Doctor Stockstill does. And you used to say nobody would ever find out about you, so you're not so smart. I don't think you're very smart.'

Within her, Bill slept.

'If you did anything bad,' she said, 'I could swallow something that would poison you. Isn't that so? So you better behave.'

She felt more and more afraid of him; she was talking to herself, trying to bolster her confidence. Maybe it would be a good thing if you did die, she thought. Only then I'd have to carry you around still, and it – wouldn't be pleasant; I wouldn't like that.

She shuddered.

'Don't worry about me,' Bill said suddenly. He had become awake again or maybe he had never been asleep at all; maybe he had just been pretending. 'I know a lot of things; I can take care of myself. I'll protect you, too. You better be glad about me because I can – well, you wouldn't understand. You know I can look at everyone who's dead, like the man I imitated. Well, there're a whole lot of them, trillions and trillions of them and they're all different. When I'm asleep I hear them muttering. They're still all around.'

'Around where?' she asked.

'Underneath us,' Bill said. 'Down in the ground.'

'Brrr,' she said.

Bill laughed. 'It's true. And we're going to be there, too. And so is Mommy and Daddy and everybody else. Everybody and everything's there, including animals. That dog's almost there, that one that talks. Not there yet, maybe; but it's the same. You'll see.'

'I don't want to see,' she said. 'I want to listen to the reading; you be quiet so I can listen. Don't you want to listen, too? You always say you like it.'

'He'll be there soon, too,' Bill said. 'The man who does the reading up in the satellite.'

'No,' she said. 'I don't believe that; are you sure?'

'Yes,' her brother said. 'Pretty sure. And even before him – do you know who the "glasses man" is? You don't, but he'll be there very soon, in just a few minutes. And then later on—' He broke off. 'I won't say.'

'No,' she agreed. 'Don't say, please. I don't want to hear.'

Guided by the tall, crooked mast of floppy's transmitter, Eldon Blaine made his way toward the phocomelus' house. It's now or never, he realized. I have only a little time. No one stopped him; they were all at the Hall, including the phocomelus himself. 'I'll get that radio and nap it, Eldon said to himself. If I can't get him at least I can return to Bolinas with something. The transmitter was now close ahead; he felt the presence of Hoppy's construction – and then all at once he was stumbling over something. He fell, floundered with his arms out. The remains of a fence, low to the ground.

Now he saw the house itself, or what remained of it. Foundations and one wall, and in the center a a patched-together cube, a room made out of debris, protected from rain by tar paper. The mast, secured by heavy guy wires, rose directly behind a little metal chimney.

The transmitter was on.

He heard the hum even before he saw the gaseous blue light of its tubes. And from the crack under the door of the tar-paper cube more light streamed out. He found the knob, paused, and then quickly turned it; the door swung open with no resistance, almost as if something inside were expecting him.

A friendly, intimate voice murmured, and Eldon Blaine glanced around, chilled, expecting to see – incredibly – the phocomelus. But the voice came from a radio mounted on a work bench on which lay tools and meters and repair parts in utter disorder. Dangerfield, still speaking, even though the satellite surely had passed on. Contact with the satellite such as no one else had achieved, he realized. They even have that, up here in West Marin. But why was the big transmitter on? What was it doing? He began to look hastily around . . .

From the radio the low, intimate voice suddenly changed; it became harsher, sharper. 'Glasses man,' it said, 'what are you doing in my house?' It was the voice of Hoppy Harrington, and Eldon stood bewildered, rubbing his head numbly, trying to understand and knowing on a deep, instinctive level that he did not – and never really would.

'Hoppy,' he managed to say. 'Where are you?'

'I'm here,' the voice from the radio said. 'I'm coming closer. Wait where you are, glasses man.' The door of the room opened and Hoppy Harrington, aboard his phocomobile, his eyes sharp and blazing, confronted Eldon. 'Welcome to my home,' Hoppy said caustically, and his voice now issued from him and from the speaker of the radio both. 'Did you think you had the satellite, there on that set?' One of his manual extensions reached out, and the radio was shut off. 'Maybe you did, or maybe you will, someday. Well, glasses man, speak up. What do you want here?'

Eldon said, 'Let me go. I don't want anything; I was just looking around.'

'Do you want the radio, is that it?' Hoppy said in an expressionless voice. He seemed resigned, not surprised in the least.

Eldon said, 'Why is your transmitter on?'

'Because I'm transmitting to the satellite.'

'If you'll let me go,' Eldon said, 'I'll give you all the glasses I have. And they represent months of scavenging all over Northern California.'

'You don't have any glasses this time,' the phocomelus said. 'I don't see your briefcase, anyhow. But you can go, though, as far as I'm concerned; you haven't done anything wrong, here. I didn't give you the chance.' He laughed in his brisk, stammering way.

Eldon said, 'Are you going to try to bring down the satellite?'

The phocomelus stared at him.

'You are,' Eldon said. 'With that transmitter you're going to set off that final stage that never fired; you'll make it act as a retro-rocket and then it'll fall back into the atmosphere and eventually come down.'

'I couldn't do that,' Hoppy said, finally. 'Even if I wanted to.'

'You can affect things at a distance.'

'I'll tell you what I'm doing, glasses man.' Wheeling his 'mobile past Eldon, the phocomelus sent an extension thrusting out to pick up an object from his work bench. 'Do you recognize this? It's a reel of recording tape. It will be transmitted to the satellite at tremendously high speed, so that hours of information are conveyed in a few moments. And at the same time, all the messages which the satellite has been receiving during its transit will be broadcast down to me the same way, at ultra high speed. This is how it was designed to work originally, glasses man. Before the Emergency, before the monitoring equipment down here was lost.'

Eldon Blaine looked at the radio on the work bench and then he stole a glance at the door. The phocomobile had moved so that the door was no longer blocked. He wondered if he could do it, if he had a chance.

'I can transmit to a distance of three hundred miles,' Hoppy was saying. 'I could reach receivers up and down Northern California, but that's all, by transmitting direct. But by sending my messages to the satellite to be recorded and then played back again and again as it moves on—'

'You can reach the entire world,' Eldon said.

'That's right,' Hoppy said. 'There's the necessary machinery aboard; it'll obey all sorts of instructions from the ground.'

'And then you'll be Dangerfield,' Eldon said.

The phocomelus smiled and stammered, 'And no one will know the difference. I can pull it off; I've got everything worked out. What's the alternative? Silence. The satellite will fall silent any day, now. And then the one voice that unifies the world will be gone and the world will decay. I'm ready to cut Dangerfield off any moment, now. As soon as I'm positive that he's really going to cease.'

'Does he know about you?'

'No,' Hoppy said.

'I'll tell you what I think,' Eldon said. 'I think Dangerfield's been dead for a long time, and it's actually been you we've been listening to.' As he spoke he moved closer to the radio on the work bench.

'That's not so,' the phocomelus said, in a steady voice. He went on, then, 'But it won't be long, now. It's amazing he's survived such conditions; the military people did a good job in selecting him.'

Eldon Blaine swept up the radio in his arms and ran toward the door.

Astonished, the phocomelus gaped at him; Eldon saw the expression on Hoppy's face and then he was outside, running through the darkness toward the parked police cart. I distracted him, Eldon said to himself. The poor damn phoce had no idea what I was going to do. All that talk – what did it mean? Nothing. Delusions of grandeur; he wants to sit down here and talk to the entire world, receive the entire world, make it his audience . . . but no one can do that except Dangerfield; no one can work the machinery in the satellite from down here. The phoce would have to be inside it, up there, and it's impossible to—

Something caught him by the back of the neck.

How? Eldon Blaine asked himself as he pitched face-forward, still clutching the radio. He's back there in the house and I'm out here. Action at a distance . . . he has hold of me. Was I wrong? Can he really reach out so far?

The thing that had hold of him by the neck squeezed.

Eleven

Picking up the first mimeographed sheet of the West Marin *News & Views*, the little twice-monthly newspaper which he put out, Paul Dietz scrutinized critically the lead item, which he had written himself.

> BOLINAS MAN DIES OF BROKEN NECK
> Four days ago Eldon Blaine, a glasses man from Bolinas, California, visiting this part of the country on business, was found by the side of the road with his neck broken and marks indicating violence by someone unknown. Earl Colvig, Chief of the West Marin Police, has begun an extensive investigation and is talking to various people who saw Blaine that night.

Such was the item in its entirety, and Dietz, reading it, felt deep satisfaction; he had a good lead for this edition of his paper – a lot of people would be interested, and maybe for the next edition he could get a few more ads. His main source of income came from Andy Gill, who always advertised his tobacco and liquor, and from Fred Quinn, the pharmacist, and of course, he had several classifieds. But it was not like the old days.

Of course, the thing he had left out of his item was the fact that the Bolinas glasses man was in West Marin for no good purpose; everyone knew that. There had even been speculation that he had come to nap their handy. But since that was mere conjecture, it could not he printed.

He turned to the next item in terms of importance.

> DANGERFIELD SAID TO BE AILING
> Persons attending the nightly broadcasts from the satellite report that Walt Dangerfield declared the other day that he 'was sick, possibly with an ulcerous or coronary condition,' and needed medical attention. Much concern was exhibited by the persons at the Foresters' Hall, it was further reported. Mr Cas Stone, who informed the *News & Views* of this, stated that as a last resort his personal specialist in San Rafael would be consulted, and it was discussed without a decision being reached that Fred Quinn, owner of the Point Reyes Pharmacy, might journey to Army Headquarters at Cheyenne to offer drugs for Dangerfield's use.

The rest of the paper consisted of local items of lesser interest; who had dined with whom, who had visited what nearby town . . . he glanced briefly at them, made sure that the ads were printed perfectly, and then began to run off further sheets.

And then, of course, there were items missing from the paper, items which could never be put into print. Hoppy Harrington terrified by seven-year-old child, for instance. Dietz chuckled, thinking of the reports he had received about the phoce's fright, his fit right out in public. Mrs Bonny Keller having another affair, this time with the new school teacher, Hal Barnes . . . that would have made a swell item. Jack Tree, local sheep rancher, accuses unnamed persons (for the millionth time) of stealing his sheep. What else? Let's see, he thought. Famous tobacco expert, Andrew Gill, visited by unknown city person, probably having to do with a merger of Gill's tobacco and liquor business and some huge city syndicate as yet unknown. At that, he frowned. If Gill moved from the area, the *News & Views* would lose its most constant ad; that was not good at all.

Maybe I ought to print that, he thought. Stir up local feeling against Gill for whatever it is he's doing. Foreign influences felt in local tobacco business . . . I could phrase it that way. Outside persons of questionable origin seen in area. That sort of talk. It might dissuade Gill; after all, he's a newcomer – he's sensitive. He's only been here since the Emergency. He's not really one of us.

Who was this sinister figure seen talking to Gill? Everyone in town was curious. No one liked it. Some said he was a Negro; some thought it was radiation burns – a war-darky, as they were called.

Maybe what happened to that Bolinas glasses man will happen to him, Dietz conjectured. Because there's too many people here who don't like outside foreign influences; it's dangerous to come around here and meddle.

The Eldon Blaine killing reminded him, naturally, of the Austurias one . . . although the latter had been done legally, out in the open, by the Citizens' Council and Jury. Still, there was in essence little difference; both were legitimate expressions of the town's sentiments. As would be the sudden disappearance from this world of the Negro or war-darky or whatever he was who now hung around Gill – and it was always possible that some retaliation might be taken out on Gill as well.

But Gill had powerful friends; for instance, the Kellers. And many people were dependent on his cigarettes and liquor; both Orion Stroud and Cas Stone bought from him in huge quantity. So probably Gill was safe.

But not the darky, Dietz realized. I wouldn't like to be in his shoes. He's from the city and he doesn't realize the depth of feeling in a small community. We have integrity, here, and we don't intend to see it violated.

Maybe he'll have to learn the hard way. Maybe we'll have to see one more killing. A darky-killing. And in some ways that's the best kind.

Gliding down the center street of Point Reyes, Hoppy Harrington sat bolt-upright in the center of his 'mobile as he saw a dark man familiar to him. It was a man he had known years ago, worked with at Modern TV Sales & Service; it looked like Stuart McConchie.

But then the phoce realized that it was another of Bill's imitations.

He felt terror, to think of the power of the creature inside Edie Keller; it could do this, in broad daylight, and what did he himself have to counter it? As with the voice of Jim Fergesson the other night he had been taken in; it had fooled him, despite his own enormous abilities. I don't know what to do, he said to himself frantically; he kept gliding on, toward the dark figure. It did not vanish.

Maybe, he thought, Bill knows I did that to the glasses man. Maybe he's paying me back. Children do things like that.

Turning his cart down a side street he picked up speed, escaping from the vicinity of the imitation of Stuart McConchie.

'Hey,' a voice said warningly.

Glancing about, Hoppy discovered that he had almost run over Doctor Stockstill. Chagrined, he slowed his 'mobile to a halt. 'Sorry.' He eyed the doctor narrowly, then, thinking that here was a man he had known in the old days, before the Emergency; Stockstill had been a psychiatrist with an office in Berkeley, and Hoppy had seen him now and then along Shattuck Avenue. Why was he here? How had he happened to decide on West Marin, as Hoppy had? Was it only coincidence?

And then the phocomelus thought, maybe Stockstill is a perpetual imitation, brought into existence the day the first bomb fell on the Bay Area; that was the day Bill was conceived, wasn't it?

That Bonny Keller, he thought; it all emanates from her. All the trouble in the community . . . the Austurias situation, which almost wrecked us, divided us into two hostile camps. She saw to it that Austurias was killed, and actually it should have been that degenerate, that Jack Tree up there with his sheep; he's the one who should have been shot, not the former school teacher.

That was a good man, a kindly person, the phoce thought, thinking of Mr Austurias. And hardly anyone – except me – supported him openly at his so-called trial.

To the phoce, Doctor Stockstill said tartly, 'Be more careful with that 'mobile of yours, Hoppy. As a personal favor to me.'

'I said I was sorry,' Hoppy answered.

'What are you afraid of?' the doctor said.

'Nothing,' Hoppy said. 'I'm afraid of nothing in the entire world.' And then he remembered the incident at the Foresters' Hall, how he had behaved. And it was all over town; Doctor Stockstill knew about it even though he had not been present. 'I have a phobia,' he admitted, on impulse. 'Is that in your line, or have you given that up? It has to do with being trapped. I was trapped once in a basement, the day the first bomb fell. It saved my life, but—' he shrugged.

Stockstill said, 'I see.'

'Have you ever examined the little Keller girl?' Hoppy said.

'Yes,' Stockstill said.

With acuity, Hoppy said, 'Then you know. There's not just one child but two. They're combined somehow; you probably know exactly how, but I don't – and I don't care. That's a funny person, that child, or rather she and her brother;

isn't that so?' His bitterness spilled out. 'They don't look funny. So they get by. People just go on externals, don't they? Haven't you discovered that in your practice?'

Stockstill said, 'By and large, yes.'

'I heard,' Hoppy said, 'that according to State law, all funny minors, all children who are in any way funny, either feral or not, have to be turned over to Sacramento, to the authorities.'

There was no response from the doctor; Stockstill eyed him silently.

'You're aiding the Kellers in breaking the law,' Hoppy said.

After a pause, Stockstill said, 'What do you want, Hoppy?' His voice was low and steady.

'N-nothing,' Hoppy stammered. 'Just justice, I mean; I want to see the law obeyed. Is that wrong? I keep the law. I'm registered with the US Eugenics Service as a—' He choked on the word. 'As a biological sport. That's a dreadful thing to do, but I do it; I comply.'

'Hoppy,' the doctor said quietly, 'what did you do to the glasses man from Bolinas?'

Spinning his 'mobile, Hoppy glided swiftly off, leaving the doctor standing there.

What did I do to him, Hoppy thought. I killed him; you know that. Why do you ask? What do you care? The man was from outside this area; he didn't count, and we all know that. And June Raub says he wanted to nap me, and that's good enough for most people – it's good enough for Earl Colvig and Orion Stroud and Cas Stone, and they run this community, along with Mrs Tallman and the Kellers and June Raub.

He knows I killed Blaine, he realized. He knows a lot about me, even though I've never let him examine me physically; he knows I can perform action at a distance . . . but everyone knows that. Yet, perhaps he's the only one who understands what it signifies. He's an educated man.

If I see that imitation of Stuart McConchie, he thought suddenly, I will reach out and squeeze it to death. I have to.

But I hope I don't see it again, he thought. I can't stand the dead; my phobia is about that, the *grave*: I was buried down in the grave with the part of Fergesson that was not disintegrated, and it was awful. For two weeks, with half of a man who had consideration for me, more so than anyone else I ever knew. What would you say, Stockstill, if you had me on your analyst's couch? Would that sort of traumatic incident interest you, or have there been too many like it in the last seven years?

That Bill-thing with Edie Keller lives somehow with the dead, Hoppy said to himself. Half in our world, half in the other. He laughed bitterly, thinking of the time he had imagined that he himself could contact the other world . . . it was quite a joke on me, he thought. I fooled myself more than anybody else. And they never knew. Stuart McConchie and the rat, Stuart sitting there munching with relish . . .

And then he understood. That meant that Stuart survived; he had not been killed in the Emergency, at least not at first, as Fergesson had. So this perhaps was not an imitation that he had seen just now.

Trembling, he halted his 'mobile and sat rapidly thinking.

Does he know anything about me? he asked himself. Can he get me into any trouble? No, he decided, because in those days – what was I? Just a helpless creature on a Government-built cart who was glad of any job he could find, any scrap tossed to him. A lot has changed. Now I am vital to the entire West Marin area, he told himself; I am a top-notch handy.

Rolling back the way he had come he emerged once more on the main street and searched about for Stuart McConchie. Sure enough, there he was, heading in the direction of

Andrew Gill's tobacco and liquor factory. The phoce started to wheel after him, and then an idea came to him.

He caused McConchie to stumble.

Seated within his 'mobile he grinned to himself as he saw the Negro trip, half-fall, then regain his footing. McConchie peered down at the pavement, scowling. Then he continued on, more slowly now, picking his way over the broken cement and around the tufts of weeds with care.

The phoce wheeled after him and when he was a pace or so behind he said, 'Stuart McConchie, the TV salesman who eats raw rats.'

As if struck the Negro tottered. He did not turn; he simply stood, his arms extended, fingers apart.

'How are you enjoying the afterlife?' Hoppy said.

After a moment the Negro said in a hoarse voice, 'Fine.' He turned, now. 'So you got by.' He looked the phoce and his 'mobile up and down.

'Yes,' the phoce said, 'I did. And not by eating rats.'

'I suppose you're the handy here,' Stuart said.

'Yes,' Hoppy said. 'No-hands Handy Hoppy; that's me. What are you doing?'

'I'm – in the homeostatic vermin trap business,' Stuart said.

The phoce giggled.

'Is that so goddam funny?' Stuart said.

'No,' the phoce said. 'Sorry. I'm glad you survived. Who else did? That psychiatrist across from Modern – he's here. Stockstill. Fergesson was killed.'

They both were silent then.

'Lightheiser was killed,' Stuart said. 'So was Bob Rubenstein. So were Connie the waitress and Tony; you remember them?'

'Yes,' the phoce said, nodding.

'Did you know Mr Crody, the jeweler?'

'No,' the phoce said, 'afraid not'

'He was maimed. Lost both arms and was blinded. But he's alive in a Government hospital in Hayward.'

'Why are you up here?' the phoce said.

'On business.'

'Did you come to steal Andrew Gill's formula for his special deluxe Gold Label cigarette?' Again the phoce giggled, but he thought, It's true. Everyone who comes sneaking up here from outside has a plan to murder or steal; look at Eldon Blaine the glasses man, and he came from Bolinas, a much closer place.

Stuart said woodenly, 'My business compels me to travel; I get all around Northern California.' After a pause he added, 'That was especially true when I had Edward Prince of Wales. Now I have a second-rate horse to pull my car, and it takes a lot longer to get somewhere.'

'Listen,' Hoppy said, 'don't tell anyone you know me from before, because if you do I'll get very upset; do you understand? I've been a vital part of this community for many years and I don't want anything to come along and change it. Maybe I can help you with your business and then you can leave. How about that?'

'Okay,' Stuart said. 'I'll leave as soon as I can.' He studied the phoce with such intensity that Hoppy felt himself squirm with self-consciousness. 'So you found a place for yourself,' Stuart said. 'Good for you.'

Hoppy said, 'I'll introduce you to Gill; that's what I'll do for you. I'm a good friend of his, naturally.'

Nodding, Stuart said, 'Fine, I'd appreciate that.'

'And don't you do anything, you hear?' The phoce heard his voice rise shrilly; he could not control it. 'Don't you nap or do any other crime, or terrible things will happen to you – understand?'

The Negro nodded somberly. But he did not appear to be frightened; he did not cringe, and the phoce felt more and more apprehensive. I wish you would go, the phoce thought to himself. Get out of here; don't make trouble for me. I wish I didn't know you; I wish I didn't know anyone from outside, from before the Emergency. I don't want even to think about that.

'I hid in the sidewalk,' Stuart said suddenly. 'When the first big bomb fell. I got down through the grating; it was a real good shelter.'

'Why do you bring up that?' the phoce squealed.

'I don't know. I thought you'd be interested.'

'I'm not,' the phoce squealed; he clapped his manual extensors over his ears. 'I don't want to hear or think any more about those times.'

'Well,' Stuart said, plucking meditatively at his lower lip, 'then let's go see this Andrew Gill.'

'If you knew what I could do to you,' the phoce said, 'you'd be afraid. I can do—' He broke off; he had been about to mention Eldon Blaine the glasses man. 'I can move things,' he said. 'From a long way off. It's a form of magic; I'm a magician!'

Stuart said, 'That's not magic.' His voice was toneless. 'We call that *freak-tapping*.' He smiled.

'N-no,' Hoppy stammered. 'What's that mean? "Freak-tapping," I never heard that word. Like table-tapping?'

'Yes, but with freaks. With funny people.'

He's not afraid of me, Hoppy realized. It's because he knew me in the old days when I wasn't anything. It was hopeless; the Negro was too stupid to understand that everything had changed – he was almost as he had been before, seven years ago, when Hoppy had last seen him. He was inert, like a rock.

Hoppy thought of the satellite, then. 'You wait,' he said

breathlessly to Stuart. 'Pretty soon even you city people will know about me; everyone in the world will, just like they do around here. It won't be long now; I'm almost ready!'

Grinning tolerantly, Stuart said, 'First impress me by introducing me to the tobacco man.'

'You know what I could do?' Hoppy said. 'I could whisk Andrew Gill's formula right out of his safe or wherever he keeps it and plunk it down in your hands. What do you say to that?' He laughed.

'Just let me meet him,' Stuart repeated. 'That's all I want; I'm not interested in his tobacco formula.' He looked weary.

Trembling with anxiety and rage, the phoce turned his 'mobile in the direction of Andrew Gill's little factory and led the way.

Andrew Gill glanced up from his task of rolling cigarettes to see Hoppy Harrington – whom he did not like – entering the factory with a Negro – whom he did not know. At once Gill felt uneasy. He set down his tobacco paper and rose to his feet. Beside him at the long bench the other rollers, his employees, continued at their work.

He employed, in all, eight men, and this was in the tobacco division alone. The distillery, which produced brandy, employed another twelve men, but they were north, in Sonoma County. They were not local people. His was the largest commercial enterprise in West Marin, not counting the farming interests such as Orion Stroud or Jack Tree's sheep ranch, and he sold his products all over Northern California; his cigarettes traveled, in slow stages, from one town to another and a few, he understood, had even gotten back to the East Coast and were known there.

'Yes?' he said to Hoppy. He placed himself in front of the phoce's cart, halting him at a distance from the work-area.

Once, this had been the town's bakery; being made of cement, it had survived the bomb blasts and made an ideal place for him. And of course he paid his employees almost nothing; they were glad to have jobs at any salary.

Hoppy stammered, 'This m-man came up from Berkeley to see you, Mr Gill; he's an important businessman, he says. Isn't that right?' The phoce turned toward the Negro. 'That's what you said to me, isn't it?'

Holding out his hand, the Negro said to Gill, 'I represent the Hardy Homeostatic Vermin Trap Corporation of Berkeley, California. I'm here to acquaint you with an amazing proposition that could well mean tripling your profits within six months.' His dark eyes blazed.

There was silence.

Gill repressed the impulse to laugh aloud. 'I see,' he said, nodding and putting his hands in his pockets; he assumed a serious stance. 'Very interesting, Mr—' He glanced questioningly at the Negro.

'Stuart McConchie,' the Negro said.

They shook hands.

'My employer, Mr Hardy,' Stuart said, 'has empowered me to describe to you in detail the design of a fully automated cigarette-making machine. We at Hardy Homeostatic are well aware that your cigarettes are rolled entirely in the old-fashioned way, by hand.' He pointed toward the employees working in the rear of the factory. 'Such a method is a hundred years out of date, Mr Gill. You've achieved superb quality in your special deluxe Gold Label Cigarettes—'

'Which I intend to maintain,' Gill said quietly.

Mr McConchie said, 'Our automated electronic equipment will in no way sacrifice quality for quantity. In fact—'

'Wait,' Gill said. 'I don't want to discuss this now.' He

glanced toward the phoce, who was parked close by, listening. The phoce flushed and at once spun his 'mobile away.

'I'm going,' Hoppy said. 'This doesn't interest me; good-bye.' He wheeled through the open door of the factory out onto the street. The two of them watched him go until he disappeared.

'Our handy,' Gill said.

McConchie started to speak, then changed his mind, cleared his throat and strolled a few steps away, surveying the factory and the men at their work. 'Nice place you have here, Gill. I want to state right now how much I admire your product; it's first in its field, no doubt of that.'

I haven't heard talk like that, Gill realized, in seven years. It was difficult to believe that it still existed in the world; so much had changed and yet here, in this man McConchie, it remained intact. Gill felt a glow of pleasure. It reminded him of happier times, this salesman's line of chatter. He felt amiably inclined toward the man.

'Thank you,' he said, and meant it. Perhaps the world, at last, was really beginning to regain some of its old forms, its civilities and customs and preoccupations, all that had gone into it to make it what it was. This, he thought, this talk by McConchie; it's authentic. It's a survival, not a simulation; this man has somehow managed to preserve his viewpoint, his enthusiasm, through all that has happened – he is still planning, cogitating, bullshitting . . . nothing can or will stop him.

He is, Gill realized, simply a good salesman. He has not let even a hydrogen war and the collapse of society dissuade him.

'How about a cup of coffee?' Gill said. 'I'll take a break for ten or fifteen minutes and you can tell me more about this automated machine or whatever it is.'

'Real coffee?' McConchie said, and the pleasant, optimistic

mask slid for an instant from his face; he gaped at Gill with naked, eager hunger.

'Sorry,' Gill said. 'It's a substitute, but not bad; I think you'll like it. Better than what's sold in the city at those so-called "coffee" stands.' He went to get the pot of water.

'Quite a place you have here,' McConchie said, as they waited for the coffee to heat. 'Very impressive and industrious.'

'Thank you,' Gill said.

'Coming here is a long-time dream fulfilled,' McConchie went on. 'It took me a week to make the trip and I'd been thinking about it ever since I smoked my first special deluxe Gold Label. It's—' He groped for words to express his thought. 'An island of civilization in these barbaric times.'

Gill said, 'What do you think of the country, as such? A small town like this, compared to life in the city . . . it's very different.'

'I just got here,' McConchie said. 'I came straight to you; I didn't take time to explore. My horse needed a new right front shoe and I left him at the first stable as you cross the little metal bridge.'

'Oh yes,' Gill said. 'That belongs to Stroud; I know where you mean. His blacksmith'll do a good job.'

McConchie said, 'Life seems much more peaceful here. In the city if you leave your horse – well, a while ago I left my horse to go across the Bay and when I got back someone had eaten it, and it's things like that that make you disgusted with the city and want to move on.'

'I know,' Gill said, nodding in agreement. 'It's brutal in the city because there're still so many homeless and destitute people.'

'I really loved that horse,' McConchie said, looking doleful.

'Well,' Gill said, 'in the country you're faced constantly

with the death of animals; that's always been one of the basic unpleasant verities of rural life. When the bombs fell, thousands of animals up here were horribly injured; sheep and cattle . . . but that can't compare of course to the injury to human life down where you come from. You must have seen a good deal of human misery, since E Day.'

The Negro nodded. 'That and the sporting. The freaks both as regards animals and people. Now Hoppy—'

'Hoppy isn't originally from this area,' Gill said. 'He showed up here after the war in response to our advertising for a handyman. I'm not from here, either; I was traveling through the day the bomb fell, and I elected to remain.'

The coffee being ready, the two of them began to drink. Neither man spoke for a time.

'What sort of vermin trap does your company make?' Gill asked, presently.

'It's not a passive type,' McConchie said. 'Being homeostatic, that is, self-instructing, it follows for instance a rat – or a cat or dog – down into the network of burrows such as now underlie Berkeley . . . it pursues one rat after another, killing one and going on to the next – until it runs out of fuel or by chance a rat manages to destroy it. There are a few brilliant rats – you know, mutations that are higher on the evolutionary scale – that know how to lame a Hardy Homeostatic Vermin Trap. But not many can.'

'Impressive,' Gill murmured.

'Now, our proposed cigarette-rolling machine—'

'My friend,' Gill said, 'I like you but – here's the problem. I don't have any money to buy your machine and I don't have anything to trade you. And I don't intend to let anyone enter my business as a partner. So what does that leave?' He smiled. 'I have to continue as I am.'

'Wait,' McConchie said instantly. 'There must be a

solution. Maybe we could lease you a Hardy cigarette-rolling machine in exchange for x-number of cigarettes, your special deluxe Gold Label variety, of course, delivered each week for x-number of weeks.' His face glowed with animation. 'The Hardy Corporation for instance could become sole licensed distributors of your cigarette; we could represent you everywhere, develop a systematic network of outlets up and down Northern California instead of the haphazard system you now appear to employ. What do you say to that?'

'Hmmmm,' Gill said. 'I must admit it does sound interesting. I admit that distribution has not been my cup of tea . . . I've thought off and on for several years about the need of getting an organization going, especially with my factory being located in a rural spot, as it is. I've even thought about moving into the city, but the napping and vandalism are too great there. And I don't want to move back to the city; this is my home, here.'

He did not say anything about Bonny Keller. That was his real reason for remaining in West Marin; his affair with her had ended years ago but he was more in love with her now than ever. He had watched her go from man to man, becoming more dissatisfied with each of them, and Gill believed in his own heart that someday he would get her back. And Bonny was the mother of his daughter; he was well aware that Edie Keller was his child.

'You're sure,' he said suddenly, 'that you didn't come up here to steal the formula for my cigarettes?'

McConchie laughed.

'You laugh,' Gill said, 'but you don't answer.'

'No, that's not why I'm here,' the Negro said. 'We're in the business of making electronic machines, not cigarettes.' But, it seemed to Gill, he had an evasive look on his face, and his voice was too full of confidence, too nonchalant. All at once Gill felt uneasy.

Or is it the rural mentality? he asked himself. The isolation getting the better of me; suspicion of all newcomers . . . of anything strange.

I had better be careful, though, he decided. I must not get carried away just because this man recalls for me the good old pre-war days. I must inspect this machine with great suspicion. After all, I could have gotten Hoppy to design and build such a machine; he seems quite capable in that direction. I could have done all these things proposed to me *entirely by myself*.

Perhaps I am lonely, he thought. That might be it; I am lonely for city people and their manner of thought. The country gets me down – Point Reyes with its *News & Views* filled up with mediocre gossip, and mimeographed!

'Since you're just up from the city,' he said aloud, 'I might as well ask you – is there any interesting national or international news, of late, that I might not have heard? We do get the satellite, but I'm frankly tired of disc jockey talk and music. And those endless readings.'

They both laughed. 'I know what you mean,' McConchie said, sipping his coffee and nodding. 'Well, let's see. I understand that an attempt is being made to produce an automobile again, somewhere around the ruins of Detroit. It's mostly made of plywood but it does run on kerosene.'

'I don't know where they're going to get the kerosene,' Gill said. 'Before they build a car they better get a few refineries operating again. And repair a few major roads.'

'Oh, something else. The Government plans to reopen one of the routes across the Rockies sometime this year. For the first time since the war.'

'That's great news,' Gill said, pleased. 'I didn't know that.'

'And the telephone companies—'

'Wait,' Gill said, rising. 'How about a little brandy in your coffee? How long has it been since you've had a coffee royal?'

'Years,' Stuart McConchie said.

'This is Gill's Five Star. My own. From the Sonoma Valley.' He poured from the squat bottle into McConchie's cup.

'Here's something else that might interest you.' McConchie reached into his coat pocket and brought out something flat and folded. He opened it up, spread it out, and Gill saw an envelope.

'What is it?' Picking it up, Gill examined it without seeing anything unusual. An ordinary envelope with an address, a cancelled stamp . . . and then he understood, and he could scarcely credit his senses. *Mail service.* A letter from New York.

'That's right,' McConchie said. 'Delivered to my boss, Mr Hardy. All the way from the East Coast; it only took four weeks. The Government in Cheyenne, the military people; they're responsible. It's done partly by blimp, partly by truck, partly by horse. The last stage is on foot.'

'Good lord,' Gill said. And he poured some of Gill's Five Star into *his* coffee, too.

Twelve

'It was Hoppy who killed the glasses man from Bolinas,' Bill said to his sister. 'And he plans to kill someone later on, too, and then I can't tell but after that it's something more like that, again.'

His sister had been playing Rock, Scissors, Paper with three other children; now she stopped, jumped to her feet and quickly ran to the edge of the school grounds, where she would be alone and could talk to Bill. 'How do you know that?' she asked, excited.

'Because I talked to Mr Blaine,' Bill said. 'He's down below now, and there's others coming. I'd like to come out and hurt Hoppy; Mr Blaine says I should. Ask Doctor Stockstill again if I can't be born.' Her brother's voice was plaintive. 'If I could be born even for just a little while—'

'Maybe I could hurt him,' Edie said thoughtfully. 'Ask Mr Blaine what I ought to do. I'm sort of afraid of Hoppy.'

'I could do imitations that would kill him,' Bill said, 'if I only could get out. I have some swell ones. You should hear Hoppy's father; I do that real good. Want to hear?' In a low, grown-up man's voice he said, 'I see where Kennedy proposes another one of those tax cuts of his. If he thinks he can fix up the economy that way he's crazier than I think he is, and that's damn crazy.'

'Do me,' Edie said. 'Imitate me.'

'How can I?' Bill said. 'You're not dead yet.'

Edie said, 'What's it like to he dead? I'm going to be someday so I want to know.'

'It's funny. You're down in a hole looking up. And you're all flat like – well, like you're empty. And, you know what? Then after a while you come back. You blow away and where you get blown away to is back again! Did you know that? I mean, back where you are right now. All fat and alive.'

'No,' Edie said. 'I didn't know that.' She felt bored; she wanted to hear more about how Hoppy had killed Mr Blaine. After a point the dead people down below weren't very interesting because they never did anything, they just waited around. Some of them, like Mr Blaine, thought all the time about killing and others just mooned like vegetables – Bill had told her many times because he was so interested. He thought it mattered.

Bill said, 'Listen, Edie, let's try the animal experiment again; okay? You catch some little animal and hold it against your belly and I'll try again and see if I can get outside and in it. Okay?'

'We tried it,' she said practically.

'Let's try again! Get something real small. What are those things that – you know. Have shells and make slime.'

'Slugs.'

'No.'

'Snails.'

'Yes, that's it. Get a snail and put it as close to me as you can. Get it right up to my head where it can hear me and I can hear it back. Will you do that?' Ominously, Bill said, 'If you don't, I'm going to go to sleep for a whole year.' He was silent, then.

'Go to sleep, then,' Edie said. 'I don't care. I have a lot of other people to talk to and you don't.'

'I'll die, then, and you won't be able to stand that, because then you'll have to carry a dead thing around forever inside you, or – I tell you what I'll do; I know what I'll do. If you don't get an animal and hold it up near me I'll grow big and pretty soon I'll be so big that you'll pop like an old – you know.'

'Bag,' Edie said.

'Yes. And that way I'll get out.'

'You'll get out,' she agreed, 'but you'll just roll around and die yourself; you won't he able to live.'

'I hate you,' Bill said.

'I hate you more,' Edie said. 'I hated you first, a long time ago when I first found out about you.'

'All right for you,' Bill said morosely. 'See if I care. I'm rubber and you're glue.'

Edie said nothing; she walked back to the girls and entered once more the game of Rock, Scissors, Paper. It was much more interesting than anything her brother had to say; he knew so little, did nothing, saw nothing, down there inside her.

But it was interesting, that part about Hoppy squeezing Mr Blaine's neck. She wondered who Hoppy was going to squeeze next, and if she should tell her mother or the policeman Mr Colvig.

Bill spoke up suddenly. 'Can I play, too?'

Glancing about, Edie made sure that none of the other girls had heard him. 'Can my brother play?' she asked.

'You don't have any brother,' Wilma Stone said, with contempt.

'He's made-up,' Rose Quinn reminded her. 'So it's okay if he plays.' To Edie she said, 'He can play.'

'One, two, three,' the girls said, each extending then one hand with all fingers, none, or two displayed.

'Bill goes scissors,' Edie said. 'So he beats you, Wilma,

because scissors cuts paper, and you get to hit him, Rose, because rock crushes scissors, and he's tied with me.'

'How do I hit him?' Rose said.

Pondering, Edie said, 'Hit me very lightly here.' She indicated her side, just above the belt of her skirt. 'Just with the side of your hand, and be careful because he's delicate.'

Rose, with care, rapped her there. Within her Bill said, 'Okay, I'll get her back the next time.'

Across the playground came Edie's father, the principal of the school, and with him walked Mr Barnes, the new teacher. They paused briefly by the three girls, smiling.

'Bill's playing, too,' Edie said to her father. 'He just got hit.'

George Keller laughed. To Mr Barnes he said, 'That's what comes of being imaginary; you always get hit.'

'How's Bill going to hit me?' Wilma said apprehensively; she drew away and glanced up at the principal and teacher. 'He's going to hit me,' she explained. 'Don't do it hard,' she said, speaking in the general direction of Edie. 'Okay?'

'He can't hit hard,' Edie said, 'even when he wants to.' Across from her Wilma gave a little jump. 'See?' Edie said. 'That's all he can do, even when he tries as hard as he can.'

'He didn't hit me,' Wilma said. 'He just scared me. He doesn't have very good aim.'

'That's because he can't see,' Edie said. 'Maybe I better hit you for him; that's more fair.' She leaned forward and swiftly rapped Wilma on the wrist. 'Now let's do it again. One, two, three.'

'Why can't he see, Edie?' Mr Barnes asked.

'Because,' she said, 'he has no eyes.'

To her father, Mr Barnes said, 'Well, it's a reasonable-enough answer.' They both laughed and then strolled on.

Inside Edie her brother said, 'If you got a snail I could

be it for a while and I could maybe crawl around and see. Snails can see, can't they? You told me once they have eyes on sticks.'

'Stalks,' Edie corrected.

'Please,' Bill said.

She thought, I know what I'll do; I'll hold a worm against me, and when he gets into it he'll be just like he is – a worm can't see or do anything but dig, and won't he be surprised.

'All right,' she said, again springing up. 'I'll get an animal and do that. Wait a minute until I find one; I have to find it first so be patient.'

'Gee, thanks a lot,' Bill said, in a voice laden with nervousness and yearning. 'I'll do something back for you; on my word of honor.'

'What can you do for me?' Edie said, searching about in the grass at the edge of the school yard for a worm; she had seen many of them, since the rains of the previous night. 'What can a thing like you do for anybody?' She searched avidly, stirring the grass with eager, swift fingers.

Her brother did not answer; she felt his mute sorrow and to herself she snickered.

'Looking for something you lost?' a man's voice said above her. She peeped up; it was Mr Barnes, standing there smiling down.

'I'm looking for a worm,' she said shyly.

'What an unsqueamish girl,' he said.

'Who are you talking to?' Bill said, in confusion. 'Who's that?'

'Mr Barnes,' she said, explaining.

'Yes?' Mr Barnes said.

'I was talking to my brother, not you,' Edie said. 'He asked who it was. He's the new teacher,' she explained to Bill.

Bill said, 'I see; I understand him, he's close so I can get him. He knows Mama.'

'Our Mama?' Edie said, surprised.

'Yes,' Bill said, in a puzzled voice. 'I don't understand but he knows her and he sees her, all the time, when nobody is looking. He and she—' He broke off. 'It's awful and bad. It's—' He choked. 'I can't say it.'

Edie stared at her teacher open-mouthed.

'There,' Bill said hopefully. 'Didn't I do something back for you? I told you something secret you never would have known. Isn't that something?'

'Yes,' Edie said slowly, nodding in a daze. 'I guess so.'

To Bonny, Hal Barnes said, 'I saw your daughter today. And I got the distinct impression that she knows about us.'

'Oh, Christ, how could she?' Bonny said. 'It's impossible.' She reached out and turned up the fat-lamp. The living room assumed a much more substantial quality as the chairs and a table and pictures became visible. 'And anyhow it doesn't matter; she wouldn't care.'

To himself, Barnes thought, But she could tell George.

Thinking about Bonny's husband made him peer past the window shade and out into the moonlit road. No one stirred; the road was deserted and only foliage, rolling hillsides and the flat farm land below were to be seen. A peaceful, pastoral sight, he thought. George, being the principal of the school, was at the PTA meeting and would not be home for several hours. Edie, of course, was in bed; it was eight o'clock.

And Bill he thought. Where is Bill, as Edie calls him? Roaming about the house somewhere, spying on us? He felt uncomfortable and he moved away from the woman beside him on the couch.

'What's the matter?' Bonny said alertly. 'Hear something?'

'No. But—' He gestured.

Bonny reached out, took hold of him and drew him down to her. 'My god, you're cowardly. Didn't the war teach you anything about life?'

'It taught me,' he said, 'to value my existence and not to throw it away; it taught me to play it safe.'

Groaning, Bonny sat up; she rearranged her clothes, buttoned her blouse back up. What a contrast this man was to Andrew Gill, who always made love to her right out in the open, in broad daylight, along the oak-lined roads of West Marin, where anyone and anything might go past. He had seized her each time as he had the first time – yanking her into it, not gabbling or quaking or mumbling . . . maybe I ought to go back to him, she thought.

Maybe, she thought, I ought to leave them all, Barnes and George and that nutty daughter of mine; I ought to go live with Gill openly, defy the community and be happy for a change.

'Well, if we're not going to make love,' she said, 'then let's go down to the Foresters' Hall and listen to the satellite.'

'Are you serious?' Barnes said.

'Of course.' She went to the closet to get her coat.

'Then all you want,' he said slowly, 'is to make love; that's all you care about in a relationship.'

'What do you care about? *Talking?*'

He looked at her in a melancholy way, but he did not answer.

'You fruit,' she said, shaking her head. 'You poor fruit. Why did you come to West Marin in the first place? Just to teach little kids and stroll around picking mushrooms?' She was overcome with disgust.

'My experience today on the playground—' Barnes began.

'You had no experience,' she interrupted. 'It was just your goddam guilty conscience catching up with you. Let's go; I want to hear Dangerfield. At least when he talks it's fun to listen.' She put on her coat, walked quickly to the front door and opened it.

'Will Edie be all right?' Barnes asked as they started down the path.

'Sure,' she said, unable at the moment to care. Let her burn up, she said to herself. Gloomily, she plodded down the road, hands thrust deep in her coat pockets; Barnes trailed along behind her, trying to keep up with her strides.

Ahead of them two figures appeared, turning the corner and emerging into sight; she stopped, stricken, thinking one of them was George. And then she saw that the shorter, heavier man was Jack Tree and the other – she strained to see, still walking as if nothing were wrong. It was Doctor Stockstill.

'Come on,' she said over her shoulder, calmly, to Barnes. He came, then, hesitantly, wanting to turn back, to run. 'Hi,' she called to Stockstill and Bluthgeld, or rather Jack Tree – she had to remember to keep calling him that. 'What's this, psychoanalysis out in the dark at night? Does that make it more effective? I'm not surprised to learn it.'

Gasping, Tree said in his hoarse, grating voice, 'Bonny, *I saw him again.* It's the Negro who understood about me that day when the war began, when I was going into Stockstill's office. Remember, you sent me?'

Jokingly, Stockstill said, 'They all look alike, as the saying goes. And anyhow—'

'No, it's the same man,' Tree said. 'He's followed me here. Do you know what this means?' He looked from Bonny to Stockstill to Barnes, his eyes rubbery and enlarged, terror-stricken. 'This means that it's going to start again.'

'What's going to start again?' Bonny said.

'The war,' Tree said to her. 'Because that's why it began last time; the Negro saw me and understood what I had done, he knew who I was and he still does. As soon as he sees me—' He broke off, wheezing and coughing in his agony. 'Pardon me,' he murmured.

To Stockstill, Bonny said, 'There's a Negro here; he's right. I saw him. Evidently he came to talk to Gill about selling his cigarettes.'

'It couldn't be the same person,' Stockstill said. He and she went off to one side slightly, talking now between themselves.

'Certainly it could,' Bonny said. 'But that doesn't matter because that's one of his delusions. I've heard him gabble about it countless times. Some Negro was sweeping the sidewalk and saw him go into your office, and that day the war began so he's got them connected in his mind. And now he'll probably completely deteriorate, don't you think?' She felt resigned; she had been expecting this to happen, eventually. 'And so the period,' she said, 'of stable maladjustment is drawing to a close.' Perhaps, she thought, for us all. Just plain all of us. We could not have gone on like this forever, Bluthgeld with his sheep, me with George . . . she sighed. 'What do you think?'

Stockstill said, 'I wish I had some Stelazine, but Stelazine ceased to exist on E Day. That would help him. I can't. I've given up; you know that, Bonny.' He sounded resigned, too.

'He'll tell everyone,' she said, watching Bluthgeld, who stood repeating to Barnes what he had just told her and Stockstill. 'They'll know who he is, and they will kill him, as he fears; he's right.'

'I can't stop him,' Stockstill said mildly.

'You don't particularly care,' she said.

He shrugged.

Going back to Bluthgeld, Bonny said, 'Listen, Jack, let's all go to Gill's and see this Negro and I'll bet he didn't notice you that day. Do you want to bet? 'I'll bet you twenty-five silver cents.'

'Why do you say you caused the war?' Barnes was saying to Bluthgeld. He turned to Bonny with a puzzled expression. 'What is this, a war psychosis? And he says the war's coming back.' Once more to Bluthgeld he said, 'It isn't possible for it to happen again; I can give you fifty reasons. First of all, there're no hydrogen weapons left. Second—'

Putting her hand on Barnes' shoulder, Bonny said, 'Be quiet.' She said to Bruno Bluthgeld, 'Let's go down, all of us together, and listen to the satellite. Okay?'

Bluthgeld muttered, 'What is the satellite?'

'Good lord,' Barnes said. 'He doesn't know what you're talking about. He's mentally ill.' To Stockstill he said, 'Listen, Doctor, isn't schizophrenia where a person loses track of their culture and its values? Well, this man has lost track; listen to him.'

'I hear him,' Stockstill said in a remote voice.

Bonny said to him, 'Doctor, Jack Tree is very dear to me. He has been in the past very much like a father to me. For God's sake, do something for him. I can't stand to see him like this; I just can't stand it.'

Spreading his hands helplessly, Stockstill said, 'Bonny, you think like a child. You think anything can be obtained if you just want it badly enough. That's magical thinking. I can't help – Jack Tree.' He turned away and walked off a few steps, toward town. 'Come on,' he said to them over his shoulder. 'We'll do as Mrs Keller suggests; we'll go sit in the Hall and listen for twenty minutes to the satellite and then we'll all feel a good deal better.'

Once more Barnes was talking with great earnestness to

Jack Tree. 'Let me point out where the error in your logic lies. You saw a particular man, a Negro, on Emergency Day. Okay. Now, seven years later—'

'Shut up,' Bonny said to him, digging her fingers into his arm. 'For God's sake—' She walked on, then, catching up with Doctor Stockstill. 'I can't stand it,' she said. 'I know this is the last of him; he won't survive past this, seeing that Negro again.'

Tears filled her eyes; she felt tears dropping, escaping her. 'Goddam,' she said bitterly, walking as fast as possible, ahead of the others, in the direction of town and the Foresters' Hall. Not even to know about the satellite. To be that cut off, that deteriorated . . . I didn't realize. How can I stand it? How can a thing like this be? And once he was brilliant. A man who talked over TV and wrote articles, taught and debated . . .

Behind her, Bluthgeld was mumbling, 'I know it's the same man, Stockstill, because I ran into him on the street – I was buying feed at the feed store – he gave me that same queer look, as if he was about to jeer at me, but then he knew if he jeered I'd make it all happen again, and this time he was afraid. He saw it once before and he knows. Isn't that a *fact*, Stockstill? He would know now. Am I correct?'

'I doubt if he knows you're alive,' Stockstill said.

'But I'd have to be alive,' Bluthgeld answered. 'Or the world—' His voice became a blur and Bonny missed the rest; she heard only the sound of her own heels striking the weedy remains of pavement beneath her feet.

And the rest of us, we're all just as insane, she said to herself. My kid with her imaginary brother, Hoppy moving pennies at a distance and doing imitations of Dangerfield, Andrew Gill rolling one cigarette after another by hand, year after year . . . only death can get us out of this and maybe not even death.

Maybe it's too late; we'll carry this deterioration with us to the next life.

We'd have been better off, she thought, if we'd all died on E Day; we wouldn't have lived to see the freaks and the funnies and the radiation-darkies and the brilliant animals – the people who began the war weren't thorough enough. I'm tired and I want to rest; I want to get out of this and go lie down somewhere, off where it's dark and no one speaks. Forever.

And then she thought, more practically, Maybe what's the matter with me is simply that I haven't found the right man yet. And it isn't too late; I'm still young and I'm not fat, and as everyone says, I've got perfect teeth. It could still happen, and I must keep watching.

Ahead lay the Foresters' Hall, the old-fashioned white wooden building with its windows boarded up – the glasses had never been replaced and never would be. Maybe Dangerfield, if he hasn't died of a bleeding ulcer yet, could run a classified ad for me, she conjectured. How would that go over with this community, I wonder? Or I could advertise in *News & Views*, let the worn-out drunk Paul Dietz run a little notice on my behalf for the next six months or so.

Opening the door of the Foresters' Hall she heard the friendly, familiar voice of Walt Dangerfield in his recorded reading; she saw the rows of faces, the people listening, some with anxiety, some with relaxed pleasure . . . she saw, seated inconspicuously in the corner, two men, Andrew Gill and with him a slender, good-looking young Negro. It was the man who had caved in the roof of Bruno Bluthgeld's fragile structure of maladaptation, and Bonny stood there in the doorway not knowing what to do.

Behind her came Barnes and Stockstill and with them

Bruno; the three men started past her, Stockstill and Barnes automatically searching for empty seats in the crowded hall. Bruno, who had never shown up before to hear the satellite, stood in confusion, as if he did not comprehend what the people were doing, as if he could make nothing out of the words emanating from the small battery-powered radio.

Puzzled, Bruno stood beside Bonny, rubbing his forehead and surveying the people in the room; he glanced at her questioningly, with a numbed look, and then he started to follow Barnes and Stockstill. And then he saw the Negro. He stopped. He turned back toward her, and now the expression on his face had changed; she saw there the eroding, dreadful suspicion – the conviction that he understood the meaning of all that he saw.

'Bonny,' he mumbled, 'you have to get him out of here.'

'I can't,' she said, simply.

'If you don't get him out of here,' Bruno said, 'I'll make the bombs fall again.'

She stared at him and then she heard herself say in a brittle, dry voice, 'Will you? Is that what you want to do, Bruno?'

'I have to,' he mumbled in his toneless way, staring at her sightlessly; he was completely preoccupied with his own thoughts, the various changes taking place within him. 'I'm sorry, but first I'll make the high-altitude test bombs go off again; that's how I started before, and if that doesn't do it then I'll bring them down here, they'll fall on everyone. Please forgive me, Bonny, but my God, I have to protect myself.' He tried to smile, but his toothless mouth did not respond beyond a distorted quiver.

Bonny said, 'Can you *really* do that, Bruno? Are you sure?'

'Yes,' he said, nodding. And he was sure; he had always been sure of his power. He had brought the war once and he could do it again if they pushed him too far; in his eyes she saw no doubt, no hesitation.

'That's an awful lot of power for one man to have,' she said to him. 'Isn't that strange, that one man would have so much?'

'Yes,' he said, 'it's all the power in the world rolled together; I am the center. God willed it to be that way.'

'What a mistake God made,' she said.

Bruno gazed at her bleakly. 'You, too,' he said. 'I thought you never would turn against me, Bonny.'

She said nothing; she went to an empty chair and seated herself. She paid no attention to Bruno. She could not; she had worn herself out, over the years, and now she had nothing left to give him.

Stockstill, seated not far away, leaned toward her and said, 'The Negro is here in the room, you know.'

'Yes.' She nodded. 'I know.' Seated bolt-upright, she concentrated on the words coming from the radio; she listened to Dangerfield and tried to forget everyone and everything around her.

It's out of my hands now, she said to herself. Whatever he does, whatever becomes of him, it's not my fault. Whatever happens – to all of us. I can't take any more responsibility; it's gone on too long, as it is, and I am glad, at last, to get out from under it.

What a relief, she thought. Thank God.

Now it must begin again. Bruno Bluthgeld thought to himself. The war. Because there is no choice; it is forced on me. I am sorry for the people. All of them will have to suffer, but perhaps out of it they will be redeemed. Perhaps in the long run it is a good thing.

He seated himself, folded his hands, shut his eyes and concentrated on the task of assembling his powers. Grow, he said to them, the forces at his command everywhere in the world. Join and become potent, as you were in former times. There is need for you again, all ye agencies.

The voice issuing from the loudspeaker of the radio, however, disturbed him and made it difficult for him to concentrate. Breaking off, he thought, I must not be distracted; that is contrary to the Plan. Who is this that's talking? They are all listening . . . are they getting their instructions from him, is that it?

To the man seated beside him he said, 'Who is that we're listening to?'

The man, elderly, turned irritably to regard him. 'Why, it's Walt Dangerfield,' he said, in tones of utter disbelief.

'I have never heard of him,' Bruno said. Because he had not wanted to hear of him. 'Where is he talking from?'

'The satellite,' the elderly man said witheringly, and resumed his listening.

I remember now, Bruno said to himself. That's why we came here; to listen to the satellite. To the man speaking from overhead.

Be destroyed, he thought in the direction of the sky above. Cease, because you are deliberately tormenting me, impeding my work. Bruno waited, but the voice went on.

'Why doesn't he stop? he asked the man on the other side of him. 'How can he continue?'

The man, a little taken aback, said, 'You mean his illness? He recorded this a long time ago, before he was sick.'

'Sick,' Bruno echoed. 'I see.' He had made the man in the satellite sick, and that was something, but not enough. It was a beginning. Be dead, he thought toward the sky satellite above. The voice, however, continued uninterrupted.

Do you have a screen of defense erected against me? Bruno wondered. Have they provided you with it? I will crush it;

obviously you have been long prepared to withstand attack, but it will do you no real good.

Let there be a hydrogen instrument, he said to himself. Let it explode near enough to this man's satellite to demolish his ability to resist. Then have him die in complete awareness of who it is that he is up against. Bruno Bluthgeld concentrated, gripping his hands together, squeezing out the power from deep inside his mind.

And yet the reading continued.

You are very strong, Bruno acknowledged. He had to admire the man. In fact, he smiled a little, thinking about it. Let a whole series of hydrogen instruments explode now, he willed. Let his satellite be bounced around; let him discover the truth.

The voice from the loudspeaker ceased.

Well, it is high time, Bruno said to himself. And he let up on his concentration of powers; he sighed, crossed his legs, smoothed his hair, glanced at the man to his left.

'It's over,' Bruno observed.

'Yeah,' the man said. 'Well, now he'll give the news – if he feels well enough.'

Astonished, Bruno said, 'But he's dead now.'

The man, startled, protested, 'He can't be dead; I don't believe it. Go on – you're nuts.'

'It's true,' Bruno said. 'His satellite has been totally destroyed and there is nothing remaining.' Didn't the man know that? Hadn't it penetrated to the world, yet?

'Doggone it,' the man said, 'I don't know who you are or why you say something like that, but you sure are a gloomy gus. Wait a second and you'll hear him; I'll even bet you five US Government metal cents.'

The radio was silent. In the room, people stirred, murmured with concern and apprehension.

Yes, it has begun, Bruno said to himself. First, high-altitude detonations, as before. And soon – for all of you here. The world itself wiped out as before, to halt the steady advance of cruelty and revenge; it must be halted before it's too late. He glanced in the direction of the Negro and smiled. The Negro pretended not to see him; he pretended to be involved in discussion with the man beside him.

You are aware, Bruno thought, I can tell; you can't fool me. You, more than anyone else, know what is beginning to happen.

Something is wrong, Doctor Stockstill thought. Why doesn't Walt Dangerfield go on? Has he suffered an embolism or something on that order?

And then he noticed the crooked grin of triumph on Bruno Bluthgeld's toothless face. At once Stockstill thought, He's taking credit for it, in his own mind. Paranoid delusions of omnipotence; everything that takes place is due to him. Repelled, he turned away, moved his chair so that he could no longer see Bluthgeld.

Now he turned his attention on the young Negro. Yes, he thought, that could well be the Negro television salesman who used to open up the TV store across from my office in Berkeley, years ago. I think I'll go over and ask him.

Rising, he made his way over to Andrew Gill and the Negro. 'Pardon me,' he said, bending over them. 'Did you ever live in Berkeley and sell TV sets on Shattuck Avenue?'

The Negro said, 'Doctor Stockstill.' He held out his hand and they shook. 'It's a small world,' the Negro said.

'What's happened to Dangerfield?' Andrew Gill said worriedly. Now June Raub appeared by the radio, fiddling with the knobs; other people began to collect around her, offering advice and murmuring with one another in small, grave clusters. 'I think this is the end. What do you say, Doctor?'

'I say,' Stockstill said, 'that if it is it's a tragedy.'

In the rear of the room, Bruno Bluthgeld rose to his feet and said in a loud, husky voice, 'The demolition of existence has begun. Everyone present will be spared by special consideration long enough to confess sins and repent if it is sincere.'

The room fell silent. The people, one by one, turned in his direction.

'You have a preacher, here?' the Negro said to Stockstill.

To Gill, Stockstill said rapidly, 'He's sick, Andy. We've got to get him out of here. Give me a hand.'

'Sure,' Gill said, following him; they walked toward Bluthgeld, who was still on his feet.

'The high-altitude bombs which I set off in 1972,' Bluthgeld was declaring, 'find reinforcement in the present act, sanctioned by God Himself in His wisdom for the world. See the Book of Revelation for verification.' He watched Stockstill and Gill approach. 'Have you cleansed yourselves?' he asked them. 'Are you prepared for the judgment which is to come?'

All at once from the speaker of the radio, came a familiar voice; it was shaky and muted, but they all recognized it. 'Sorry for the pause, folks,' Dangerfield said. 'But I sure felt giddy there for a while; I had to lie down and I didn't notice the tape had ended. Anyhow—' He laughed his old, familiar laugh. 'I'm back. At least for a while. Now, what was I about to do? Does anybody remember? Wait, I've got a red light on; somebody's calling me from below. Hold on.'

The people in the room buzzed with joy and relief; they turned back to the radio, and Bluthgeld was forgotten. Stockstill himself walked toward the radio, and so did Gill and the

Negro TV salesman; they joined the circle of smiling people and stood waiting.

'I've got a request for "Bei Mir Bist Du Schön," ' Dangerfield said. 'Can you beat that? Anybody remember the Andrews Sisters? Well, the good old US Government had the kindness to provide me with, believe it or not, a tape of the Andrews Sisters singing this corny but well-loved number . . . I guess they figured I was going to be some sort of time capsule on Mars, there.' He chuckled. 'So it's "Bei Mir Bist Du Schön," for some old codger in the Great Lakes Area. Here we go.' The music, tinny and archaic, began, and the people in the room gratefully, joyfully, moved one by one back to their seats.

Standing by his chair rigidly, Bruno Bluthgeld listened to the music and thought, I can't believe it. The man up there is gone; I myself caused him to be destroyed. *This must be a fake of some kind. A deception. I know that it is not real.*

In any case, he realized, I must exert myself more fully; I must begin again and this time with utmost force. No one was paying attention to him – they had all turned their attention back to the radio – so he left his chair and made his way quietly from the Hall, outside into the darkness.

Down the road the tall antenna at Hoppy Harrington's house glowed and pulsed and hummed; Bruno Bluthgeld, puzzled, noted it as he walked along toward his horse, where he had left the beast tied up. What was the phocomelus doing? Lights blazed behind the windows of the tar-paper house; Hoppy was busy at work.

I must include him, too, Bluthgeld said to himself. He must cease to exist along with the others, for he is as evil as they are. Perhaps more so.

As he passed Hoppy's house he sent a stray, momentary

thought of destruction in Hoppy's direction. The lights, however, remained on and the antenna mast continued to hum. It will take more mind-force, Bluthgeld realized, and I don't have the time right now. A little later.

Meditating profoundly, he continued on.

Thirteen

Bill Keller heard the small animal, the snail or slug, near him and at once he got into it. But he had been tricked; it was sightless. He was out but he could not see or hear, he could only move.

'Let me back,' he called to his sister in panic. 'Look what you did, you put me into something wrong.' You did it on purpose, he said to himself as he moved. He moved on and on, searching for her.

If I could reach out, he thought. Reach – upward. But he had nothing to reach with, no limbs of any sort. What am I now that I'm finally out? he asked himself as he tried to reach up. What do they call those things up there that shine? Those lights in the sky . . . can I see them without having eyes? No, he thought, I can't.

He moved on raising himself now and then as high as possible and then sinking back, once more to crawl, to do the one thing possible for him in his new life, his born, outside life.

In the sky, Walt Dangerfield moved, in his satellite, although he was resting with his head in his hands. The pain inside him grew, changed, absorbed him until, as before, he could imagine nothing else.

And then he thought he saw something. Beyond the window of the satellite – a flash far off, along the rim of the

Earth's darker edge. What was that? he asked himself. An explosion, like the ones he had seen and cringed from several years ago . . . the flares ignited over the surface of the Earth. Were they beginning again?

On his feet he stood peering out, hardly breathing. Seconds passed and there were no further explosions. And the one he had seen; it had been peculiarly vague and shadowy, with a diffuseness that had made it seem somehow unreal, as if it was only imagined.

As if, he thought, it was more a recollection of a fact than the fact itself. It must be some sort of sidereal echo, he concluded. A remnant left over from E Day, still reverberating in space somehow . . . but harmless, now. More so all the time.

And yet it frightened him. Like the pain inside him, it was too odd to be dismissed; it seemed to be dangerous and he could not forget it.

I feel ill, he repeated to himself, resuming his litany based on his great discomfort. Can't they get me down? Do I have to stay up here, creeping across the sky again and again – forever?

For his own needs he put on a tape of the Bach B Minor Mass; the giant choral sound filled the satellite and made him forget. The pain inside, the dull, elderly explosion briefly outlined beyond the window – both began to leave his mind.

'Kyrie eleison,' he murmured to himself. Greek words, embedded in the Latin text; strange. Remnants of the past . . . still alive, at least for him. I'll play the B Minor Mass for the New York area, he decided. I think they'll like it; a lot of intellectuals, there. Why should I only play what they request anyhow? I ought to be teaching them, not following. And especially, he thought, if I'm not going to be around much longer. . . I better get going and do an especially bang-up job, here at the end.

All at once his vehicle shuddered. Staggering, he caught hold of the wall nearest him; a concussion, series of shock waves, passing through. Objects fell and collided and burst; he looked around amazed.

Meteor? he wondered.

It seemed to him almost as if someone were attacking him.

He shut off the B Minor Mass and stood, listening and waiting. Far off through the window he saw another dull explosion and he thought, they may get me. But why? It won't be long anyhow before I'm finished . . . why not wait? And then the thought came to him, But damn it, I'm alive now, and I better act alive; I'm not utterly dead yet.

He snapped on his transmitter and said into the mike, 'Sorry for the pause, folks. But I sure felt giddy there for a while; I had to lie down and I didn't notice the tape had ended. Anyhow—'

Laughing his laugh, he watched through the window of the satellite for more of the strange explosions. There was one, faint and farther off . . . he felt a measure of relief. Maybe they wouldn't get him after all; they seemed to be losing track of the range, as if his location were a mystery to them.

I'll play the corniest record I can think of, he decided, as an act of defiance. 'Bei Mir Bist Du Schön'; that ought to do it. Whistling in the dark, as they say, and he laughed again, thinking about it; what an act of defiance it was, by God. It would certainly come as a surprise to whoever was trying to eradicate him – if that was in fact what they wanted to do.

Maybe they're just plain tired of my corny talk and my corny readings, Dangerfield conjectured. Well, if so – this will fix them.

'I'm back,' he said into his mike. 'At least for a while. Now, what was I about to do? Does anybody remember?'

There were no more concussions. He had a feeling that, for the time being, they had ceased.

'Wait,' he said, I've got a red light on; somebody's calling me from below. Hold on.'

From his tape library he selected the proper tape, carried it to the transport and placed it on the spindle.

'I've got a request for "Bei Mir Bist Du Schön," ' he said, with grim relish, thinking of their dismay down below. 'Can you beat that?' No, you can't, he said to himself. And – by the Andrews Sisters. Dangerfield is striking back. Grinning, he started the tape into motion.

Edie Keller, with a delicious shiver of exultation, watched the angle worm crawling slowly across the ground and knew with certitude that her brother was in it.

For inside her, down in her abdomen, the mentality of the worm now resided; she heard its monotonous voice. 'Boom, boom, boom,' it went, in echo of its nondescript biological processes.

'Get out of me, worm,' she said, and giggled. What did the worm think about its new existence? Was it as dumbfounded as Bill probably was? I have to keep my eye on him, she realized, meaning the creature wriggling across the ground. For he might get lost. 'Bill,' she said, bending over him, 'you look funny. You're all red and long; did you know that?' And then she thought, What I should have done was put him in the body of another human being. Why didn't I do that? Then it would be like it ought to be; I would have a real brother, outside of me, who I could play with.

But, on the other hand, she would have a strange, new person inside her. And that did not sound like much fun.

Who would do? she asked herself. One of the kids at school? An adult? I bet Bill would like to be in an adult. Mr

Barnes, maybe. Or Hoppy Harrington, who was afraid of Bill anyhow. Or – she screeched with delight, Mama. It would be so easy; I could snuggle up close to her, lay against her . . . and Bill could switch, and I'd have my own Mama inside me – and wouldn't that be wonderful? I could make her do anything I wanted. And she couldn't tell me what to do.

And Edie thought, She couldn't do any more unmentionable things with Mr Barnes anymore, or with anybody else. I'd see to that. I know Bill wouldn't behave that way; he was as shocked as I was.

'Bill,' she said, kneeling down and carefully picking up the angleworm; she held it in the palm of her hand. 'Wait until you hear my plan – you know what? We're going to fix Mama for the bad things she does.' She held the worm against her side, where the hard lump within lay. 'Get back inside now. You don't want to be a worm anyhow; it's no fun.'

Her brother's voice once more came to her. 'You pooh-pooh; I hate you, I'll never forgive you. You put me in a blind thing with no legs or nothing; all I could do was drag myself around!'

'I know,' she said, rocking back and forth, cupping the now-useless worm in her hand still. 'Listen, did you hear me? You want to do that, Bill, what I said? Shall I get Mama to let me lie against her so you can do you-know-what? You'd have eyes and ears; you'd be a full-grown person.'

Nervously, Bill said, 'I don't know. I don't think I want to walk around being Mama; it sort of scares me.'

'Sissy,' Edie said. 'You better do it or you may never get out ever again. Well, who do you want to be if not Mama? Tell me and I'll fix it up; I cross my heart and promise to fall down black and hard.'

'I'll see,' Bill said. 'I'll talk to the dead people and see what they say about it. Anyhow I don't know if it'll work; I had trouble getting out into that little thing, that worm.'

'You're afraid to try,' she laughed; she tossed the worm away, into the bushes at the end of the school grounds. 'Sissy! My brother is a big baby sissy!'

There was no answer from Bill; he had turned his thoughts away from her and her world, into the regions which only he could reach. Talking to those old crummy, sticky dead, Edie said to herself. Those empty pooh-pooh dead that never have any fun or nothing.

And then a really stunning idea came to her. I'll fix it so he gets out and into that crazy man Mr Tree who they're all talking about right now, she decided. Mr Tree stood up in the Foresters' Hall last night and said those dumb religious things about repenting, and so if Bill acts funny and doesn't know what to do or say, *nobody will pay any attention.*

Yet that posed the awful problem of her finding herself containing a crazy man. Maybe I could take poison like I'm always saying, she decided. I could swallow a lot of oleander leaves or castor beans or something and get rid of him; he'd be helpless, he couldn't stop me.

Still, it was a problem; she did not relish the idea of having that Mr Tree – she had seen him often enough not to like him – inside herself. He had a nice dog, and that was about all . . .

Terry, the dog. That was it. She could lie down against Terry and Bill could get out and into the dog and everything would be fine.

But dogs had a short life. And Terry was already seven years old; according to her mother and father. He had been born the same time almost as she and Bill.

Darn it, she thought. It's hard to decide; it's a real problem, what to do with Bill who wants so bad to get out and see and hear things. And then she thought, Who of all the people I know would I like most to have living inside my stomach? And the answer was: her father.

'You want to walk around as Daddy?' she asked Bill But Bill did not answer; he was still turned away, conversing with the great majority beneath the ground.

I think, she decided, that Mr Tree would be the best because he lives out in the country with sheep and doesn't see too many people, and it would be easier on Bill that way because he wouldn't have to know very much about talking. He'd just have Terry out there and all the sheep, and then with Mr Tree being crazy now it's really perfect. Bill could do a lot better with Mr Tree's body than Mr Tree is doing, I bet, and all I have to worry about really is chewing the right number of poisonous oleander leaves – enough to kill him but not me. Maybe two would do. Three at the most, I guess.

Mr Tree went crazy at the perfect time, she decided. He doesn't know it, though. But wait'll he finds out; won't he be surprised. I might let him live for a while inside me, just so he'd realize what happened; I think that would be fun. I never liked him, even though Mama does, or says she does. He's creepy. Edie shuddered.

Poor, poor Mr Tree, she thought delightedly. You aren't going to ruin any more meetings at the Foresters' Hall because where you'll be you won't be able to preach to anybody, except maybe to me and I won't listen.

Where can I do it? she asked herself. Today; I'll ask Mama to take us out there after school. And if she won't do it, I'll hike out there by myself.

I can hardly wait, Edie said to herself, shivering with anticipation.

The bell for class rang, and, together with the other children, she started into the building. Mr Barnes was waiting at the door of the single classroom which served all the children from first grade to sixth; as she passed him, deep in thought, he said to her, 'Why so absorbed, Edie? What's on your weighty mind today?'

'Well,' she said, halting, 'you were for a while. Now it's Mr Tree instead.'

'Oh yes,' Mr Barnes said, nodding. 'So you heard about that.'

The other children had passed on in, leaving them alone. So Edie said, 'Mr Barnes, don't you think you ought to stop doing what you're doing with my mama? It's wrong; Bill says so and he knows.'

The school teacher's face changed color, but he did not speak. Instead he walked away from her, into the room and up to his desk, still darkly flushed. Did I say it wrong? Edie wondered. Is he mad at me now? Maybe he'll make me stay after, for punishment, and maybe he'll tell Mama and she'll spank me.

Feeling discouraged, she seated herself and opened the precious, ragged, fragile, coverless book to the story of *Snow White*; it was their reading assignment for the day.

Lying in the damp rotting leaves beneath the old live oak trees, in the shadows, Bonny Keller clasped Mr Barnes to her and thought to herself that this was probably the last time; she was tired of it and Hal was scared, and that, she had learned from long experience, was a fatal combination.

'All right,' she murmured, 'so she knows. But she knows on a small child's level; she has no real understanding.'

'She knows it's wrong,' Barnes answered.

Bonny sighed.

'Where is she now?' Barnes asked.

'Behind that big tree over there. Watching.'

Hal Barnes sprang to his feet as if stabbed; he whirled around, wide-eyed, then sagged as he comprehended the truth. 'You and your malicious wit,' he muttered. But he did not return to her; he stayed on his feet, a short distance off, looking glum and uneasy. 'Where is she really?'

'She hiked out to Jack Tree's sheep ranch.'

'But—' He gestured. 'The man's insane! Won't he be – well, isn't it dangerous?'

'She just went out to play with Terry, the verbose canine.' Bonny sat up and began picking bits of humus from her hair. 'I don't think he's even there. The last time anybody saw Bruno, he—'

'Bruno,' Barnes echoed. He regarded her queerly.

'I mean Jack.' Her heart labored.

'He said the other night something about having been responsible for the high-altitude devices in 1972.' Barnes continued to scrutinize her; she waited, her pulse throbbing in her throat. Well, it was bound to come out sooner or later.

'He's insane,' she pointed out. 'Right? He believes—'

'He believes,' Hal Barnes said, 'that he's Bruno Bluthgeld, isn't that right?'

Bonny shrugged. 'That, among other things.'

'And he is, isn't he? And Stockstill knows it, you know it – that Negro knows it.'

'No,' she said, 'that Negro doesn't know it, and stop saying "that Negro".' His name is Stuart McConchie; I talked to Andrew about him and he says he's a very fine, intelligent, enthusiastic and alive person.'

Barnes said, 'So Doctor Bluthgeld didn't die in the Emergency. He came here. He's been here, living among us. The man most responsible for what happened.'

'Go murder him,' Bonny said.

Barnes grunted.

'I mean it,' Bonny said. 'I don't care any more. Frankly I wish you would.' It would be a good manly act, she said to herself. It would be a distinct change.

'Why have you tried to shield a person like, that?'

'I don't know.' She did not care to discuss it. 'Let's go back to town,' she said. His company wearied her and she had begun to think once again about Stuart McConchie. 'I'm out of cigarettes,' she said. 'So you can drop me off at the cigarette factory.' She walked toward Barnes' horse, which, tied to a tree, complacently cropped the long grass.

'A darky,' Barnes said, with bitterness. 'Now you're going to shack up with him. That certainly makes me feel swell.'

'Snob,' she said. 'Anyhow, you're afraid to go on; you want to quit. So the next time you see Edie you can truthfully say, "I am not doing anything shameful and evil with your mama, scout's honor." Right?' She mounted the horse, picked up the reins and waited. 'Come on, Hal.'

An explosion lit up the sky.

The horse bolted, and Bonny leaped from it, throwing herself from its side to roll, sliding, into the shrubbery of the oak forest. Bruno, she thought; can it be him really? She lay clasping her head, sobbing with pain; a branch had laid her scalp open and blood dripped through her fingers and ran down her wrist. Now Barnes bent over her; he tugged her up, turned her over. 'Bruno,' she said. 'Goddamn him. Somebody *will* have to kill him; they should have done it long ago – they should have done it in 1970 because he was insane then.' She got her handkerchief out and mopped at her scalp. 'Oh dear,' she said. 'I really am hurt. That was a real fall.'

'The horse is gone, too,' Barnes said.

'It's an evil god,' she said, 'who gave him that power,

whatever it is. I know it's him, Hal. We've seen a lot of strange things over the years, so why not this? The ability to recreate the war, to bring it back, like he said last night. Maybe he's got us snared in time. Could that be it? We're stuck fast; he—' She broke off as a second white flash broke overhead, traveling at enormous speed; the trees around them lashed and bent and she heard, here and there, the old oaks splinter.

'I wonder where the horse went,' Barnes murmured, rising cautiously to his feet and peering around.

'Forget the horse,' she said. 'We'll have to walk back; that's obvious. Listen, Hal. Maybe Hoppy can do something; he has funny powers, too. I think we ought to go to him and tell him. He doesn't want to be incinerated by a lunatic. Don't you agree? I don't see anything else we can do at this point.'

'That's a good idea,' Barnes said, but he was still looking for the horse; he did not seem really to be listening.

'Our punishment.' Bonny said.

'What?' he murmured.

'You know. For what Edie calls our "shameful, evil doings." I thought the other night . . . maybe we should have been killed with the others; maybe it's a good thing this is happening.'

'There's the horse,' Barnes said, walking swiftly from her. The horse was caught; his reins had become tangled in a bay limb.

The sky, now, had become sooty black. She remembered that color; it had never entirely departed anyhow. It had merely lessened.

Our little fragile world, Bonny thought, that we labor to build up, after the Emergency . . . this puny society with our tattered school books, our 'deluxe' cigarettes, our wood-burning trucks – it can't stand much punishment; it can't stand this that Bruno is doing or appears to be doing. One blow again directed at us and we will be gone; the brilliant animals will perish, all the new, odd species will disappear as suddenly as they arrived. Too bad, she thought with grief. It's unfair; Terry, the verbose dog – him, too. Maybe we were too ambitious; maybe we shouldn't have dared to try to rebuild and go on.

I think we did pretty well, she thought, all in all. We've been alive; we've made love and drunk Gill's Five Star, taught our kids in a peculiar-windowed school building, put out *News & Views*, cranked up a car radio and listened daily to W. Somerset Maugham. What more could be asked of us? Christ, she thought. *It isn't fair*, this thing now. It isn't right at all. We have our horses to protect, our crops, our lives . . .

Another explosion occurred, this time further off. To the south, she realized. Near the site of the old ones. San Francisco.

Wearily, she shut her eyes. And just when this McConchie has shown up, too, she thought. What lousy, stinking luck.

The dog, placing himself across the path, barring her way, groaned in his difficult voice, 'Treezzz bizzzeeeeee. Stoppppp.' He woofed in warning. She was not supposed to continue on to the wooden shack.

Yes, Edie thought, I know he's busy. She had seen the explosions in the sky. 'Hey, you know what?' she said to the dog.

'Whuuuuut?' the dog asked, becoming curious; he had a simple mind, as she well knew; he was easily taken in.

'I learned how to throw a stick so far nobody can find it,' she said. She bent, picked up a nearby stick. 'Want me to prove it?'

Within her Bill said, 'Who're you talking to?' He was agitated, now that the time was drawing near. 'Is it Mr Tree?'

'No,' she said, 'just the dog.' She waved the stick. 'Bet you a paper ten dollar bill if I throw it you can't find it.'

'Surrrrre I cannnnnn,' the dog said, and whined in eagerness; this was his favorite sort of sport. 'Buuuut I cannnn't betttttt,' he added. 'I haaaaave no monnnnnneyyyy.'

From the wooden shack walked Mr Tree, all at once; taken by surprise, both she and the dog stopped what they were doing. Mr Tree paid no attention to them; he continued on up a small hill and disappeared down the far side, out of sight.

'Mr Tree!' Edie called. 'Maybe he isn't busy now,' she said to the dog. 'Go ask him, okay? Tell him I want to talk to him a minute.'

Within her Bill said restlessly, 'He's not far off now, is he? I know he's there. I'm ready; I'm going to try real hard this time. He can do almost anything, can't he? See and walk and hear and smell – isn't that right? It's not like that worm.'

'He doesn't have any teeth,' Edie said, 'but he has everything else that most people have.' As the dog obediently loped off in pursuit of Mr Tree she began walking along the path once more. 'It won't be long,' she said. 'I'll tell him—' She had it all worked out. 'I'll say, "Mr Tree, you know what? Well, I swallowed one of those duck-callers hunters use, and if you can lean close you can hear it." How's that?'

'I don't know,' Bill said desperately. 'What's a "duck-caller"? What's a duck, Edie? Is it alive?' He sounded more and more confused, as if the situation were too much for him.

'You sissy,' she hissed. 'Be quiet.' The dog had reached Tree and now the man had turned; he was starting back toward her, frowning.

'I am very busy, Edie,' Mr Tree called. 'Later – I'll talk to you later; I can't be interrupted now.' He raised his arms and made a bizarre motion toward her, as if he were keeping time to some music; he scowled and swayed, and she felt like laughing, he looked so foolish.

'I just want to show you something,' she called back.

'Later!' He started away, then spoke to the dog.

'Yessirr,' the dog growled, and loped back toward the girl. 'Nooo,' the dog told her. 'Stoppppp.'

Darn it, Edie thought. We can't do it today; we'll have to come back maybe tomorrow.

'Gooo awayyyy,' the dog was saying to her, and it bared its fangs; it had been given the strongest possible instructions.

Edie said, 'Listen, Mr Tree—' And then she stopped, because there was no longer any Mr Tree there. The dog turned, whined, and within her Bill moaned.

'Edie,' Bill cried, 'he's gone; I can feel it. Now where'll I go to get out? What'll I do?'

High up in the air, a tiny black speck blew and tumbled; the girl watched it drift as if it were caught in some violent spout of wind. It was Mr Tree and his arms stuck out as he rolled over and over, dropping and rising like a kite. What's happened to him? she wondered dismally, knowing that Bill was right; their chance, their plan, was gone forever now.

Something had hold of Mr Tree and it was killing him. It lifted him higher and higher, and then Edie shrieked. Mr Tree suddenly dropped. He fell like a stone straight at the ground; she shut her eyes and the dog, Terry, let out a howl of stark dismay.

'What is it?' Bill was clamoring in despair. 'Who did it to him? They took him away, didn't they?'

'Yes,' she said, and opened her eyes.

Mr Tree lay on the ground, broken and crooked, with his legs and arms sticking up at all angles. He was dead; she knew that and so did the dog. The dog trotted over to him, halted, turned to her with a stricken, numbed look. She said nothing; she stopped, too, a distance away. It was awful, what they – whoever it was – had done to Mr Tree. It was like the glasses man from Bolinas, she thought; it was a killing.

'Hoppy did it,' Bill moaned. 'Hoppy killed Mr Tree from a distance because he was afraid of him; Mr Tree's down with the dead, now, I can hear him talking. He's saying that; he says Hoppy reached out all the way from his house where he is and grabbed Mr Tree and picked him up and flung him everywhere!'

'Gee,' Edie said. I wonder how come Hoppy did that, she wondered. Because of the explosions Mr Tree was making in the sky, was that it? Did they bother Hoppy? Make him sore?

She felt fright. That Hoppy, she thought; he can kill from so far off; nobody else can do that. We better be careful. Very careful. Because he could kill all of us; he could fling us all around or squeeze us.

'I guess *News & Views* will put this on the first page,' she said, half to herself, half to Bill.

'What's *News & Views*?' Bill protested in anguish, 'I don't understand what's going on; can't you explain it to me? *Please.*'

Edie said, 'We better go back to town now.' She started slowly away, leaving the dog sitting there beside the squashed remains of Mr Tree. I guess, she thought, it's a good thing you didn't switch, because if you had been inside Mr Tree you would have been killed.

And, she thought, he would be alive inside me. At least until I got the oleander leaves chewed and swallowed. And maybe he would have found a way to stop that. He had funny powers; he could make those explosions, and he might have done that inside me.

'We can try somebody else,' Bill said, hopefully. 'Can't we? Do you want to try that – what do you call it again? That dog?

I think I'd like to be that dog; it can run fast and catch things and see a long way, can't it?'

'Not now,' she said, still frightened, wanting to get away. 'Some other time. You'd better wait.' And she began to run back along the path, in the direction of town.

Fourteen

Orion Stroud, seated in the center of the Foresters' Hall where he could clearly be heard by everyone, rapped for order and said:

'Mrs Keller and Doctor Stockstill asked that the West Marin Official Jury and also the West Marin Governing Citizens' Council convene to hear a piece of vital news regarding a killing that just took place today.'

Around him, Mrs Tallman and Cas Stone and Fred Quinn and Mrs Lully and Andrew Gill and Earl Colvig and Miss Costigan – he glanced from one to the next, satisfied that everyone was present. They all watched with fixed attention, knowing that this was really important. Nothing like this had ever happened in their community before. This was not a killing like that of the glasses man or of Mr Austurias.

'I understand,' Stroud said, 'that it was discovered that Mr Jack Tree who's been living among us—'

From the audience a voice said, 'He was Bluthgeld.'

'Right,' Stroud said, nodding. 'But he's dead now so there's nothing to worry about; you have to get that through your heads. And it was Hoppy that done it. Did it, I mean.' He glanced at Paul Dietz apologetically. 'Have to use proper grammar,' he said, 'because this is all going to be in *News & Views* – right Paul?'

'A special edition,' Paul said, nodding in agreement.

'Now you understand, we're not here to decide if Hoppy ought to be punished for what he did. There's no problem there because Bluthgeld was a noted war criminal and what's more he was beginning to use his magical powers to restart some of the old war. I guess everybody in this room knows that, because you all saw the explosions. Now—' He glanced toward Gill. 'There's a newcomer, here, a Negro named Stuart McConchie, and ordinarily I have to admit we don't welcome darkies to West Marin, but I understand that McConchie was tracking down Bluthgeld, so he's going to be allowed to settle in West Marin if he so desires.'

The audience rustled with approval.

'Mainly what we're here for,' Stroud continued, 'is to vote some sort of reward to Hoppy to show our appreciation. We probably would all have been killed, due to Bluthgeld's magical powers. So we owe him a real debt of gratitude. I see he isn't here, because he's busy at work in his house, fixing things; after all, he's our handy and that's a pretty big responsibility, right there. Anyhow, has anybody got an idea of how the people here can express their appreciation for Hoppy's timely killing of Doctor Bluthgeld?' Stroud looked around questioningly.

Rising to his feet, Andrew Gill cleared his throat and said, 'I think it's appropriate for me to say a few words. First, I want to thank Mr Stroud and this community for welcoming my new business associate, Mr McConchie. And then I want to offer one reward that might be appropriate regarding Hoppy's great service to this community and to the world at large. I'd like to contribute a hundred special deluxe Gold Label cigarettes.' He paused, starting to reseat himself, and then added, 'And a case of Gill's Five Star.'

The audience applauded, whistled, stamped in approval.

'Well,' Stroud said, smiling, 'that's really something. I guess Mr Gill is aware of what Hoppy's action spared us all. There's a whole lot of oak trees knocked over along blasts Bluthgeld was setting off. Also, you may know, I understand that he was beginning to turn his attention south toward San Francisco—'

'That's correct,' Bonny Keller spoke up.

'So,' Stroud said, 'maybe those people down there will want to pitch in and contribute something to Hoppy as a token of appreciation. I guess the best we can do, and it's good but I wish there was more, is turn over Mr Gill's gift of the hundred special deluxe Gold Label cigarettes and the case of brandy . . . Hoppy will appreciate that, but I was actually thinking of something more in the line of a memorial, like a statue or a park or at least a plaque of some sort. And – I'd be willing to donate the land, and I know Cas Stone would, too.'

'Right,' Cas Stone declared emphatically.

'Anybody else got an idea?' Stroud asked. 'You, Mrs Tallman; I'd like to hear from you.'

Mrs Tallman said, 'It would be fitting to elect Mr Harrington to an honorary public office, such as President of the West Marin Governing Citizens' Council, for instance, or as clerk of the School Trustees Board. That, of course, in addition to the park or memorial and the brandy and cigarettes.'

'Good idea,' Stroud said. 'Well? Anybody else? Because let's be realistic, folks; Hoppy saved our lives. That Bluthgeld had gone out of his mind, as everybody who was at the reading last night knows . . . he would have put us right back where we were seven years ago, and all our hard work in rebuilding would have gone for nothing. Nothing at all.'

The audience murmured its agreement.

'When you have magic like he had,' Stroud said, 'a physicist like Bluthgeld with all that knowledge . . . the world never was in such danger before; am I right? It's just lucky Hoppy can move objects at a distance; it's lucky for us that Hoppy's been practicing that all these years now because nothing else would have reached out like that, over all that distance, and mashed that Bluthgeld like it did.'

Fred Quinn spoke up, 'I talked to Edie Keller who witnessed it and she tells me that Bluthgeld got flung right up into the air before Hoppy mashed him; tossed all around.'

'I know,' Stroud said. 'I interviewed Edie about it.' He looked around the room, at all the people. 'If anybody wants details, I'm sure Edie would give them. Right, Mrs Keller?'

Bonny, seated stiffly, her face pale, nodded.

'You still scared, Bonny?' Stroud asked.

'It was terrible,' Bonny said quietly.

'Sure it was,' Stroud said, 'but Hoppy got him.' And then he thought to himself, That makes Hoppy pretty formidable, doesn't it? Maybe that's what Bonny's thinking. Maybe that's why she's so quiet.

'I think the best thing to do,' Cas Stone said, 'is to go right to Hoppy and say, "Hoppy, what do you want that we can do for you in token of our appreciation?" We'll put it right to him. Maybe there's something he wants very badly that we don't know about.'

Yes, Stroud thought to himself. You have quite a point there, Cas. Maybe he wants many things we don't know about, and maybe one day – not too far off – he'll want to get them. Whether we form a delegation and go inquire after that or not.

'Bonny,' he said to Mrs Keller, 'I wish you'd speak up; you're sitting there so quiet.'

Bonny Keller murmured, 'I'm just tired.'

'Did you know Jack Tree was Bluthgeld?'

Silently, she nodded.

'Was it you, then,' Stroud asked, 'who told Hoppy?'

'No,' she said. 'I intended to; I was on my way. But it had already happened. He knew.'

I wonder how he knew, Stroud asked himself.

'That Hoppy,' Mrs Lully said in a quavering voice, 'he seems to be able to do almost anything . . . why, he's even more powerful than that Mr Bluthgeld, evidently.'

'Right,' Stroud agreed.

The audience murmured nervously.

'But he's put all his abilities to use for the welfare of our community,' Andrew Gill said. 'Remember that. Remember he's our handy and he helps bring in Dangerfield when the signal's weak, and he does tricks for us, and imitations when we can't get Dangerfield at all – he does a whole lot of things, including saving our lives from another nuclear holocaust. So I say, God bless Hoppy and his abilities. I think we should thank God that we have a funny here like him.'

'Right,' Cas Stone said.

'I agree,' Stroud said, with caution. 'But I think we ought to sort of put it to Hoppy that maybe from now on—' He hesitated. 'Our killings should be like with Austurias, done legally, by our Jury. I mean, Hoppy did right and he had to act quickly and all . . . but the Jury is the legal body that's supposed to decide. And Earl here should do the actual act. In the future, I mean. That doesn't include Bluthgeld because having all that magic he was different.' You can't kill a man with powers like that through the ordinary methods, he realized. Like Hoppy, for instance . . . suppose someone tried to kill him; it would be next to impossible.

He shivered.

'What's the matter, Orion?' Cas Stone asked, acutely.

'Nothing,' Orion Stroud said. 'Just thinking what we can do to reward Hoppy to show our appreciation; it's a weighty problem because we owe him so much.'

The audience murmured, as the individual members discussed with one another how to reward Hoppy.

★

George Keller, noticing his wife's pale, drawn features, said, 'Are you okay?' He put his hand on her shoulder but she leaned away.

'Just tired,' she said. 'I ran for a mile, I think, when those explosions began. Trying to reach Hoppy's house.'

'How did you know Hoppy could do it?' he asked.

'Oh,' she said, 'we all know that; we all surely know he's the only one of us who has anything remotely resembling that land of strength. It came into our—' she corrected herself, 'my mind right away, as soon as I saw the explosions.' She glanced at her husband.

'Who were you with?' he said.

'Barnes. We were hunting chanterelle mushrooms under the oaks along Bear Valley Ranch Road.'

George Keller said, 'Personally I'm afraid of Hoppy. Look – he isn't even here. He has a sort of contempt for us all. He's always late getting to the Hall; do you know what I mean? Do you sense it? And it gets more true all the time, perhaps as he sharpens his abilities.'

'Perhaps,' Bonny murmured.

'What do you think will happen to us now?' George asked her. 'Now that we've killed Bluthgeld? We're better off, a lot safer. It's a load off everybody's mind. Someone should notify Dangerfield so he can broadcast it from the satellite.'

'Hoppy could do that,' Bonny said in a remote voice. 'He can do anything. Almost anything.'

In the speaker's chair, Orion Stroud rapped for order. 'Who wants to be in the delegation that goes down to Hoppy's house and confers the reward and notification of honor on him?' He looked all around the room. 'Somebody start to volunteer.'

'I'll go,' Andrew Gill spoke up.

'Me, too,' Fred Quinn said.

Bonny said, 'I'll go.'

To her, George said, 'Do you feel well enough to?'

'Sure.' She nodded listlessly. 'I'm fine, now. Except for the gash on my head.' Automatically she touched the bandage.

'How about you, Mrs Tallman?' Stroud was saying.

'Yes, I'll go,' Mrs Tallman answered, but her voice trembled.

'Afraid?' Stroud asked.

'Yes,' she said.

'Why?'

Mrs Tallman hesitated. 'I – don't know, Orion.'

'I'll go, too,' Orion Stroud announced. 'That's five of us, three men and two women; that's just about right. We'll take the brandy and the cigaboos along and announce the rest – about the plaque, and him being President of the Council and clerk and all that.'

'Maybe,' Bonny said in a low voice, 'we ought to send a delegation there that will stone him to death.'

George Keller sucked in his breath, and said, 'For God's sake, Bonny.'

'I mean it,' she said.

'You're behaving in an incredible way,' he said, furious and surprised; he did not understand her. 'What's the matter?'

'But of course it wouldn't do any good,' she said. 'He'd mash us before we got near his house. Maybe he'll mash me now.' She smiled. 'For saying that.'

'Then shut up!' He stared at her in great fear.

'All right,' she said. 'I'll be quiet. I don't want to be flung up into the air and then dropped all the way to the ground, the way Jack was.'

'I should think not.' He was trembling.

'You're a coward,' she said mildly. 'Aren't you? I wonder

why I in all this time didn't realize it before. Maybe that's why I feel the way I do about you.'

'And what way's that?'

Bonny smiled. And did not answer. It was a hard, hateful and rigidly cold smile and he did not understand it; he glanced away, wondering once again if all the rumors he had heard about his wife, over the years, could be true after all. She was so cold, so independent. George Keller felt miserable.

'Christ,' he said, 'you call me a coward because I don't want to see my wife mashed flat.'

'It's my body and my existence,' Bonny said. 'I'll do with it what I want. I'm not afraid of Hoppy; actually I am, but I don't intend to act afraid, if you can comprehend the difference. I'll go down there to that tar-paper house of his and face him honestly. I'll thank him but I think I'll tell him that he must be more careful in the future. We insist on it.'

He couldn't help admiring her. 'Do that,' he urged. 'It would be a good thing, dear. He should understand that, how we feel.'

'Thank you,' she said remotely. 'Thanks a lot, George, for your encouragement.' She turned away, then, listening to Orion Stroud.

George Keller felt more miserable than ever.

First it was necessary to visit Andrew Gill's factory to pick up the special deluxe Gold Label cigarettes and the Five Star brandy; Bonny, along with Orion Stroud and Gill, left the Foresters' Hall and walked up the road together, all of them conscious of the gravity of their task.

'What's this business relationship you're going into with McConchie?' Bonny asked Andrew Gill.

Gill said, 'Stuart is going to bring automation to my factory.'

Not believing him she said, 'And you're going to advertise over the satellite, I suppose. Singing commercials, as they used to be called. How will they go? Can I compose one for you?'

'Sure,' he said, 'if it'll help business.'

'Are you serious, about this automation?' It occurred to her now that perhaps he actually was.

Gill said, 'I'll know more when I've visited Stuart's boss in Berkeley. Stuart and I are going to make the trip very shortly. I haven't seen Berkeley in years. Stuart says it's building up again – not as it was before, of course. But even that may eventually come some day.'

'I doubt that,' Bonny said. 'But I don't care anyhow; it wasn't so good as all that. Just so it builds back some.'

Glancing back to make sure that Orion could not hear him, Gill said to her, 'Bonny, why don't you come along with Stuart and me?'

Astonished, she said, 'Why?'

'It would do you good to break with George. And maybe you could manage to make the break with him final. You should, for his sake and yours.'

Nodding, she said, 'But—' It seemed to her out of the question; it went too far. Appearances would not be maintained. 'Then, everyone would know,' she said. 'Don't you think?'

Gill said, 'Bon, they know already.'

'Oh.' Chastened, she nodded meekly. 'Well, what a surprise. I've been living under a delusion, evidently.'

'Come to Berkeley with us,' Gill said, 'and start over. In a sense that's what I'm going to be doing; it marks the end of rolling cigarettes by hand, one at a time, on a little cloth and rod machine. It means I'll have a true factory in the old sense, the pre-war sense.'

' "The pre-war sense",' she echoed. 'Is that good?'

'Yes,' Gill said. 'I'm damn sick and tired of rolling them by hand. I've been trying to free myself for years; Stuart has shown me the way. At least, I hope so.' He crossed his fingers.

They reached his factory, and there were the men at work in the rear, rolling away. Bonny thought, So this portion of our lives is soon to be over with forever. I must be sentimental because I cling to it. But Andrew is right. This is no way to produce goods; it's too tedious, too slow. And too few cigarettes are made, really, when you get right down to it. With authentic machinery, Andrew can supply the entire country – assuming that the transportation, the means of delivery, is there.

Among the workmen Stuart McConchie crouched by a barrel of Gill's fine ersatz tobacco, inspecting it. Well, Bonny thought, he either has Andrew's special deluxe formula by now or he isn't interested in it. 'Hello,' she said to him. 'Can you sell his cigarettes once they start rolling off the assembly line in quantity? Have you worked that part out?'

'Yes,' McConchie said. 'We've set up plans for distribution on a mass basis. My employer, Mr Hardy—'

'Don't give me a big sales pitch,' she interrupted. 'I believe you if you say so; I was just curious.' She eyed him critically. 'Andy wants me to travel to Berkeley with you. What do you say?'

'Sure,' he said vaguely.

'I could be your receptionist,' Bonny said. 'At your central offices. Right in the center of the city. Correct?' She laughed, but neither Stuart McConchie nor Gill joined her. 'Is this sacred?' she asked. 'Am I treading on holy topics when I joke? I apologize, if I am.'

'It's okay,' McConchie said. 'We're just concerned; there're still a number of details to work out.'

'Maybe I will go along,' Bonny said. 'Maybe it'll solve my problems, financially.'

Now it was McConchie's turn to scrutinize her. 'What problems do you have? This seems a nice environment here, to bring up your daughter in; and your old man being principal of—'

'Please,' she said. 'I don't care to hear a summary of my blessings. Spare me.' She walked off, to join Gill who was packaging cigarettes in a metal box for presentation to the phocomelus.

The world is so innocent, she thought to herself. Even yet, even after all that's happened to us. Gill wants to cure me of my – restlessness. Stuart McConchie can't imagine what I could wish for that I don't have right here. But maybe they're right and I'm wrong. Maybe I've made my life unduly complicated . . . maybe there's a machine in Berkeley that will save me, too. Perhaps my problems can be automated out of existence.

Off in a corner, Orion Stroud was writing out a speech which he intended to deliver to Hoppy. Bonny smiled, thinking of the solemnity of it all. Would Hoppy be impressed? Would he perhaps be amused or even filled with bitter contempt? No, she thought, he will like it – I have an intuition. It is just the sort of display that he yearns for. Recognition of him; that will please him terribly.

Is Hoppy preparing to receive us? she wondered. Has he washed his face, shaved, put on an especially clean suit . . . is he waiting expectantly for us to arrive? Is this the achievement of his life, the pinnacle?

She tried to imagine the phocomelus at this moment. Hoppy had, a few hours ago, killed a man, and she knew from what Edie said the people all believed he had killed the glasses man. The town rat catcher, she said to herself, and shivered. Who will be next? And will he get a presentation next time – for each one, from now on?

Maybe we will be returning again and again to make one presentation after another, she thought. And she thought, *I will go to Berkeley; I want to get as far away from here as possible.*

And, she thought, as soon as possible. Today, if I can. Right now. Hands in her coat pockets, she walked quickly back to join Stuart McConchie and Gill; they were conferring, now, and she stood as close to them as she could, listening to their words with complete raptness.

Doubtfully, Doctor Stockstill said to the phocomelus, 'Are you sure he can hear me? This definitely transmits all the way to the satellite?' He touched the mike button again, experimentally.

'I can't possibly assure you that he can hear you,' Hoppy said with a snigger. 'I can only assure you that this is a five hundred-watt transmitter; that's not very much by old standards but it's enough to reach him. I've reached him with it a number of times.' He grinned his sharp, alert grin, his intelligent gray eyes alive with splinters of light. 'Go ahead. Does he have a couch up there, or can that be skipped?' The phocomelus laughed, then.

Doctor Stockstill said, 'The couch can be skipped.' He pressed the mike button and said, 'Mr Dangerfield, this is a – doctor, down below here in West Marin. I'm concerned with your condition. Naturally. Everyone down here is. I, um, thought maybe I could help you.'

'Tell him the truth,' Hoppy said. 'Tell him you're an analyst.'

Cautiously, Stockstill said into the microphone, 'Formerly I was an analyst, a psychiatrist. Of course, now I'm a GP. Can you hear me?' He listened to the loudspeaker mounted in the corner but heard only static. 'He's not picking me up,' he said to Hoppy, feeling discouragement.

'It takes time to establish contact,' Hoppy said. 'Try again.' He giggled. 'So you think it's just in his mind. Hypochondria. Are you sure? Well, you might as well assume that because if it's not, there is practically nothing you can do anyhow.'

Doctor Stockstill pressed the mike button and said, 'Mr Dangerfield, this is Stockstill, speaking from Marin County, California; I'm a doctor.' It seemed to him absolutely hopeless; why go on? But on the other hand—

'Tell him about Bluthgeld,' Hoppy said suddenly.

'Okay,' Stockstill said. 'I will.'

'You can tell him my name,' Hoppy said. 'Tell him I did it; listen, Doctor – this is how he'll sound when he tells it.' The phocomelus assumed a peculiar expression and from his mouth, as before, issued the voice of Walt Dangerfield. 'Well, friends, I have a bit of good, good news here . . . I think you'll all enjoy this. Seems as if—' The phocomelus broke off, because from the speaker came a faint sound.

'. . . hello, Doctor. This is Walt Dangerfield.'

Doctor Stockstill said instantly into the microphone, 'Good. Dangerfield, what I want to talk to you about is the pains you've been having. Now, do you have a paper bag up there in the satellite? We're going to try a little carbon dioxide therapy, you and I. I want you to take the paper bag and blow into it. You keep blowing into it and inhaling from it, so that you're finally inhaling pure carbon dioxide. Do you understand? It's just a little idea, but it has a sound basis behind it. You see, too much oxygen triggers off certain diencephalic responses which set up a vicious cycle in the autonomic nervous system. One of the symptoms of a too-active autonomic nervous system is hyperperistalsis, and you may be suffering from that. Fundamentally, it's an anxiety symptom.'

The phocomelus shook his head, turned and rolled away.

'I'm sorry . . .' the voice from the speaker came faintly. 'I don't understand, Doctor. You say breathe into a paper bag? What about a polyethylene container? Couldn't asphyxiation result?' The voice, querulous and unreasonable, stumbled uncertainly on, 'Is there any way I can synthesize phenobarbital out of the constituents available to me up here? I'll give you an inventory list and possibly—' Static interrupted Dangerfield; when he next was audible he was talking about something else. Perhaps, Doctor Stockstill thought, the man's faculties were wandering.

'Isolation in space,' Stockstill broke in, 'breeds its own disruptive phenomena, similar to what once was termed "cabin fever." Specific to this is the feedback of free-floating anxiety so that it assumes a somatic consequence.' He felt, as he talked, that he was doing it all wrong; that he had failed already. The phocomelus had retired, too disgusted to listen – he was off somewhere else entirely, puttering. 'Mr Dangerfield,' Stockstill said, 'what I want to do is interrupt this feedback and the carbon dioxide trick might do just that. Then when tension symptoms have eased, we can begin a form of psychotherapy, including recall of forgotten traumatic material.'

The disc jockey said dryly, 'My traumatic material isn't forgotten, Doctor; I'm experiencing it right now. It's all around me. It's a form of claustrophobia and I have it very, very bad.'

'Claustrophobia,' Doctor Stockstill said, 'is a phobia directly traceable to the diencephalon in that it's a disturbance of the sense of spaciality. It's connected with the panic reaction to the presence or the imagined presence of danger; it's a repressed desire to flee.'

Dangerfield said, 'Well, where can I flee to, Doctor? Let's

be realistic. What in Christ's name can psychoanalysis do for me? I'm a sick man; I need an operation, not the crap you're giving me.'

'Are you sure?' Stockstill asked, feeling ineffective and foolish. 'Now, this will admittedly take time, but you and I have at least established basic contact; you know I'm down here trying to help you and I know that you're listening.' You are listening, aren't you? he asked silently. 'So I think we've accomplished something already.'

He waited. There was only silence.

'Hello, Dangerfield?' he said into the microphone.

Silence.

From behind him the phocomelus said, 'He's either cut himself off or the satellite's too far, now. Do you think you're helping him?'

'I don't know,' Stockstill said. 'But I know it's worth trying.'

'If you had started a year ago—'

'But nobody knew.' We took Dangerfield for granted, like the sun, Stockstill realized. And now, as Hoppy says, it's a little late.

'Better luck tomorrow afternoon,' Hoppy said, with a faint – almost sneering – smile. And yet Stockstill felt in it a deep sadness. Was Hoppy sorry for him, for his futile efforts? Or for the man in the satellite passing above them? It was difficult to tell.

'I'll keep trying,' Stockstill said.

There was a knock at the door.

Hoppy said, 'That will be the official delegation.' A broad, pleased smile appeared on his pinched features; his face seemed to swell, to fill with warmth. 'Excuse me.' He wheeled his 'mobile to the door, extended a manual extensor, and flung the door open.

There stood Orion Stroud, Andrew Gill, Cas Stone, Bonny Keller and Mrs Tallman, all looking nervous and ill-at-ease. 'Harrington,' Stroud said, 'we have something for you, a little gift.'

'Fine,' Hoppy said, grinning back at Stockstill. 'See?' he said to the doctor. 'Didn't I tell you? It's their appreciation.' To the delegation he said, 'Come on in; I've been waiting.' He held the door wide and they passed on inside his house.

'What have you been doing?' Bonny asked Doctor Stockstill, seeing him standing by the transmitter and microphone.

Stockstill said, 'Trying to reach Dangerfield.'

'Therapy?' she said.

'Yes.' He nodded.

'No luck, though.'

'We'll try again tomorrow,' Stockstill said.

Orion Stroud, his presentation momentarily forgotten, said to Doctor Stockstill, 'That's right; you used to be a psychiatrist.'

Impatiently, Hoppy said, 'Well, what did you bring me?' He peered past Stroud, at Gill; he made out the sight of the container of cigarettes and the case of brandy. 'Are those mine?'

'Yes,' Gill said. 'In appreciation.'

The container and the case were lifted from his hands; he blinked as they sailed toward the phoce and came to rest on the floor directly in front of the 'mobile. Avidly, Hoppy plucked them open with his extensors.

'Uh,' Stroud said, disconcerted, 'we have a statement to make. Is it okay to do so now, Hoppy?' He eyed the phocomelus with apprehension.

'Anything else?' Hoppy demanded, the boxes open, now. 'What else did you bring me to pay me back?'

To herself as she watched the scene Bonny thought, I had

no idea he was so childish. Just a little child . . . we should have brought much more and it should have been wrapped gaily, with ribbons and cards, with as much color as possible. *He must not be disappointed*, she realized. Our lives depend on it, on his being – placated.

'Isn't there more?' Hoppy was saying peevishly.

'Not yet,' Stroud said. 'But there will be.' He shot a swift, flickering glance at the others in the delegation. 'Your *real* presents, Hoppy, have to be prepared with care. This is just a beginning.'

'I see,' the phocomelus said. But he did not sound convinced.

'Honest,' Stroud said. 'It's the truth, Hoppy.'

'I don't smoke,' Hoppy said, surveying the cigarettes; he picked up a handful and crushed them, letting the bits drop. 'It causes cancer.'

'Well,' Gill began, 'there're two sides to that. Now—'

The phocomelus sniggered. 'I think that's all you're going to give me,' he said.

'No, there will certainly be more,' Stroud said.

The room was silent, except for the static coming from the speaker.

Off in the corner an object, a transmitter tube, rose and sailed through the air, burst loudly against the wall, sprinkling them all with fragments of broken glass.

' "More," ' Hoppy mimicked, in Stroud's deep, portentous voice. ' "There will certainly be more." '

Fifteen

For thirty-six hours Walt Dangerfield had lain on his bunk in a state of semi-consciousness, knowing now that it was not an ulcer; it was cardiac arrest which he was experiencing, and it was probably going to kill him in a very short time. In spite of what Stockstill, the analyst, had said.

The transmitter of the satellite had continued to broadcast a tape of light concert music over and over again; the sound of soothing strings filled his ears in a travesty of unavailing comfort. He did not even have the strength to get up and make his way to the controls to shut it off.

That psychoanalyst, he thought bitterly. Talking about breathing into a paper bag. It had been like a dream . . . the faint voice, so full of self-confidence. So utterly false in its premises.

Messages were arriving from all over the world as the satellite passed through its orbit again and again; his recording equipment caught them and retained them, but that was all. Dangerfield could no longer answer.

I guess I have to tell them, he said to himself. I guess the time – the time we've been expecting, all of us – has finally come at last.

On his hands and knees he crept until he reached the seat by the microphone, the seat in which for seven years he had broadcast to the world below. After he had sat there for a time resting he turned on one of the many tape recorders, picked up the mike, and began dictating a message which, when it had been completed, would play endlessly, replacing the concert music.

'My friends, this is Walt Dangerfield talking and wanting to thank you all for the times we have had together, speaking back and forth, us all keeping in touch. I'm afraid though that this complaint of mine makes it impossible for me to go on any longer. So with great regret I've got to sign off for the last time—' He went on, painfully, picking his words with care, trying to make them, his audience below, as little unhappy as possible. But nevertheless he told them the truth; he told them that it was the end for him and that they would have to find some way to communicate without him, and then he rang off, shut down the microphone, and in a weary reflex, played the tape back.

The tape was blank. There was nothing on it, although he had talked for almost fifteen minutes.

Evidently the equipment had for some reason broken down, but he was too ill to care; he snapped the mike back on, set switches on the control panel, and this time prepared to deliver his message live to the area below. Those people there would just have to pass the word on to the others; there was no other way.

'My friends,' he began once more, 'this is Walt Dangerfield. I have some bad news to give you but—' And then he realized that he was talking into a dead mike. The loudspeaker above his head had gone silent; nothing was being transmitted. Otherwise he would have heard his own voice from the monitoring system.

As he sat there, trying to discover what was wrong, he noticed something else, something far stranger and more ominous.

Systems on all sides of him were in motion. Had been in motion for some time, by the looks of them. The highspeed recording and playback decks which he had never used – all at once the drums were spinning, for the first time in seven years. Even as he watched he saw relays click on and off; a drum halted, another one began to turn, this time at slow speed.

'I don't understand,' he said to himself. *What's happening?*

Evidently the systems were receiving at high speed, recording, and now one of them had started to play back, but what had set all this in motion? Not he. Dials showed him that the satellite's transmitter was on the air, and even as he realized that, realized that messages which had been picked up and recorded were now being played over the air, he heard the speaker above his head return to life.

'Hoode hoode hoo,' a voice – his voice – chuckled. 'This is your old pal, Walt Dangerfield, once more, and forgive that concert music. Won't be any more of that.'

When did I say that? he asked himself as he sat dully listening. He felt shocked and puzzled. His voice sounded so vital, so full of good spirits; how could I sound like that now? he wondered. That's the way I used to sound, years ago, when I had my health, and when *she* was still alive.

'Well,' his voice murmured on, 'that bit of indisposition I've been suffering from . . . evidently mice got into the supply cupboards, and you'll laugh to think of Walt Dangerfield fending off mice up here in the sky, but 'tis true. Anyhow, part of my stores deteriorated and I didn't happen to notice . . . but it sure played havoc with my insides. However—' And he heard himself give his familiar chuckle. 'I'm okay now. I know you'll be glad to hear that, all you people down there who were so good as to transmit your get-well messages, and for that I give you thanks.'

Getting up from the seat before the microphone, Walt Dangerfield made his way unsteadily to his bunk; he lay down, closing his eyes, and then he thought once more of the pain in his chest and what it meant. Angina pectoris, he thought, is supposed to be more like a great fist pressing down; this is more a burning pain. If I could look at the medical data on the microfilm again . . . maybe there's some fact I failed to read. For instance, this is directly under the breastbone, not off to the left side. Does that mean anything?

Or maybe there's nothing wrong with me, he thought to himself as he struggled to get up once more. Maybe Stockstill, that psychiatrist who wanted me to breathe carbon dioxide, was right; maybe it's just in my mind, from the years of isolation here.

But he did not think so. It felt far too real for that.

There was one other fact about his illness that bewildered him. For all his efforts, he could not make a thing out of that fact, and so he had not even bothered to mention it to the several doctors and hospitals below. Now it was too late, because now he was too sick to operate the controls of the transmitter.

The pain seemed always to get worse when his satellite was passing over Northern California.

In the middle of the night the din of Bill Keller's agitated murmurings woke his sister up. 'What is it?' Edie said sleepily, trying to make out what he wanted to tell her. She sat up in her bed now, rubbing her eyes as the murmurings rose to a crescendo.

'Hoppy Harrington!' he was saying, deep down inside her. 'He's taken over the satellite! Hoppy's taken over Dangerfield's satellite!' He chattered on and on excitedly, repeating it again and again.

'How do you know?'

'Because Mr Bluthgeld says so; he's down below now but he can still see what's going on above. He can't do anything and he's mad. He still knows all about us. He hates Hoppy because Hoppy mashed him.'

'What about Dangerfield?' she asked. 'Is he dead yet?'

'He's not down below,' her brother said after a long pause. 'So I guess not.'

'Who should I tell?' Edie said, 'About what Hoppy did?'

'Tell Mama,' her brother said urgently. 'Go right in now.'

Climbing from the bed, Edie scampered to the door and up the hall to their parents' bedroom; she flung the door open, calling, 'Mama, I have to tell you something—' And then her voice failed her, because her mother was not there. Only one sleeping figure lay in the bed, her father, alone. Her mother – she knew instantly and completely – had gone and she would not be coming back.

'Where is she?' Bill clamored from within her. 'I know she's not here; I can't feel her.'

Slowly, Edie shut the door of the bedroom. What'll I do? she asked herself. She walked aimlessly, shivering from the night cold. 'Be quiet,' she said to Bill, and his murmurings sank down a little.

'You have to find her,' Bill was saying.

'I can't,' she said. She knew it was hopeless. 'Let me think what to do instead,' she said, going back into her bedroom for her robe and slippers.

To Ella Hardy, Bonny said, 'You have a very nice home here. It's strange to be back in Berkeley after so long, though.' She felt overwhelmingly tired. 'I'm going to have to turn in,' she said. It was two in the morning. Glancing at Andrew Gill and Stuart she said, 'We made awfully good time getting here, didn't we? Even a year ago it would have taken another three days.'

'Yes,' Gill said, and yawned. He looked tired, too; he had

done most of the driving because it was his horsecar they had taken.

Mr Hardy said, 'Along about this time, Mrs Keller, we generally tune in a very late pass by the satellite.'

'Oh,' she said, not actually caring but knowing it was inevitable; they would have to listen at least for a few moments to be polite. 'So you get two transmissions a day, down here.'

'Yes,' Mrs Hardy said, 'and frankly we find it worth staying up for this late one, although in the last few weeks . . .' She gestured. 'I suppose you know as well as we do. Dangerfield is such a sick man.'

They were all silent, for a moment.

Hardy said, 'To face the brutal fact, we haven't been able to pick him up at all the last day or so, except for a program of light opera that he has played over and over again automatically . . . so—' He glanced around at the four of them. 'That's why we were pinning so many hopes on this late transmission tonight.'

To herself, Bonny thought, there's so much business to conduct tomorrow, but he's right; we must stay up for this. We must know what is going on in the satellite; it's too important to us all. She felt sad. Walt Dangerfield, she thought, are you dying up there alone? Are you already dead and we don't know yet?

Will the light opera music go on forever? she wondered. At least until the satellite at last falls back to the Earth or drifts off into space and finally is attracted to the sun?

'I'll turn it on,' Hardy said, inspecting his watch. He crossed the room to the radio, turned it on carefully. 'It takes it a long time to warm up,' he apologized. 'I think there's a weak tube; we asked the West Berkeley Handyman's Association to inspect it but they're so busy, they're too tied up, they said.

I'd look at it myself, but—' He shrugged ruefully. 'Last time I tried to fix it, I broke it worse.'

Stuart said, 'You're going to frighten Mr Gill away.'

'No,' Gill said. 'I understand. Radios are in the province of the handies. It's the same up in West Marin.'

To Bonny, Mrs Hardy said, 'Stuart says you used to live here.'

'I worked at the radiation lab for a while,' Bonny said. 'And then I worked out at Livermore, also for the University. Of course—' She hesitated. 'It's so changed. I wouldn't know Berkeley, now. As we came through I saw nothing I recognized except perhaps San Pablo Avenue itself. All the little shops – they look new.'

'They are,' Dean Hardy said. Now static issued from the radio and he bent attentively, his ear close to it. 'Generally we pick up this late transmission at about 640 kc. Excuse me.' He turned his back to them, intent on the radio.

'Turn up the fat-lamp,' Gill said, 'so he can see better to tune it.'

Bonny did so, marveling that even here in the city they were still dependent on the primitive fat-lamp; she had supposed that their electricity had long since been restored, at least on a partial basis. In some ways, she realized, they were actually behind West Marin. And in Bolinas—

'Ah,' Mr Hardy said, breaking into her thoughts. 'I think I've got him. And it's not light opera.' His face glistened, beamed.

'Oh dear,' Ella Hardy said, 'I pray to heaven he's better.' She clasped her hands together with anxiety.

From the speaker a friendly, informal, familiar voice boomed out loudly, 'Hi, there, all you night people down below. Who do you suppose this is, saying hello, hello and hello.' Dangerfield laughed. 'Yes, folks, I'm up and around, on my two feet once more. And just twirling all these little old knobs and controls like crazy . . . yes sir.' His voice was warm, and around Bonny the faces in the room relaxed, too, and smiled in company with the pleasure contained in the voice. The faces nodded, agreed.

'You hear him?' Ella Hardy said. 'Why, he's better. He is; you can tell. He's not just saying it, you can tell the difference.'

'Hoode hoode hoo,' Dangerfield said. 'Well, now, let us see; what news is there? You heard about that public enemy number one, that one-time physicist we all remember so well. Our good buddy Doctor Bluthgeld, or should I say Doctor Bloodmoney? Anyhow, I guess you all know by now that dear Doctor Bloodmoney is no longer with us. Yes, that's right.'

'I heard a rumor about that,' Mr Hardy said excitedly. 'A peddler who hitched a balloon ride out of Marin County—'

'Shhh,' Ella Hardy said, listening.

'Yes indeed,' Dangerfield was saying. 'A certain party up in Northern California took care of Doctor B. For good. And we owe a debt of sheer unadulterated gratitude to that certain little party because – well, just consider this, folks; that party's a bit handicapped. And yet he was able to do what no one else could have done.' Now Dangerfield's voice was hard, unbending; it was a new sound which they had not heard from him ever before. They glanced at one another uneasily. 'I'm talking about Hoppy Harrington, my friends. You don't know that name? You should, because without Hoppy not one of you would be alive.'

Hardy, rubbing his chin and frowning, shot a questioning look at Ella.

'This, Hoppy Harrington,' Dangerfield continued, 'mashed Doctor B. from a good four miles away, and it was easy. Very easy. You think it's impossible for someone to reach out and touch a man four miles off? That's miiiiighty long arms, isn't it, folks? And mighty strong hands. Well, I'll tell you something even more remarkable.' The voice became confidential; it dropped to an intimate near-whisper. 'Hoppy has no arms and no hands *at all*.' And Dangerfield, then, was silent.

Bonny said quietly, 'Andrew, it's him, isn't it?'

Twisting around in his chair to face her, Gill said, 'Yes, dear. I think so.'

'Who?' Stuart McConchie said.

Now the voice from the radio resumed, more calmly this time, but also more bleakly. The voice had become chilly and stark. 'There was an attempt made,' it stated, 'to reward Mr Harrington. It wasn't much. A few cigarettes and some bad whiskey – If you can call that a 'reward.' And some empty phrases delivered by a cheap local politico. That was all – that was it for the man who saved us all. I guess they figured—'

Ella Hardy said, 'That is not Dangerfield.'

To Gill and Bonny, Mr Hardy said, 'Who is it? Say.'

Bonny said, 'It's Hoppy.' Gill nodded.

'Is he up there?' Stuart said. 'In the satellite?'

'I don't know,' Bonny said. But what did it matter? 'He's got control of it; that's what's important.' And we thought by coming to Berkeley we would get away, she said to herself. That we would have left Hoppy. 'I'm not surprised,' she said. 'He's been preparing a long time; everything else has been practice, for this.'

'But enough of that,' the voice from the radio declared, in a lighter tone now. 'You'll hear more about the man who saved us all; I'll keep you posted, from time to time . . . old Walt isn't going to forget. Meanwhile, let's have a little music. What about a little authentic five-string banjo music, friends? Genuine authentic US American old-time folk music. . . "Out on

Penny's Farm", played by Pete Seeger, the greatest of the folk music men.'

There was a pause, and then, from the speaker, came the sound of a full symphony orchestra.

Thoughtfully, Bonny said, 'Hoppy doesn't have it down quite right. There're a few circuits left he hasn't got control of.'

The symphony orchestra abruptly ceased. Silence obtained again, and then something spilled out at the incorrect speed; it squeaked frantically and was chopped off. In spite of herself Bonny smiled. At last, belatedly, there came the sound of the five-string banjo.

Hard times in the country,
Out on Penny's farm.

It was a folksy tenor voice twanging away, along with the banjo. The people in the room sat listening, obeying out of long habit; the music emanated from the radio and for seven years they had depended on this; they had learned this and it had become a part of their physical bodies, this response. And yet – Bonny felt the shame and despair around her. No one in the room fully understood what had happened; she herself felt only a numbed confusion. They had Dangerfield back and yet they did not; they had the outer form, the appearance, but was it really, in essence? It was some labored apparition, like a ghost; it was not alive, not viable. It went through the motions but it was empty and dead. It had a peculiar *preserved* quality, as if somehow the cold, the loneliness, had combined to form around the man in the satellite a new shell. A case which fitted over the living substance and snuffed it out.

The killing, the slow destruction of Dangerfield, Bonny thought, was deliberate, and it came – not from space, not from beyond – but from below, from the familiar landscape.

Dangerfield had not died from the years of isolation; he had been stricken by careful instruments issuing up from the very world which he struggled to contact. If he could have cut himself off from us, she thought, he would be alive now. At the very moment he listened to us, received us, he was being killed – and did not guess.

He does not guess even now, she decided. It probably baffles him, if he is capable of perception at this point, capable of any form of awareness.

'This is terrible,' Gill was saying in a monotone.

'Terrible,' Bonny agreed, 'but inevitable. He was too vulnerable up there. If Hoppy hadn't done it someone else would have, one day.'

'What'll we do?' Mr Hardy said. 'If you folks are so sure of this, we better—'

'Oh,' Bonny said, 'we're sure. There's no doubt. You think we ought to form a delegation and call on Hoppy again? Ask him to stop? I wonder what he'd say.' I wonder, she thought, how near we would get to that familiar little house before we were demolished. Perhaps we are too close even now, right here in this room.

Not for the world, she thought, would I go any nearer. I think in fact I will move farther on; I will get Andrew Gill to go with me and if not him then Stuart, if not Stuart then someone. I will keep going; I will not stay in one place and maybe I will be safe from Hoppy. I don't care about the others at this point, because I am too scared; I only care about myself.

'Andy' she said to Gill, 'listen. I want to go.'

'Out of Berkeley, you mean?'

'Yes.' She nodded. 'Down the coast to Los Angeles. I know we could make it; we'd get there and we'd be okay there. I know it.'

Gill said, 'I can't go, dear. I have to return to West Marin; I have my business – I can't give it up.'

Appalled, she said, 'You'd go back to West Marin?'

'Yes. Why not? We can't give up just because Hoppy has done this. That's not reasonable to ask of us. Even Hoppy isn't asking that.'

'But he will,' she said. 'He'll ask everything, in time; I know it, I can foresee it.'

'Then we'll wait,' Gill said. 'Until then. Meanwhile, let's do our jobs.' To Hardy and Stuart McConchie he said, 'I'm going to turn in, because Christ – we have plenty to discuss tomorrow.' He rose to his feet. 'Things may work themselves out. We mustn't despair.' He whacked Stuart on the back. 'Right?'

Stuart said, 'I hid once in the sidewalk. Do I have to do that again?' He looked around at the rest of them, seeking an answer.

'Yes,' Bonny said.

'Then I will,' he said. 'But I came up out of the sidewalk; I didn't stay there. And I'll come up again.' He, too, rose. 'Gill, you can stay with me in my place. Bonny, you can stay with the Hardys.'

'Yes,' Ella Hardy said, stirring. 'We have plenty of room for you, Mrs Keller. Until we can find a more permanent arrangement.'

'Good,' Bonny said, automatically. 'That's swell.' She rubbed her eyes. A good night's sleep, she thought. It would help. And then what? We will just have to see.

If, she thought, we are alive tomorrow.

To her, Gill said suddenly, 'Bonny, do you find this hard to believe about Hoppy? Or do you find it easy? Do you know him that well? Do you understand him?'

'I think,' she said, 'it's very ambitious of him. But it's what we should have expected. Now he has reached out farther than any of us; as he says, he's now got long, long arms. He's compensated beautifully. You have to admire him.'

'Yes,' Gill admitted. 'I do. Very much.'

'If I only thought this would satisfy him,' she said, 'I wouldn't be so afraid.'

'The man I feel sorry for,' Gill said, 'is Dangerfield. Having to lie there passively, sick as he is, and just listen.'

She nodded, but she refused to imagine it; she could not bear to.

Hurrying down the path in her robe and slippers, Edie Keller groped her way toward Hoppy Harrington's house.

'Hurry,' Bill said, from within her. 'He knows about us, they're telling me; they say we're in danger. If we can get close enough to him I can do an imitation of someone dead that'll scare him, because he's afraid of dead people. Mr Blaine says that's because to him the dead are like fathers, lots of fathers, and—'

'Be quiet,' Edie said. 'Let me think.' In the darkness she had gotten mixed up. She could not find the path through the oak forest now, and she halted, breathing deeply, trying to orient herself by the dull light of the partial moon overhead.

It's to the right, she thought. Down the hill. I must not fall; he'd hear the noise, he can hear a long way, almost everything. Step by step she descended, holding her breath.

'I've got a good imitation ready,' Bill was mumbling; he would not be quiet. 'It's like this: when I get near him I switch with someone dead, and you won't like that because it's – sort of squishy, but it's just for a few minutes and then they can talk to him direct, from inside you. Is that okay, because once he hears—'

'It's okay,' she said, 'just for a little while.'

'Well, then you know what they say? They say "We have been taught a terrible lesson for our folly. This is God's way of making us see." And you know what that is? That's the minister who used to make sermons when Hoppy was a baby and got carried on his dad's back to church. He'll remember that, even though it was years and years ago. It was the most awful moment in his life; you know why? Because that minister, he was making everybody in the church look at Hoppy and that was wrong, and Hoppy's father never went back after that. But that's a lot of the reason why Hoppy is like he is today, because of that minister. So he's really terrified of that minister, and when he hears his voice again—'

'Shut up,' Edie said desperately. They were now above Hoppy's house; she saw the lights below. 'Please, Bill, *please*.'

'But I have to explain to you,' Bill went on. 'When I—'

He stopped. Inside her there was nothing. She was empty.

'Bill,' she said.

He had gone.

Before her eyes, in the dull moonlight, something she had never seen before bobbed. It rose, jiggled, its long, pale hair streaming behind it like a tail; it rose until it hung directly before her face. It had tiny, dead eyes and a gaping mouth, it was nothing but a little hard round head, like a baseball. From its mouth came a squeak, and then it fluttered upward once more, released. She watched as it gained more and more height, rising above the trees in a swimming motion, ascending in the unfamiliar atmosphere which it had never known before.

'Bill,' she said, 'he took you out of me. He put you outside.' And you are leaving, she realized; Hoppy is making you go. 'Come back,' she said, but it didn't matter because he could not live outside of her. She knew that. Doctor Stockstill had said that. He could not be born, and Hoppy had heard him and made him born, knowing that he would die.

You won't get to do your imitation, she realized. I told you to be quiet and you wouldn't. Straining, she saw – or thought she saw – the hard little object with the streamers of hair now above her . . . and then it disappeared, silently.

She was alone.

Why go on now? It was over. She turned, walked back up the hillside, her head lowered, eyes shut, feeling her way. Back to her house, her bed. Inside she felt raw; she felt the tearing loose. If you only could have been quiet, she thought. He would not have heard you. I told you, I told you so.

She plodded on back.

Floating in the atmosphere, Bill Keller saw a little, heard a little, felt the trees and the animals alive and moving among them. He felt the pressure at work on him, lifting him, but he remembered his imitation and he said it. His voice came out tiny in the cold air; then his ears picked it up and he exclaimed.

'We have been taught a terrible lesson for our folly,' he squeaked, and his voice echoed in his ears, delighting him.

The pressure on him let go; he bobbed up, swimming happily, and then he dove. Down and down he went and just before he touched the ground he went sideways until, guided by the living presence within, he hung suspended above Hoppy Harrington's antenna and house.

'This is God's way!' he shouted in his thin, tiny voice. 'We can see that it is time to call a halt to high-altitude nuclear testing. I want all of you to write letters to President Johnson!' He did not know who President Johnson was. A living person, perhaps. He looked around for him but he did not see him; he saw oak forests of animals, he saw a bird with noiseless wings that drifted, huge-beaked, eyes staring. Bill squeaked in fright as the noiseless, brown-feathered bird glided his way.

The bird made a dreadful sound, of greed and the desire to rend.

'All of you,' Bill cried, fleeing through the dark, chill air. 'You must write letters in protest!'

The glittering eyes of the bird followed behind him as he and it glided above the trees, in the dim moonlight.

The owl reached him. And crunched him, in a single instant.

Sixteen

Once more he was within. He could no longer see or hear; it had been for a short time and now it was over.

The owl, hooting, flew on.

Bill Keller said to the owl, 'Can you hear me?'

Maybe it could, maybe not; it was only an owl, it did not have any sense, as Edie had had. It was not the same. Can I live inside you? he asked it, hidden away in here where no one knows . . . you have your flights that you make, your passes. With him, in the owl, were the bodies of mice and a thing that stirred and scratched, big enough to keep on trying to live.

Lower, he told the owl. He saw, by means of the owl, the oaks; he saw clearly, as if everything were full of light. Millions of individual objects lay immobile and then he spied one that crept – it was alive and the owl turned that way. The creeping thing, suspecting nothing, hearing no sound, wandered on, out into the open.

An instant later it had been swallowed. The owl flew on.

Good, he thought. And, is there more? This goes on all night, again and again, and then there is bathing when it rains, and the long, deep sleeps. Are they the best part? They are.

He said, 'Fergesson don't allow his employees to drink; it's against his religion, isn't it?' And then he said, 'Hoppy, what's the light from? Is it God? You know, like in the Bible. I mean, is it true?'

The owl hooted.

'Hoppy,' he said, from within the owl, 'you said last time it was all dark. Is that right? No light at all?'

A thousand dead things within him yammered for attention. He listened, repeated, picked among them.

'You dirty little freak,' he said. 'Now listen. Stay down here; we're below street-level. You moronic jackass, stay where you are, you are, you are. I'll go upstairs and get those. People. Down here you clear. Space. Space for them.'

Frightened, the owl flapped; it rose higher, trying to evade him. But he continued, sorting and picking and listening on.

'Stay down here,' he repeated. Again the lights of Hoppy's house came in to view; the owl had circled, returned to it, unable to get away. He made it stay where he wanted it. He brought it closer and closer in its passes to Hoppy. 'You moronic jackass,' he said. 'Stay where you are.'

The owl flew lower, hooting in its desire to leave. It was caught and it knew it. The owl hated him.

'The president must listen to our pleas,' he said, 'before it is too late.'

With a furious effort the owl performed its regular technique; it coughed him up and he sank in the direction of the ground, trying to catch the currents of air. He crashed among humus and plant-growth; he rolled, giving little squeaks until finally he came to rest in a hollow.

Released, the owl soared off and disappeared.

'Let man's compassion be witness to this,' he said as he lay in the hollow; he spoke in the minister's voice from long ago. 'It is ourselves who have done this; we see here the results of mankind's own folly.'

Lacking the owl eyes he saw only vaguely; the illumination seemed to be gone and all that remained were several nearby shapes. They were trees.

He saw, too, the form of Hoppy's house outlined against the dim night sky. It was not far off.

'Let me in,' Bill said, moving his mouth. He rolled about in the hollow; he thrashed until the leaves stirred. 'I want to come in.'

An animal, hearing him, moved further off, warily.

'In, in, in,' Bill said. 'I can't stay out here long; I'll die. Edie, where are you?' He did not feel her nearby; he felt only the presence of the phocomelus within the house.

As best he could, he rolled that way.

Early in the morning, Doctor Stockstill arrived at Hoppy Harrington's tar-paper house to make his fourth attempt at treating Walt Dangerfield. The transmitter, he noticed, was on, and so were lights here and there; puzzled, he knocked on the door.

The door opened and there sat Hoppy Harrington in the center of his 'mobile. Hoppy regarded him in an odd, cautious, defensive fashion.

'I want to make another try,' Stockstill said, knowing how useless it was but wanting to go ahead anyhow. 'Is it okay?'

'Yes sir,' Hoppy said. 'It's okay'

'Is Dangerfield still alive?'

'Yes sir. I'd know if he was dead.' Hoppy wheeled aside to admit him. 'He must still be up there.'

'What's happened?' Stockstill said. 'Have you been up all night?'

'Yes,' Hoppy said. 'Learning to work things.' He wheeled the 'mobile about, frowning. 'It's hard,' he said, apparently preoccupied.

'I think that idea of carbon dioxide therapy was a mistake, now that I look back on it,' Stockstill said as he seated himself at the microphone. 'This time I'm going to try some free association with him, if I can get him to.'

The phocomelus continued to wheel about; now the 'mobile bumped into the end of a table. 'I hit that by mistake,' Hoppy said. 'I'm sorry; I didn't mean to.'

Stockstill said, 'You seem different.'

'I'm the same; I'm Bill Keller,' the phocomelus said. 'Not Hoppy Harrington.' With his right manual extensor he pointed. 'There's Hoppy. That's him, from now on.'

In a corner lay a shriveled dough-like object several inches long; its mouth gaped in congealed emptiness. It had a human-like quality to it, and Stockstill went over to pick it up.

'That was me,' the phocomelus said. 'But I got close enough last night to switch. He fought a lot, but he was afraid, so I won. I kept doing one imitation after another. The minister one got him.'

Stockstill, holding the wizened little homunculus, said nothing.

'Do you know how to work the transmitter?' the phocomelus asked presently. 'Because I don't. I tried, but I can't. I got the lights to work; they turn on and off. I practiced that all night.' To demonstrate, he rolled his 'mobile to the wall, where with his manual extensor he snapped the light switch up and down.

After a time Stockstill said, looking down at the dead, tiny form he held in his hand, 'I knew it wouldn't survive.'

'It did for a while,' the phocomelus said. 'For around an hour; that's pretty good, isn't it? Part of that time it was in an owl; I don't know if that counts.'

'I – better get to work trying to contact Dangerfield,' Stockstill said finally. 'He may die any time.'

'Yes,' the phocomelus said, nodding. 'Want me to take that?' He held out an extensor and Stockstill handed him the homunculus. 'That owl ate me,' the phoce said. 'I didn't like that, but it sure had good eyes; I liked that part, using its eyes.'

'Yes,' Stockstill said reflexively. 'Owls have tremendously good eyesight; that must have been quite an experience.' This, that he had held in his hand – it did not seem at all possible to him. And yet, it was not so strange; the phoce had moved Bill only a matter of a few inches – that had been enough. And what was that in comparison to what he had done to Doctor Bluthgeld? Evidently after that the phoce had lost track because Bill, free from his sister's body, had mingled with first one substance and then another. And at last he had found the phoce and mingled with him, too; had, at the end, supplanted him in his own body.

It had been an unbalanced trade. Hoppy Harrington had gotten the losing end of it, by far; the body which he had received in exchange for his own had lasted only a few minutes, at the most.

'Did you know,' Bill Keller said, speaking haltingly as if it was still difficult for him to control the phocomelus' body, 'that Hoppy got up in the satellite for a while? Everybody was excited about that; they woke me up in the night to tell me and I woke Edie. That's how I got here,' he added, with a strained, earnest expression on his face.

'And what are you going to do now?' Stockstill asked.

The phoce said, 'I have to get used to this body; it's heavy. I feel gravity . . . I'm used to just floating about. You know what? I think these extensors are swell. I can do a lot with them already.' The extensors whipped about, touched a picture on the wall, flicked in the direction of the transmitter. 'I have to go find Edie,' the phoce said. 'I want to tell her I'm okay; I bet she probably thinks I died.'

Turning on the microphone, Stockstill said, 'Walter Dangerfield, this is Doctor Stockstill in West Marin. Can you hear me? If you can, give me an answer. I'd like to resume the therapy we were attempting the other day.' He paused, then repeated what he had said.

'You'll have to try a lot of times,' the phoce said, watching him. 'It's going to be hard because he's so weak; he probably can't get up to his feet and he didn't understand what was happening when Hoppy took over.'

Nodding, Stockstill pressed the microphone button and tried again.

'Can I go?' Bill Keller asked. 'Can I look for Edie now?'

'Yes,' Stockstill said, rubbing his forehead; he drew his faculties together and said, 'You'll be careful, what you do . . . you may not be able to switch again.'

'I don't want to switch again,' Bill said. 'This is fine, because for the first time there's no one in here but me.' In explanation, he added, 'I mean, I'm alone; I'm not just part of someone else. Of course, I switched before, but it was to that blind thing – Edie tricked me into it and it didn't do at all. This is different.' The thin phoce-face broke into a smile.

'Just be careful,' Stockstill repeated.

'Yes sir,' the phoce said dutifully. 'I'll try; I had bad luck with the owl but it wasn't my fault because I didn't want to get swallowed. That was the owl's idea.'

Stockstill thought, But this was yours. There is a difference; I can see that. And it is very important. Into the microphone he repeated, 'Walt, this is Doctor Stockstill down below; I'm still trying to reach you. I think we can do a lot to help you pull through this, if you'll do as I tell you. I think we'll try some free association, today, in an effort to get at the root causes of your tension. In any case, it won't do any harm; I think you can appreciate that.'

From the loudspeaker came only static.

Is it hopeless? Stockstill wondered. Is it worth keeping on?

He pressed the mike button once more, saying, 'Walter, the one who usurped your authority in the satellite – he's dead, now, so you don't have to worry regarding him. When you feel strong enough I'll give you more details. Okay? Do you agree?' He listened. Still only static.

The phoce, rolling about the room on his 'mobile, like a great trapped beetle, said, 'Can I go to school now that I'm out?'

'Yes,' Stockstill murmured.

'But I know a lot of things already,' Bill said, 'from listening with Edie when she was in school; I won't have to go back and repeat, I can go ahead, like her. Don't you think so?'

Stockstill nodded.

'I wonder what my mother will say,' the phoce said.

Jarred, Stockstill said, 'What?' And then he realized who was meant 'She's gone,' he said. 'Bonny left with Gill and McConchie.'

'I know she left,' Bill said plaintively. 'But won't she be coming back sometime?'

'Possibly not,' Stockstill said. 'Bonny's an odd woman, very restless. You can't count on it.' It might be better if she didn't know, he said to himself. It would be extremely difficult for her; after all, he realized, she never knew about you at all. Only Edie and I knew. And Hoppy. And, he thought, the owl. 'I'm going to give up,' he said suddenly, 'on trying to reach Dangerfield. Maybe some other time.'

'I guess I bother you,' Bill said.

Stockstill nodded.

'I'm sorry,' Bill said. 'I was trying to practice and I didn't know you were coming by. I didn't mean to upset you; it happened suddenly in the night – I rolled here and got in under the door before Hoppy understood, and then it was too late because I was close.' Seeing the expression on the doctor's face, he ceased.

'It's – just not like anything I ever ran into before,' Stockstill said. 'I knew you existed But that was about all.'

Bill said, with pride, 'You didn't know I was learning to switch.'

'No,' Stockstill agreed.

'Try talking to Dangerfield again,' Bill said. 'Don't give up, because I know he's up there. I won't tell you how I know because if I do you'll get more upset.'

'Thank you,' Stockstill said. 'For not telling me.'

Once more he pressed the mike button. The phoce opened the door and rolled outside, onto the path; the 'mobile stopped a little way off, and the phoce looked back indecisively.

'Better go find your sister,' Stockstill said. 'It'll mean a great deal to her, I'm sure.'

When next he looked up, the phoce had gone. The 'mobile was nowhere in sight.

'Walt Dangerfield,' Stockstill said into the mike, 'I'm going to sit here trying to reach you until either you answer or I know you're dead. I'm not saying you don't have a genuine physical ailment, but I am saying that part of the cause lies in your psychological situation, which in many respects is admittedly bad. Don't you agree? And after what you've gone through, seeing your controls taken away from you—'

From the speaker a far-off, laconic voice said, 'Okay, Stockstill. I'll make a stab at your free association. If for no other reason than to prove to you by default that I actually am desperately physically ill.'

Doctor Stockstill sighed and relaxed. 'It's about time. Have you been picking me up all this time?'

'Yes, good friend,' Dangerfield said. 'I wondered how long

you'd ramble on. Evidently forever. You guys are persistent, if nothing else.'

Leaning back, Stockstill shakily tit up a special deluxe Gold Label cigarette and said, 'Can you lie down and make yourself comfortable?'

'I *am* lying down,' Dangerfield said tartly. 'I've been lying down for five days, now.'

'And you should become thoroughly passive, if possible. Become supine.'

'Like a whale,' Dangerfield said. 'Just lolling in the brine – right? Now, shall I dwell on childhood incest drives? Let's see . . . I think I'm watching my mother and she's combing her hair at her vanity table. She's very pretty. No, sorry, I'm wrong. It's a movie and I'm watching Norma Shearer. It's the late-late show on TV.' He laughed faintly.

'Did your mother resemble Norma Shearer?' Stockstill asked; he had pencil and paper out now, and was making notes.

'More like Betty Grable,' Dangerfield said. 'If you can remember her. But that probably was before your time. I'm old, you know. Almost a thousand years . . . it ages you, to be up here, alone.'

'Just keep talking,' Stockstill said. 'Whatever comes into your mind. Don't force it, let it direct itself instead.'

Dangerfield said, 'Instead of reading the great classics to the world maybe I can free-associate as to childhood toilet traumas, right? I wonder if that would interest mankind as much. Personally, I find it pretty fascinating.'

Stockstill, in spite of himself, laughed.

'You're human,' Dangerfield said, sounding pleased. 'I consider that good. A sign in your favor.' He laughed his old, familiar laugh. 'We both have something in common; we both consider what we're doing here as being very funny indeed.'

Nettled, Stockstill said, 'I want to help you.'

'Aw, hell,' the faint, distant voice answered, 'I'm the one who's helping you, Doc. You know that, deep down in your unconscious. You need to feel you're doing something worthwhile again, don't you? When do you first remember ever having had that feeling? Just lie there supine, and I'll do the rest from up here' He chuckled. 'You realize, of course, that I'm recording this on tape; I'm going to play our silly conversations every night over New York – they love this intellectual stuff, up that way.'

'Please,' Stockstill said. 'Let's continue.'

'Hoode hoode hoo,' Dangerfield chortled. 'By all means. Can I dwell on the girl I loved in the fifth grade? That was where my incest fantasies really got started.' He was silent for a moment and then he said in a reflective voice, 'You know, I haven't thought of Myra for years. Not in twenty years.'

'Did you take her to a dance or some such thing?'

'In the *fifth grade*?' Dangerfield yelled. 'Are you some kind of a nut? Of course not. But I did kiss her.' His voice seemed to become more relaxed, more as it had been in former times. 'I never forgot that,' he murmured.

Static for a moment supervened.

'. . . and then,' Dangerfield was saying when next Stockstill could make his words out, 'Arnold Klein rapped me on the noggin and I shoved him over, which is exactly what he deserved. Do you follow? I wonder how many hundreds of my avid listeners are getting this; I see lights lit up – they're trying to contact me on a lot of frequencies. Wait, Doc. I have to answer a few of these calls. Who knows, some of them might be other, better analysts.' He added, in parting, 'And at lower rates.'

There was silence. Then Dangerfield was back.

'Just people telling me I did right to rap Arnold Klein on

the noggin,' he said cheerfully. 'So far the votes are in favor four to one. Shall I continue?'

'Please do,' Stockstill said, scratching notes.

'Well,' Dangerfield said, 'and then there was Jenny Linhart. That was in the low sixth.'

The satellite, in its orbit, had come closer; the reception was now loud and clear. Or perhaps it was that Hoppy Harrington's equipment was especially good. Doctor Stockstill leaned back in his chair, smoked his cigarette, and listened, as the voice grew until it boomed and echoed in the room.

How many times, he thought, Hoppy must have sat here receiving the satellite. Building up his plans, preparing for the day. And now it is over. Had the phocomelus – Bill Keller – taken the wizened, dried-up little thing with him? Or was it still somewhere nearby?

Stockstill did not look around; he kept his attention on the voice which came to him so forcefully, now. He did not let himself notice anything else in the room.

In a strange but soft bed in an unfamiliar room, Bonny Keller woke to sleepy confusion. Diffuse light, yellow and undoubtedly the early-morning sun, poured about her, and above her a man whom she knew well bent over her, reaching down his arms. It was Andrew Gill and for a moment she imagined – she deliberately allowed herself to imagine – that it was seven years ago, E Day again.

'Hi,' she murmured, clasping him to her. 'Stop,' she said, then. 'You're crushing me and you haven't shaved yet. What's going on?' She sat up, all at once, pushing him away.

Gill said, 'Just take it easy.' Tossing the covers aside, he picked her up, carried her across the room, toward the door.

'Where are we going?' she asked. 'To Los Angeles? This way – with you carrying me in your arms?'

'We're going to listen to somebody.' With his shoulder he pushed the door open and carried her down the small, low-ceilinged hall.

'Who?' she demanded. 'Hey, I'm not dressed.' All she had on was her underwear, which she had slept in.

Ahead, she saw the Hardys' living room, and there, at the radio, their faces suffused with an eager, youthful joy, stood Stuart McConchie, the Hardys, and several men whom she realized were employees of Mr Hardy.

From the speaker came the voice they had heard last night, or was it that voice? She listened, as Andrew Gill seated himself with her on his lap. '. . . and then Jenny Linhart said to me,' the voice was saying, 'that I resembled, in her estimation, a large poodle. It had to do with the way my big sister was cutting my hair, I think. I did look like a large poodle. It was not an insult. It was merely an observation; it showed she was aware of me. But that's some improvement over not being noticed at all, isn't it?' Dangerfield was silent, then, as if waiting for an answer.

'Who's he talking to?' she said, still befuddled by sleep, still not fully awake. And then she realized what it meant 'He's alive,' she said. And Hoppy was gone. 'Goddamn it,' she said loudly, 'will somebody tell me what happened?' She squirmed off Andrew's lap and stood shivering; the morning air was cold.

Ella Hardy said, 'We don't know what happened. He apparently came back on the air sometime during the night. We hadn't turned the radio off, and so we heard it; this isn't his regular time to transmit to us.'

'He appears to be talking to a doctor,' Mr Hardy said. 'Possibly a psychiatrist who's treating him.'

'Dear God,' Bonny said, doubling up. 'It isn't possible – he's being psychoanalyzed.' But, she thought, *Where did Hoppy go? Did he give up?* Was the strain of reaching out that far too much for him, was that it? Did he, after all, have limitations, like every other living thing? She returned quickly to her bedroom, still listening, to get her clothes. No one noticed; they were all so intent on the radio.

To think, she said to herself as she dressed, that the old witchcraft could help him. It was incredibly funny; she trembled with cold and merriment as she buttoned her shirt. Dangerfield, on a couch up in his satellite, gabbling away about his childhood . . . oh God, she thought, and she hurried back to the living room to catch it all.

Andrew met her, stopping her in the hall. 'It faded out,' he said. 'It's gone, now.'

'Why?' Her laughter ceased; she was terrified.

'We were lucky to get it at all. He's all right, I think.'

'Oh,' she said, 'I'm so scared. Suppose he isn't?'

Andrew said, 'But he is.' He put his big hands on her shoulders. 'You heard him; you heard the quality of his voice.'

'That analyst,' she said, 'deserves a Hero First Class medal.'

'Yes,' he said gravely. 'Analyst Hero First Class, you're entirely right.' He was silent then, still touching her but standing a little distance from her. 'I apologize for barging in on you and dragging you out of bed. But I knew you'd want to hear.'

'Yes,' she agreed.

'Is it still essential to you that we go further on? All the way to Los Angeles?'

'Well,' she said, 'you do have business here. We could stay here a while at least. And see if he remains okay.' She was still apprehensive, still troubled about Hoppy.

Andrew said, 'One can never be really sure, and that's what makes life a problem, don't you agree? Let's face it – he is mortal; someday he has to perish anyhow. Like the rest of us.' He gazed down at her.

'But not *now*,' she said. 'If it only can be later, a few years from now – I could stand it then.' She took hold of his hands and then leaned forward and kissed him. Time, she thought. The love we left for each other in the past; the love we have for Dangerfield right now, and for him in the future. Too bad it is a powerless love; too bad it can't automatically knit him up whole and sound once more, this feeling we have for one another – and for him.

'Remember E Day?' Andrew asked.

'Oh yes, I certainly do,' she said.

'Any further thoughts on it?'

Bonny said, 'I've decided I love you.' She moved quickly away from him flushing at having said such a thing. 'The good news,' she murmured. 'I'm carried away; please excuse me, I'll recover.'

'But you mean it,' he said, perceptively.

'Yes.' She nodded.

Andrew said, 'I'm getting a little old, now.'

'We all are,' she said. 'I creak, when I first get up . . . perhaps you noticed, just now.'

'No,' he said. 'Just so long as your teeth stay in your head, as they are.' He looked at her uneasily. 'I don't know exactly what to say to you, Bonny. I feel that we're going to achieve a great deal here; I hope so, anyhow. Is it a base, onerous thing, coming here to arrange for new machinery for my factory? Is that—' He gestured. 'Crass?'

'It's lovely,' she answered.

Coming into the hall, Mrs Hardy said, 'We picked him up again for just a minute, and he was still talking about his childhood. I would say now we won't hear again until the regular time at four in the afternoon. What about breakfast? We have three eggs to divide among us; my husband managed to pick them up from a peddler last week.'

'Eggs,' Andrew Gill repeated 'What kind? Chicken?'

'They're large and brown,' Mrs Hardy said. 'I'd guess so, but we can't be positive until we open them.'

Bonny said, 'It sounds marvelous.' She was very hungry, now. 'I think we should pay for them, though; you've already given us so much – a place to stay and dinner last night.' It was virtually unheard of, these days, and certainly it was not what she had expected to find in the city.

'We're in business together,' Mrs Hardy pointed out. 'Everything we have is going to be pooled, isn't it?'

'But I have nothing to offer.' She felt that keenly, all at once, and she hung her head. I can only take, she thought. Not give.

However, they did not seem to agree. Taking her by the hand, Mrs Hardy led her toward the kitchen area. 'You can help fix,' she explained. 'We have potatoes, too. You can peel them. We serve our employees breakfast; we always eat together – it's cheaper, and they don't have kitchens, they live in rooms, Stuart and the others. We have to watch out for them.'

You're very good people, Bonny thought. So this is the city – this is what we've been hiding from, throughout these years. We heard the awful stories, that it was only ruins, with predators creeping about, derelicts and opportunists and nappers, the dregs of what it had once been . . . and we had fled from that, too, before the war. We had already become too afraid to live here.

As they entered the kitchen she heard Stuart McConchie saying to Dean Hardy, '. . . and besides playing the nose-flute this rat—' He broke off, seeing her. 'An anecdote about life here,' he apologized. 'It might shock you. It has to do with a brilliant animal, and many people find them unpleasant.'

'Tell me about it,' Bonny said. 'Tell me about the rat who plays the nose-flute.'

'I may be getting two brilliant animals mixed together,' Stuart said as he began heating water for the imitation coffee. He fussed with the pot and then, satisfied, leaned back against the wood-burning stove, his hands in his pockets. 'Anyhow, I think the veteran said that it also had worked out a primitive system of bookkeeping. But that doesn't sound right.' He frowned.

'It does to me,' Bonny said.

'We could use a rat like that working here,' Mr Hardy said. 'We'll be needing a good bookkeeper, with our business expanding, as it's going to be.'

Outside, along San Pablo Avenue, horse-drawn cars began to move; Bonny heard the sharp sound of the hoofs striking. She heard the stirrings of activity, and she went to the window to peep out. Bicycles, too, and a mammoth old wood-burning truck. And people on foot, many of them.

From beneath a board shack an animal emerged and with caution crossed the open to disappear beneath the porch of a building on the far side of the street. After a moment it reappeared, this time followed by another animal, both of them short-legged and squat, perhaps mutations of bulldogs. The second animal tugged a clumsy sleigh-like platform after it; the platform, loaded with various valuable objects, most of them food, slid and bumped on its runners over the irregular pavement after the two animals hurrying for cover.

At the window, Bonny continued to watch attentively, but the two short-legged animals did not reappear. She was just about to turn away when she caught sight of something else moving into its first activity of the day. A round metal hull, splotched over with muddy colors and bits of leaves and twigs, shot into sight, halted, raised two slender antennae quiveringly into the early morning sun.

What in the world is it? Bonny wondered. And then she

realized that she was seeing a Hardy Homeostatic trap in action.

Good luck, she thought.

The trap, after pausing and scouting in all directions, hesitated and then at last doubtfully took off on the trail of the two bulldog-like animals. It disappeared around the side of a nearby house, solemn and dignified, much too slow in its pursuit, and she had to smile.

The business of the day had begun. All around her the city was awakening, back once more into its regular life.

Afterword

Philip K. Dick

Well, I predicted wrong when I wrote *Dr Bloodmoney* back in 1964. Events that I foresaw never came about, and as you read this novel you will see what I mean. But it is not the job, really, of science fiction to predict. Science fiction only *seems* to predict. It's like the aliens on Star Trek all of whom speak English. A literary convention is involved here. Nothing more.

I am amused, however, to see what specifically I got wrong. Worst of all, I totally misread the future of the manned space program. But this only shows how rapidly history unfolds. In *Dr Bloodmoney* I have one American circling the world forever. This is obvious nonsense; either there would be many Americans – and many Russians, for that matter – or none at all.

Of course the major item that I got wrong is the End of the World. Back in 1964 I was expecting it any time; I kept checking my watch. Horace Gold, who edited *Galaxy* magazine, once chided me for anticipating global wipeout within the next week. That was back around 1954; I anticipated it by 1964. Well, such were the fears of the times. Right now we have other worries. Our problem seems to be paying our debts with incredibly inflated dollars, finding gas for our cars – much more mundane worries. Less cosmic.

Oddly, these are the sort of worries that assail the characters in *Dr Bloodmoney* in their post-World War Three world. There are horses pulling cars. Eyeglasses are rare and treasured.

A man who manufactures cigarettes is honored wherever he goes. Of supreme value is someone who can fix things. Society has reverted, but not to the brutal level that we might expect. Rather, it has become rural in nature. The vast cities are gone, and in their place a sort of countryside exists that is not awful at all. I must add, however, that in no sense does it resemble any world that we actually have.

But then, of course, we haven't had World War Three.

In my opinion this is an extremely hopeful novel. It does not posit the end of human civilization as a result of the next war. People are still around and they are still coping. Those who survive, anyhow, are fairly lucky in their new lives. What is interesting is the subtle change in the relative power status of the survivors. Take Hoppy Harrington, who has no arms or legs. Before the bomb hits, Hoppy is marginal in terms of power. He is fortunate if he can get any kind of job at all. But in the postwar world this is not the case. Hoppy is elevated by stealthy increments until, at last, he is a menace to a man not even on the planet's surface; Hoppy has become a demigod, and a complex one at that. He is not really evil, in the usual sense . . . but here is an instance of the abuse of power: evil emanating from power per se. It is not so much that Hoppy is evil but that his *power* is evil.

In the satellite, Walt Dangerfield is transformed from a man assisting the fragmented postwar society, giving it unity and strength, raising its morale, to a man desperate for help from it, a man who is becoming weaker day by day. He signifies isolation, which is the horror of the many down below: isolation and a loss of the objects and values that comprised their original world. As time passes, Walt Dangerfield must gain strength from those on the planet's surface, rather than giving strength to them. And into the vacuum created comes Hoppy Harrington, who epitomizes the monster in us: the person who is hungry. Not hungry for food, but hungry for coercive control over others. This drive in Hoppy stems from a physical deprivation. It is compensation for what he lacked from birth. Hoppy is incomplete, and he will complete himself at the expense of the entire world; he will psychologically devour it.

You will note in *Dr Bloodmoney* an account of a test conducted in 1972 that turned out to be a catastrophe, and of course there was in fact no such test and no such catastrophe. But then, there was no such person as Doctor Bluthgeld. This is a work of fiction. And yet at a certain level it is not. The West Marin County area, where much of the novel is set, is an area that I knew well. When I wrote the novel I lived in that area. Many of the features that I describe are real. So a great deal of the veridical is blended in with the fiction. As do some of the characters, I searched for wild mushrooms in West Marin, and I found the varieties they find (and avoided the varieties they avoid). It is one of the most beautiful areas in the United States, and is called by the Sierra Club 'The Island in Time.' When I lived there in the late fifties and early sixties it was set apart from the rest of California and therefore seemed to me a natural locus for a postwar microcosm of society. Already, in fact, West Marin was a little world. When I read over *Dr Bloodmoney* I discover, to my pleasure, that I have captured in words much of that little world that I so loved – a little world from which I am now separated by time and distance.

My favorite character in the novel is the TV salesman Stuart McConchie, who happens to be black. In 1964, when I wrote *Dr Bloodmoney*, it was daring to have a major character be a black man. My God, how much change has taken place in these recent years! But what an excellent change, one we can be proud of. In my first novel, *Solar Lottery*, I had a black man as captain of a spaceship – daring indeed for a novel published in 1955. Stuart is in my opinion the focus of the novel, and he appears first. It is through his eyes that we initially see Doctor Bluthgeld, which is to say, Doctor Bloodmoney. Stuart's reaction is simple; he is seeing a lunatic and that is that. Bonny Keller, however, knowing Doctor Bluthgeld more intimately, holds a more complex view of the man. Frankly, I tend to see Bluthgeld as Stuart McConchie sees him. I am, so to speak, Stuart McConchie, and at one time *I* was a TV salesman at a store on Shattuck Avenue in Berkeley. Like Stuart, I used to sweep the sidewalk in front of the store in the early morning, noticing the cute girls on their way to work. So I have to confess to an overly simple view of Doctor Bluthgeld: I hate him and I hate everything he stands for. He is the alien and he is the enemy. I cannot fathom his mind; I cannot understand his hates. It is not the Russians I fear; it is the Doctor Bluthgelds, the Doctor Bloodmoneys, in our own society, that terrify me. I am sure that to the extent that they know me, or would know me, they hate me back and would do exactly to me what I would do to them.

'And, sure enough as Stuart watched, leaning on his broom, the furtive first nut of the day sidled guiltily toward the psychiatrist's office.'

This is our initial glimpse of Doctor Bloodmoney: through the eyes of a man pushing a broom. I am with the man pushing the broom, here at the beginning of the novel and all the way to the end. Stuart McConchie is an astute man, and in seeing Doctor Bloodmoney he has experienced a moment of instant insight that Bonny Keller in her years of personal, intimate knowledge lacks. I admit to prejudice, here. I think the first response by the man pushing the broom can be trusted. Doctor Bloodmoney is sick, and sick in a way that is dangerous to the rest of us. And much of the evil in our world now emanates from such men, because such men do exist.

So in writing *Dr Bloodmoney* in 1964 I may have erred in many of my predictions, but upon rereading the novel recently I sensed a basic accuracy in it – an accuracy about human beings and their power to survive. Not survive as beasts, either, but as genuine humans doing genuinely human things. There are no supermen in this novel. There are no heroic deeds. There are some very poor predictions on my part, I must admit; but about the people themselves and their strength and tenacity and vitality . . . there I think I foresaw accurately. Because, of course, I was not predicting; I was only describing what I saw around me: the men and women and children and animals, the life of this planet that has been, is, and will be, no matter what happens.

I am proud of the people in this novel. And, as I say, I would like to number myself as one of them. I once pushed a broom on the sidewalk of Shattuck Avenue in Berkeley and I felt the joy and sense of busy activity and industry that Stuart feels, the excitement, the sense of the future.

And, as the novel depicts, despite the war – the war that did not in fact happen – it is a good future. I would have enjoyed being there with them in their microcosm, their postwar West Marin world.

Philip K. Dick was born in the USA in 1928. His twin sister Jane died in infancy. He started his writing career publishing short stories in magazines. The first of these was 'Beyond Lies the Wub' in 1952. While publishing SF prolifically during the fifties, Dick also wrote a series of mainstream novels, only one of which, *Confessions of a Crap Artist*, achieved publication during his lifetime. These included titles such as *Mary and the Giant* and *In Milton Lumky Territory*. During the 1960s Dick produced an extraordinary succession of novels, including *The Man in the High Castle*, which won a Hugo award, *Martian Time-Slip, Dr Bloodmoney, The Three Stigmata of Palmer Eldritch, Do Androids Dream of Electric Sheep?* and *Ubik*. In the 1970s, Dick started to concern himself more directly with metaphysical and theological issues, experiencing a moment of revelation – or breakdown – in March 1974 which became the basis for much of his subsequent writing, in particular *Valis*, as he strove to make sense of what had happened. He died in 1982, a few weeks before the film *Blade Runner* opened and introduced his vision to a wider audience.